MAKE ME BURN

Isle of the Forgotten
Book One

᭥᭜

A Novel

Tiffany Roberts

Pilar,
Thank you for
being such an amazing,
supportive reader!

We dedicate this book to each other, for finally having the courage and determination to make it a reality.

Special thanks to our editor, Lora Gasway, for helping us realize the full potential of this book, and to Isis Sousa for bringing our characters to life so vibrantly on the cover. Another thank you to authors Grace Draven and Mel Sterling for their willingness to provide advice, wisdom, and support to us as we start on this journey.

Thanks to all the family and friends who have supported us in the pursuit of our dreams.

Chapter One

"There will be no escape this time, demon."

The five mages spread out in a line, shoulder-to-shoulder. Their bared swords pulsed with reflections of the fire all around, their figures dark against the intense light. This village would be visible for miles around tonight, and people would see the smoke for days to come as they crossed the grasslands.

Morthanion sneered, lips pulling back to display his fangs. He could smell the sweat on the mages, even over the aroma of burning wood and flesh. It would have been comforting if he didn't know what the men before him were. If they didn't know what *he* was.

"Starting to feel warm, mortals?" he asked, laughter bubbling from his throat.

He sensed their magical onslaught just before they launched it; a faint tingling on the surface of his skin that raised the little hairs on his arms and the back of his neck. That was all the warning he needed. With a pump of his shadowy wings, he cast himself aside. The air where he'd been standing rippled with arcane energy, and the flames behind him wavered as though caught in a great wind, flaring high with a roar.

Three of the five moved forward. Their attacks were fast and unified, setting Morthanion on the defensive. The demon growled, the fire in his eyes intensifying. He wouldn't be upstaged by mortals. He wouldn't be defeated by things that lived and died over the course of a single heartbeat, in the space of a breath.

Flames sparked in his palms, roiling up his arms like flowing water to sheath them completely. The demon lashed out with flaming claws, the air wavering with the heat of his hands. His attack was fiercer than anything the mages could mount, his vision crimson and orange, his blood molten in his veins.

Two of the mages dropped back, leaving a single comrade to fend off the demon's blows in a flurry of flesh, steel, and claw. Morthanion gladly channeled all of his fury at the lone mageling, knowing the others would not be able to flee fast enough to save them from their fate.

There was another instant of that light prickling on his skin, and his arm was mid-swing when the flames swirling around it abruptly went out. Stumbling, he shifted his gaze to the other mages, and could see the faint sheen of their spell. They were channeling their abilities to nullify the magic around him – the magic *in* him!

They could not take away his claws, his strength, his speed. Shifting his momentum, he turned toward the other mages. He preferred burning his enemies, but perhaps fire was too good for these mages. Disembowelment might be more fitting.

As he turned, a hand clamped over his wrist. It was enough to disrupt his movement, to flare his rage.

"Now!" the mage holding Morthanion's arm yelled.

The demon felt the flood of power as the suppression on his magic was lifted. It surged back into him, a sweetly blazing storm in his gut, spreading throughout his entire being. He spun back to the mortal who had dared place a hand on him and buried his claws in the man's throat.

Crimson gushed down the front of the man's tunic, but his eyes remained steady. The mage brought his other hand up and pressed a metal disc to the hand that had torn into his neck.

Fire had never felt as cold as it did to Morthanion in that moment. The delightful heat he'd known for more than four millennia fled as his flesh bubbled and charred beneath the scalding brand. Such a paltry wound shouldn't have fazed him. Shouldn't have left him feeling so empty. The nullification barrier was down, but he was devoid of the power that had always been his.

Jaw clenched, he heaved the mage's body aside. Any glee he might have taken in slaughtering these mages vanished. He turned toward the others and charged them.

Morthanion recognized the fear in the eyes of the four remaining mortals, who had grouped together twenty or thirty feet from their fallen brother-in-arms. That was enough to turn his sneer into a wild grin. They'd pay, and it would be as painful as he could make it.

This time, it wasn't a prickle across the surface of his skin. It was a crackle, a charge like lightning. All four mages gestured at him simultaneously, and the magic struck him with the force of a charging bull. His stomach lurched and twisted and writhed on itself.

When he hit the ground, sand filled his mouth. He pushed himself up, spitting, snapping his gaze back to the mages.

They weren't there. None of it was. Instead of the heat of burning huts, there was a warm, moist breeze. The soft sighing of the ocean. A beach stretched out before him, curving around to rocky cliffs several hundred yards away. To the other side, it was flanked by thick, green jungle.

Anger surged through him, its molten waves quickly cooling to lead in his limbs. They'd stripped him of his power and banished him. There were no trees like this near the plains. Not even in distant Feloshia, where everything was green and alive. The air was thick with the smell of wet vegetation, of rotting leaves and alien fruits, all punctuated by the ocean's briny mist.

He didn't know where he'd been sent, only that it was far away from anywhere he'd ever been.

Dropping his gaze to the symbol burned onto the back of his right hand, he bared his fangs. A pair of snakes in a circle, devouring one another. They were bisected by a sword, before which was centered an eye. It was the mark of

The Order of the Justicars, the hand of the High Council of Mages. Their purveyors of law and justice.

He knew it robbed him of his power, forcefully wrenched his birthright from him. The skin around it was charred and ash-blackened, but the mark itself was raw and red. Clenching his teeth, he used the claws of his other hand to shred the patch of skin off, flicking it to the sand.

He willed fire to his hands, willed it to consume the entire damned jungle, to spread over the water and swallow up the whole world. The open wound sizzled, blood boiling away to reveal the Order's mark charred into the exposed tendons and muscle. It was a surge of pain more intense than removing the skin had produced, and left only emptiness in its wake.

"Fuck!"

Nearby lay a piece of gnarled gray driftwood. He buried his claws in it, spun, and hurled it out into the ocean with a growl that strengthened to a roar. Spewing more oaths, he kicked at the sand repeatedly, sending a cloud of it after the wood. His fury was as impotent as his magic; he'd allowed himself to be bested by a pack of mortals.

He would find a way back, and he would find the four surviving mages. Then, one by one, he would make them suffer, make them beg for their lives. Make them beg for their deaths.

*****

Morthanion clenched his fists and stared out toward the beach through the gap in the smooth-barked trees. He forced himself to watch the moonlight dance on the dark water, glittering like countless diamonds scattered across the surface. Otherwise, he'd drop his gaze back to his hand.

The part of his mind that had given in fully to his rage had demanded the brand be removed. After tearing it off four times, he knew the symbol had grown back for a fifth, the flesh now raised and pinkish. A fruitless endeavor, but even now a part of him longed to shred it again. He'd even considered cutting his whole damned hand off, but the thought had been fleeting. Such spells tended to be more resilient than that, and he'd just be out a perfectly good hand.

Two days of wandering had told him little. There were other people – he'd heard them from a distance – but he didn't know how many, and he'd yet to actually see anyone. All the better for them. His temper had cooled, but was otherwise undiminished, and he needed an outlet for it. Having to proceed with caution and walk around like some helpless mortal didn't improve his disposition. It irritated him to admit that he was more vulnerable now than he'd ever been.

The waves swept up onto the sand, sighing softly, reaching a little farther onto land as the tide steadily rose. Within that sound, he thought there was something else, but it was too distant, too faint. It sounded like a woman singing. It was likely the wind moving around the rocks just off the shoreline, jutting up from the water like broken teeth from a jawbone.

He stretched his fingers, longing for flames to engulf them, for the sweet, thrilling heat that had been so much a part of him. Beyond the rocks, the water was choppy, rising in brief white crests and falling again abruptly. He could fly past them, but there was only water as far as he could see. How far could he hope to get?

Though the brand hadn't nullified the shadow magic in him – that was the core of his very being – it had been dulled. The shroud that masked his demonic features was thin; would that extend to his other abilities, as well?

The breeze shifted, carrying the salt air directly to him. The singing became clearer; not a trick of the wind at all. There could be no mistaking it for anything but a woman's voice. Silently, he stepped through the undergrowth and out onto the sand, the full expanse of the beach opening up as he walked toward the voice.

The song ensnared him, drawing him westward, to a group of rocks that marched into the water like soldiers off to war. The sound grew more distinct with each step. There were words, but he could not understand them. Still, they were somehow…calming.

His frustration peaked again. He would not be pacified, and refused to let an outside force control him. All he needed was within. He had to hold on to anger and contempt; he could not let their heat fade. They were the only emotions that could rekindle his fire. Distractions would delay the vengeance he craved.

Shadows enveloped his form as he reached the rocks, dropping forward to crawl over them like a stalking beast. At the crest, he paused, his eyes immediately falling upon the source of the song.

The woman was sitting in the sand with her back to Morthanion. Her voice, the most haunting thing he'd ever heard, rose and fell with the whispering waves. There was a loneliness woven through her words, though they were foreign to him, that evoked an oddly soothing melancholy.

He climbed down onto the sand, walking slowly toward her. All he could hear apart from her voice was the dull thumping of his own heart. A great weight settled over him, freezing him in place as he stared at her. For a fleeting moment, he had the disorienting sense that every decision in his life had inexorably led him here.

Her dark hair shimmered in the silver light, the ends shifting as the tide swept up gently around her. The tips of her slender fingers skated over the surface of the water. Her skin was pale, and seemed to glow with the moonlight.

A wholly feminine aroma drifted to him: fragrant sands and sun-drenched flowers, all the sweetness of the sea.

Her song stopped abruptly, replaced by the hissing retreat of the waves from the shore. There was tension in her back, across her shoulders, and her fingers stilled their little dance. Her sudden quiet jarred him from his reverie, quelling any foolish contemplation of destiny.

This was no convergence of fate. It was merely an opportunity for entertainment.

She looked over her shoulder, and he met her eyes. They were the blue-green of clear ocean waters, wide with fear, and for a moment he could feel himself drowning in them. He'd seen that fear in the eyes of countless others, had relished in it and laughed in the face of it. But in those eyes, it made his insides twist, and the muscles of his jaw clenched in response. It was unexplainable.

Her fear disturbed him.

Chapter Two

The woman rose quickly and started to move backwards, water kicking up around her calves.

"Don't go," he said, raising his hands to show they were empty. That was supposed to be a non-threatening gesture, wasn't it?

He'd never seen so alluring a creature. Her lithe limbs accentuated the enticing flare of her hips, and the wet scrap of clothing she wore hid nothing from his hungry gaze.

She made a soft sound of distress, calling his eyes back up to hers as she took several quick steps backward.

"I mean you no harm." He curled his lips into what he considered a charming smile and took another step closer.

Her eyes flared in panic before she turned and ran toward the ocean.

The smile he wore split into a grin, his blood heating with the thrill of a predator scenting prey. This was a decidedly different feeling, however, a lust like he'd never known.

Even without using his wings, his steps felt light as he chased her, boots splashing in the surf. He wrapped his arms around her and drew her against him.

"No, no," he purred, his mouth near her ear, "no running. Please. I don't want to hurt you."

He could feel her draw in air as though she was about to scream. Who would come to her aid?

"Let me go!" she demanded instead, arching her back and twisting to escape his hold.

He relished her struggles and the sweet sound of her voice. Inhaling her unique scent deeply, he brushed his face in her long, damp hair. His head spun with the sensation of it. "You are unlike anything," he said huskily, his heart pounding. His cock throbbed painfully against the curve of her ass.

She was clearly no demon, which meant she was a plaything, an object to be used for the pleasure of a superior being. A perfect outlet for any urges that might overcome him, once she came to her senses and realized how much she'd enjoy it, too. He just needed to convince her.

Her struggles ceased.

"That's a good girl."

Before he realized what happened, seawater splashed like a wave over his arms and torso. He stumbled back a step, spreading his suddenly empty arms, and looked down to the foamy water at his feet. Floating on the retreating tide was the scrap of cloth she'd been wearing.

The girl was gone. He laughed in disbelief. If he had his sanity before they'd sent him here, it was certainly gone now.

Something tugged at the edge of his consciousness, an inexplicable urge that drew his attention up to scan the water. There she was, her hair streaming around her as she turned to look back. She was a few dozen yards out already. Even he couldn't swim so far in that time. He laughed harder; why not enjoy being insane? She couldn't be swimming as fast as his eyes were telling him.

He dropped the last of the thinning shroud, shadowy wings blossoming from his back. With a leap, he propelled himself into the air, heading for the same rocks that the girl was. His blood was still pumping with scalding heat. His unhinged mind had made a female for him, and he'd take her tonight – even if she was a figment of his imagination.

Morthanion swept past her, dropping to the rocks just before she reached them. He heard her gasp as he turned around, and watched her swim backwards a few strokes, her wide eyes locked on him.

"Why must you run?" he asked, his voice full of mirth as he raised it over the sound of the waves. The water gave him a faint, distorted glimpse of her pale, naked form, teasing at slender limbs and supple curves. "Whether you're a hallucination or flesh and blood, I've never seen anyone so exquisite."

"Why do you pursue me?"

"Because I am compelled to," he replied, baring his ivory fangs in a grin. Had he simply gone so long without finding his mate that he had the urge to chase a delusion?

He eased into a crouch, his clawed hands on his knees. She backed away again.

"I frighten you?" Still he wore that grin, but he was beginning to feel a weight in his stomach; her distress seemed only to cause him apprehension.

"How can you not?"

"You just turned to water in my arms. Why should you be afraid?"

She pressed her lips together, offering him no reply. Unwilling to let loose any more information? Perhaps charm would work, if he applied a little more.

He was willing the shroud back into place, his demonic features fading, when something struck the water in front of him. The girl inhaled sharply, wrenching back, and a moment later a spear floated to the surface.

Morthanion looked to the shoreline. A tall man with broad shoulders stood on the beach, several spears stuck in the sand beside him.

Something in his chest tightened, and he shifted his attention back to the girl. Crimson spread in the water around her. She was hurt. His nostrils flared as he tried to control his surge of anger at that discovery. Leaning forward, he reached out to her.

"Give me your hand."

She looked to his clawed fingers, and then dipped her head under the waves. Morthanion swiped down to grab at her, managing only to catch a handful of water. She'd disappeared again; even with his superior night vision, he could see no trace of her. *No!* Growling, his other hand clenched the rock beneath him, and it crumbled in his grasp.

A second spear clattered onto the rocks a few feet away from the demon. His hand darted out to catch its shaft before it fell into the water. He would have had the woman, were it not for the spearman. He sprang from the rock like a coiled snake striking, his wings carrying him low over the water.

Several moments later, his feet touched down on the sand again. "I do not appreciate things being thrown at me."

"Get used to it, demon," the spearman laughed. He was taller than Morthanion, with cords of muscle wrapped around his athletic frame. On the right side of the man's thick neck was the Order's mark, pale against dark skin. A wound long since healed but never faded. The spearman had been banished by the mages, too.

"I should like to know your name before I kill you," the demon said, twirling the spear casually as he advanced on the human. "I'd add it to my list, if I'd thought to bring it with me."

"You won't be needing my name once you're dead." The spearman grinned, pulling two of the weapons out of the sand. "I'd bind you to me so I could use you like the filth you are if there were magic here, but killing you will do just as well."

If there were magic here. Where had they been banished to? There was an answer to that question buried somewhere in his memory.

"Your claws will make decent trophies, demon." The spearman swung his weapons in fluid arcs, halting their momentum with one tip pointed at Morthanion.

There would be time to think later. The demon hefted his spear, testing its feel. It was clearly made with whatever materials could be found on the island. The wooden shaft was heavy, but sturdy, and the head was a shard of sharpened metal. The tip had bent slightly when it hit the rocks, but the edge was good.

It had been a long time since he'd used a weapon to kill someone. Magic had always come more naturally to him.

"Get on with it, then," he said, affecting an air of polite boredom that was in direct opposition to the fury flowing inside of him, "I've got a fish to catch."

The spearman began to circle Morthanion. "Too bad the other two didn't hit you."

"Yes. You would've lasted a few moments longer with me injured," the demon replied, watching the spearhead as he twirled the shaft over his palm again. The first spear had hit the girl. He didn't know how badly she'd been wounded, only that her blood had darkened the water. Closing his fingers around the haft, he nearly splintered the wood in his grip. Morthanion had thought her a potential outlet to relieve his boredom, but this man offered a new one.

The distance between the two of them shrank gradually, the human still circling. When he attacked, it came faster than Morthanion anticipated. The demon batted aside the thrusting head of his opponent's spear with the shaft of his own weapon an instant before it would have cut him.

"Did you make these yourself?" he asked.

"Like them, do you?" The spearman lunged forward with another thrust. Morthanion knocked it away with a twist of his own spear, and shifted his weapon back around to parry the jab from the human's other hand.

"Heavy, but well balanced. Not much to look at, though," the demon said conversationally. He offered an attack of his own, slashing horizontally at the man's throat.

The spearman jerked back. "Borgeln's blackened balls," he growled, a thin line of blood welling near his collarbone. He clenched his teeth, glaring at the demon. "They're not for looking at!"

"If you paid them more attention, you might not be the one bleeding."

Charging forward, the human launched into a flurry of blows, attacking with both spears in rapid succession. Morthanion moved backwards, letting the crimson battle-haze fall into place over his vision. Instinct guided him, his body twisting to avoid thrusts, his hands moving in a blur to deflect and block blows. The shaft of his spear flexed and moaned under the onslaught; the human was nothing if not powerful, and the demon knew his weapon would not hold for long.

All the while, his fury grew hotter, its smoldering spark igniting into a fire in his gut. This mortal had harmed the girl in the water. Morthanion had seen her blood in the ocean, had *smelled* it.

The man swung with both spears, and the demon raised his own to block them, their shafts clacking together furiously.

"I just remembered something," Morthanion said, and shoved his enemy's weapons aside, throwing the large man off-balance.

"What's that?" the man demanded, his shoulders rising and falling rapidly. A sheen of sweat glistened on his sun-darkened skin.

The spearman thrust again, wildly this time, throwing his considerable weight behind it. Morthanion stepped aside, the spearhead cutting the fabric of his shirt. Missing his attack, the human stumbled past, carried by his own momentum. The demon whipped around, burying the head of his weapon in the man's kidney.

"I'm not very happy with you."

The man spun, his mouth open and eyes bulging. For a moment, Morthanion was reminded of a gaping fish. The spearman swung high with his right arm, but the demon caught the shaft of the weapon with one hand and forced it down to the sand. Staggering, the human attempted another feeble strike.

Morthanion twisted the spear in the man's back, causing the dying fighter to rear back, yelling in pain. In that moment, his foe's throat exposed, the demon released everything. The rage that had built up over the last few days exploded in a torrent of slashing claws as he tackled the man, shadow and blood mingling in the night air. His fury at the mages for sending him here, for taking his magic. Frustration for finding the most alluring woman he'd ever encountered and losing her not once, but twice; having seen her come to harm, seen that look upon her face. Her fear had troubled him, but her pain had moved him to violence.

There was nothing subtle about his actions. By the end, the sand couldn't absorb anymore blood, and it started to pool and run toward the ocean in rivulets. Little of the spearman's upper body was recognizable when the demon finally rose.

Morthanion wiped gore from his face with his upper sleeve, his hands shaking. Any mirth he'd worn on his face during the fight, any dry, mocking politeness, was gone. His dark, sharply angling brows were low over the bridge of his nose, his eyes flaming embers.

"And these, my only clothes," he growled, dipping to grab hold of the corpse by a leg. It left a crimson trail as he dragged it into the incoming tide, staining the water red as it was pulled out to sea. Then the demon waded in up to his chest, dunking his head beneath the water, and scrubbed the blood from his skin.

A short while later, he found himself near the rocks where he'd first encountered the girl. The spearman's gory demise had not lightened his mood. Was the girl all right?

Was she even real? Perhaps he'd imagined her, but could he have imagined her fragrance as well? Imagined the tang of her blood?

He scanned the wet sand for any sign of her, knowing it to be futile. Whatever trace she might have left behind was long since claimed by the ocean, leaving him to doubt her existence even more.

Damn them all for this.

Chapter Three

Aria reached out, sea foam splashing around her, and slapped her palms down on the sloped rock ledge. Her arms trembled as she pulled herself from the water. Once she was on solid ground, she collapsed. She lay there, breathing rapidly, her body close to exhaustion. Nearly every part of her screamed in pain. Pushing past her endurance, Aria had swum faster than she ever had before, motivated by fear.

That her blood could attract predators within the sea was the least of her concerns.

She had been seen.

She wanted to laugh and weep. All of Laudine's work to keep her safe had been undone. She had kept them hidden for more than twenty years. A mere two months after the woman's death was all it took for Aria to be spotted by the islanders.

She had seen people before, but only at a distance. Never had she imagined that a man could look like the one who had found her. His eyes were fire, glowing from within the shadows of his face, and there had been fangs in his smile. It was more the grin of a hungry shark than that of a man. Panic had urged her to run; she hadn't expected that he would have claws, much less wings!

He was dangerous, everything Laudine had warned her about and more. And yet there was something about him. The way he looked at her — as though her terror had stricken a chord deep inside of him — and the open fury on his face when he discovered she'd been hurt had caught her off-guard.

Recalling the injury sent a fresh wave of pain through her leg. Aria opened her eyes and pushed herself to her feet. When she glanced down at her thigh, she cringed at the open gash and the bright red blood that had stained the small pool of seawater on the rock beneath her.

Keeping her hands on the face of the cliff, she stepped up the ledge to the entrance of the cave. Her home.

She found scraps of linen within and tied one around her thigh over the gash to stop the bleeding. It would heal quick enough; they always did. Faster than any wound Laudine had ever suffered. She sat upon the furs of her makeshift bed, and washed away the remaining blood on her leg. Once dry, she pulled another short dress over her head.

She had been discovered. There had been no one on this part of the island that she knew of, until now. Her sanctuary, her place of solace, had been taken from her, and Aria could only hope that her home wouldn't be as well. She had nowhere else to go.

*****

For three days, Aria remained within the cliff-side cave. She was too scared to leave, tense with worry that at any moment she would be found, and with her leg wounded, she was too vulnerable on land. It needed time to heal.

As the third day came, Aria knew she was overreacting. For as long as she could remember, no one had discovered the cave, much less seen Aria and Laudine. The older woman had often left to find food and supplies, and sometimes spoke of seeing others. But the cave faced away from the rest of the island, and the rocky, unforgiving terrain kept all the other inhabitants from even getting near. There was nothing to gain. No food, no shelter, just harsh, exposed ground.

If they'd found her home, they would already have come for her.

With her water supply dwindling, she knew she had to go out. They'd used hollow reeds to channel rainfall from the rocks above, but the skies had been clear for days. Besides, Laudine had taught her how to remain unseen, to creep through the jungle under cover of darkness. Cowering in the cave like a frightened animal was not going to help her survive.

She waited until nightfall, and then secured a pair of water skins to her waist. Lowering herself into the sea, she swam slowly, ducking beneath the rougher waves and moving parallel to the shoreline. When she felt she'd gone far enough, she turned for land, and remained low as she came out of the water. Crouching near a group of large rocks, she scanned the beach carefully. The sky was clear and the moon more than half full, leaving the sand pale silver. She was further down the beach than she'd been the first time she encountered the stranger, but she was still worried.

If two of them had come to this part of the island in the same night, why wouldn't there be more around now?

After watching for a time and seeing sign of no one, she walked inland, following the rocks and sticking to whatever shadows the moon cast. Nearer to the open stretch of land between the beach and the forest, she paused again, pressing herself against the last of the rocks. All was silent save for the heavy sighing of the waves, and the only movement she could see was the gentle sway of vegetation in the night breeze.

She pushed herself up and broke into a run, feeling slow as her feet sank into the soft sand. Aria knew she was entirely exposed, and all she could do was keep running and hope that no one was nearby.

After crossing the tree line, she dropped into the undergrowth. She waited for any indication that someone might have followed, and soon even the sound of her rapidly beating heart faded away, leaving only the familiar song of the sea and the hum of insects. Slowly standing up, she continued on, avoiding the patches of moonlight that came through the canopy and trying to keep her steps silent.

The gentle babbling of the stream was another familiar sound, a comforting one, but it was so different from the seemingly endless ocean. Still, she stopped once more before she approached it, waiting until she was as sure as she could be that no one else was around. Then she hurriedly knelt at the stream's bank, filling her cupped hands and drinking deeply.

The exertion made her leg ache. The gash opened by the spear had healed enough to leave her movements unrestricted, though she wondered if this one would actually scar. She'd always healed faster than Laudine, and her wounds rarely left any trace that they'd existed.

Once she quenched her thirst, she untied the water skins from her belt and began to fill them.

"You ran from me," spoke a familiar voice.

Aria started with a gasp and leapt to her feet, retreating several steps. There, directly across the stream, was the man with fire eyes. He remained crouched, drinking leisurely from his own hands, those eyes on her.

"It was not I that harmed you," he said, raising his chin to motion vaguely toward her. "Though, you seem little worse for wear."

"What do you want?" It was a ridiculous question. Everyone on the island wanted the same. Food, water, supplies.

And *entertainment*.

"To leave this place," he said, eyes intent on her. "Though you've rather piqued my curiosity."

"I do not want to 'pique' your curiosity." She watched as he moved a little bit closer, though he didn't rise from his crouch. His head tilted as he studied her further, and Aria shifted uncomfortably under such scrutiny.

"What are you?" he asked.

"What are *you*?" Aria returned, taking another step back. Before her was a man once more. While his eyes were still fire, there was no sign of the horns, fangs, or claws. Even though she couldn't see them, she somehow knew they were still there.

"Very interested in getting to know you."

Aria searched his expression, confused by his meaning. The unsettling flash of teeth he gave her was at odds with the sincerity in his voice. Get to know her? While he was attempting to appear harmless, there was something more beneath the surface.

"The man with the spears cannot hurt you anymore. I've protected you." With this announcement, his chin rose, his jaw set firm.

Her eyes widened. "You killed him." It was no question. How else could he no longer hurt her? Even though she should be frightened, the pride in the man's voice brought her a sense of security. She wasn't supposed to feel that when it came to other islanders. They were not to be trusted. Especially after admittedly murdering someone.

"People tend to die when they poke each other with sharp objects."

She longed to look behind her, to run, but she was too frightened to take her eyes off him. She knew he was fast. He could even fly! And she was nowhere near the ocean, the one place she might lose him again.

"Yes, you are far away from the sea," he said, almost gently, as if reading her mind. He rose, his movements slow, but fluid. "And I might like chasing you again just a little too much. But do we really need to let it get to that?"

Aria took another step away when he stood, glancing at his open hands. They were empty, his fingers curled slightly. The memory of the black claws they'd ended in was still fresh in her mind. "Stay away."

"What is your name?"

She eyed him warily. Not counting animals and sea creatures, she'd never spoken to anyone besides Laudine. The older woman had always warned her of the violence the people here were capable of. Was this one just trying to put her at ease before he made another move?

Still, Laudine had been one of the people sent here, and had shown Aria nothing but kindness. The woman had told many stories about Jasper and Xani; Aria's father had also been a prisoner, but had earned her mother's trust and love. Didn't that mean that some of the people on the island were capable of goodness?

Before she could think more on it, she gave him her name. "Aria"

"*Aria*," he repeated, grinning at the sound of it. Short and simple and utterly exquisite. "I am called Morthanion Ulthander, Keeper of the Flame...but Morthanion will suffice. It is a *pleasure*." He ran his gaze over her body, top to bottom, and drank in her form. All at once, his blood was ablaze again.

The girl – *Aria* – inhaled sharply and moved back. His natural response was to move that much closer to her. His eyes narrowed. She still feared him, perhaps more so now than before. He couldn't have that. There was a compulsion in him to learn about her, to know every intimate detail. That would be difficult if he kept frightening her away. This creature was so enticing that he guessed he might be chasing after her forever, if he didn't change his approach.

"I'm sorry. Perhaps my appearance is somewhat unsettling?"

Morthanion closed his eyes, reaching inwardly for the innate magic that could mask his demonic features from onlookers. When he opened them again a moment later, they were a clear, bright blue, not unlike the sky on a cloudless day.

Aria hadn't moved any farther, but her eyes were wide. "What *are* you?" she asked again.

"After all you've seen of me, do you not know?" Though to most mortals, his kind were legends, whispers from a distant past, most folk still knew enough to tell a demon when they saw one.

"I know you fly on shadows, that you have claws upon your hands and fangs for teeth. And that your eyes burn like fire." She was searching him with her gaze. "I've spent my entire life on this island and know little of the world, or even the others that live here."

"You were born here?" he asked, and for once it was he that was surprised. "How...unfortunate." The girl was inexperienced and young, at least by the way she looked and behaved. He knew better than most, however, that looks could often be quite deceiving. "I am a demon."

Dropping the shroud, he fully revealed himself. He spread his claw-tipped fingers, stretched feathery wings formed from writhing shadow. Let his true eyes linger on her again.

She stepped back, bringing her arms up as though to defend herself. As though she *could* defend herself. "Demon," she whispered, and he could tell by the look on her face that she had heard stories, after all.

"Yes." He smiled, willing the shroud back into place.

Morthanion couldn't read her expression; there was still that fear there, but something else crossed her features, too. She looked past him, to something behind and above.

"There is food, if you've been searching." She met his gaze again. "Food is...scarce, at times."

The demon turned to look over his shoulder, catching sight of the bright red fruit in the tree overhead. He'd spent three days wandering the island, trying to focus on finding a way off. In that time, he'd discovered several groups, and it hadn't taken much to tell that they were all vying for survival, killing and stealing so they had something to eat.

"So I've surmised," he said. "You've some place to hide, haven't you? To stay out of all the fun here."

Aria just pressed her lips together.

"Very well. I won't pry all your secrets from you, sweet Aria." He inhaled deeply, taking in her scent. It was intoxicating even from several feet away, and he could feel himself harden. "At least, not yet." He needed to claim her. The irrational, insatiable necessity was growing inside of him with each passing moment, threatening to overwhelm his logical mind – if there was any of that left.

She caught her lower lip between her teeth, and looked up to the fruit again. "Would you be able to get some of that down for me?"

"Can you promise you won't run while I do?" he asked, his attention fixated on the way she worried her lip. It was somehow seductive, and his heart fluttered at it.

"I promise not to run. Unless you give me reason to."

Morthanion's mouth tilted up to one side in a smile. The tension in her was almost palpable. He knew she was waiting for an opportune moment to flee. As much as he enjoyed the allure of her shapely legs stretching and tightening while she ran, he'd not let the chase go on long. He was far too interested in her to give up that much time. Still, perhaps the extension of trust on his part would help put her at ease.

Shadows sprouted from his back, coalescing into wings. Turning away from her, he leapt, and with a few beats of his wings he was high enough to pick a few of the fist-sized fruits. Their fragrance was unlike anything he'd ever smelled, sweet and exotic, but they could not compare to her.

"You make it appear so easy," she said as he returned to her, and there was a faint smile on her lips.

"Things that appear easy rarely are," he replied, his eyes narrowed at her again. Her smile was beautiful, and sight of it made something in his chest tighten. Part of him was wondering why she hadn't tried to run, was suspicious of her still being here.

"Would you have one with me?" she asked.

Morthanion held one of the fruits to her. Her change of attitude was too convenient, too sudden. Perhaps she had just realized that he truly meant her no harm? And why should he be suspicious? Didn't he want to get close to her, to come to know her more? She posed no threat to him.

She accepted the food from him, and for an instant, their fingers touched. A shock ran up his arm, through his entire body – it was a tantalizing taste of what could be. Her eyes widened for the space of a heartbeat, and she jerked the fruit out of his hand. He knew she'd felt it, too.

"To new friends?" he offered, though he only had a vague sense of what a friend was.

Resisting the urge to touch her again – but just barely – he raised the fruit to his mouth and took a bite, its juice running down his chin. Its skin was crisp, but it was soft inside, and it washed over his tongue with a foreign, overpowering sweetness. She brought hers to her mouth, but did not bite it, watching him swallow.

"What else can demons do that others cannot?" she asked.

Morthanion bit off another chunk of the fruit, chewing it thoughtfully. He wasn't sure that he liked it.

"Anything we want to," he replied, his brows falling low as he felt a tingling start on the surface of his tongue. It spread, very slowly, radiating out toward his limbs. He blinked, trying to shake off the sensation. "Are you not hungry?"

Slowly, she lowered the fruit from her lips, its skin unbroken.

He locked gazes with her, his own heartbeat growing loud in his ears. This was why she hadn't run.

"I am sorry," she said desperately, backing away from him. As his body began to go numb, the only strong feeling remaining was the fiery rage welling inside of him, sparked by her betrayal, even though her expression told him she was, indeed, sorry. He'd let himself get tricked by this girl. This sheltered girl.

He grabbed her wrist, raising a foot that felt as heavy as a pillar of stone. She pulled away, and he could not muster enough strength in his hand to prevent her arm from slipping out of his grasp. It set him to stumbling forward, his feet hitting the ground hard as he fought to maintain his balance.

Aria turned and ran. Morthanion willed his body onward, straining for the speed he had known all his life and achieving none of it. A soft laugh escaped him; he laughed at himself, at the world, at life, and the gods.

Bested by a slip of a girl! She grew only more fascinating each time he encountered her.

He didn't know how far he chased her. Moving so sluggishly, each step felt like an eternity. It may only have been ten or twenty feet when his knees gave out. He reeled forward, shoulder slamming into the trunk of a tree. His body slid down it, legs crumpled beneath him, ultimately tipping backwards to land face-up.

The canopy was thick overhead, with little specks of starlight shining through. Strange animals called elsewhere, and alien insects chirruped. The nearby stream trickled softly. Not far, the foliage rustled, the sound drawing cautiously closer.

Aria leaned into his view, frowning down at him. She stepped away, and more plants rustled, stalks snapping. When she returned, she was dragging a pile of large leaves. There was apology in her eyes as she settled it over him. She'd managed to incapacitate him, and instead of capitalizing on his helplessness, she was *hiding* him? Everything he'd known over the long millennia of his life could not help him understand this simple action.

"I will find you," he whispered, the words slurring through numbed lips, "no matter where you run."

She flinched before she dropped the leaves over his face. He listened to her footfalls fade as she ran, until he couldn't hear them anymore. That sweet scent of hers lingered for a little longer before it, too, fled.

Every fiber of his will was driving him to go after her, to turn onto his belly and crawl if he had to. He hadn't claimed her yet, and now she was once again without his protection. But his limbs refused to respond. She'd deceived him, and he'd ignored the obvious signs. Just like the mages had done, she'd rendered him helpless, taken away the gifts that he was born with.

Time lost meaning, and drifted past unnoticed. The stars shifted overhead in their slow dance, some vanishing behind the cover of the leaves while others slowly peeked through other gaps in the canopy.

Voices drifted to him through the trees, and soon footsteps accompanied them, all growing steadily louder. There were at least three of them, by the sound of it, and their footsteps slowed when they drew near.

Morthanion's heart thundered. He would not be killed like this, especially not by mortals.

"What's this?" The demon could hear someone splash into the water. "It would seem someone dropped a water skin."

"A trap?"

"Not likely," replied the first.

"Don't touch those!" the second said.

"I'm hungry," a third grumbled.

"Eat those, and you'll be helpless. Then I might just kill you myself."

There was another growl, and the scuffling of feet. Morthanion could do nothing but wait.

"Looks like someone was fool enough to eat it already," the first man said, interrupting whatever fight had been about to erupt. "See here? Probably ate some, dropped their water when they went down, and then got dragged off by some night prowler."

Leaves rustled as one of them drew nearer to where Morthanion lay. He tried to move, but could manage only a slight flex of his fingers.

"Someone ran away from here," Tracker said, very close now. "They were fleeing something."

Morthanion could feel his body tensing. He could not let them go after her. There were very few things that men on this island would be interested in, and he'd allow none of those to befall Aria. She was *his*. A sensation like thousands of hot, stabbing needles spread across his skin, but his limbs were still too heavy to move.

"An animal most likely, or maybe some of those cannibals that've been creeping about." There was a loud slap. "I told you no!" Bossy spat.

Hungry growled again. "Bugger off."

"Fine. Eat it, and we'll see if anything's interested in eating you."

The demon could sense the nearness of Tracker, could almost feel the man's eyes scanning his immediate surroundings.

"Come," Bossy ordered. "We're not following that trail tonight. Back to camp. He expects word from us come sun up."

Tracker hesitated. Morthanion clenched his jaw, still slowly regaining feeling and control, his mouth dry as the sands of the Hemrisk.

Finally, the three started walking again, back in the direction they'd come from. The demon eased somewhat, exhaling through his teeth. He'd have to find them when he was able to move. They had her water skin, and she would need it back. She could have left him exposed, left him to die, but she'd come back to hide him. Why? He managed to curl his hands into fists, and smiled. She was an enigmatic little woman, and he would find her and puzzle her out. He had no doubts about that.

Chapter Four

Dark clouds had swept in with the setting sun, leaving the night darker than any since Morthanion's arrival on the island. The shadows could not hinder his vision, but rather settled a comfortable shroud over him. They were familiar. Still, they did little to ease his frustrations.

He moved down the length of the beach, sticking to the darkness that gathered around the tree line, and watched the water. Aria was hiding out there somewhere, evading him, an affront to everything he was, everything he'd seen and done. For two days he'd sought sign of her. He'd picked up traces of her scent, but they had been faint and fleeting. For all he knew, it was just part of the island's aroma. It was becoming enough to almost make him doubt her existence again.

The clarity of his memory told him she was real. Up close, her fragrance had made his blood quicken, and the thrill that had run through him at her touch had been too intense to have been a figment of his imagination.

There was the water skin, too. He dropped a hand to it, running the tips of his fingers over its tight-stretched but uneven surface. He'd spared the men that had taken it, unwilling to draw any more attention to himself, but the vessel had been physical proof that she was real. She had dropped it at the stream, and they'd found it. Could he have imagined that?

Breaking into a run, he spread his wings and sent himself airborne, invisible against the dark sky. The joy of flying never faded for him, but it was overpowered by his need to locate this woman.

The air was cool, in stark contrast to the impotent fire in his blood. Below, the waves rolled endlessly ashore and then back again, churning around the rocks he'd chased her to that first night. When she had been hurt, he'd offered her his hand. Had she taken it, he would have protected her. Instead, she'd ducked beneath the surface and fled him like he'd been the one to harm her.

In the jungle, he'd gone to pains to be civil and soothing. He had fetched the fruit for her like he was some servant, so blinded by his craving for her that he fell easily into her trap. She'd made a fool of him.

He, who had flown wing-to-wing with the most powerful, terrible beings the world had ever known, who had burned cities and toppled kingdoms, had been bested by a girl who'd never left this gods-forsaken island.

And where was his rage? Where was his fire? He should be furious with Aria, should be seeking her to inflict punishment.

All he could find was anger for letting himself be tricked by her, for allowing her to escape him twice. *Not again*. There would be no more civility. It was time he took what he wanted, just as he always had.

He inhaled deeply the salty night air and closed his eyes as something tingled up his spine and radiated out to the surface of his skin. It was *her*, he knew. The instinct guided him, urged him to find her, to claim her. She was close.

Following the sensation, he turned for a large, rocky outcropping, tucking his wings against his back and dropping rapidly. He landed atop the stone, perching at the edge and casting his gaze out into the water. Sea spray splashed up around him, but he ignored it, listening for anything beyond the regular din of the waves, anything within it that seemed out of place. Could he detect just a hint of her scent on the air? Concentrating, he reached out with that new sense, feeling for her. The tingling grew stronger, focusing at the base of his skull.

Slowly, he became aware of a sound that was not quite in rhythm with the ocean's, just irregular enough to rouse his suspicion. He turned his head in its direction, narrowing his eyes.

It was her. Even with his excellent night vision, he might not have spotted her if her passage had been silent. Only her head was exposed, dark hair against dark water. It was the pale skin of her face that gave her away, and the occasional flash of a slender arm breaking the surface.

He pumped his wings, positioning himself directly above her, that sensation pulsing through him urgently. *Take her*, it said, *she is yours!*

Gliding on the wind, he tipped to one side and circled slowly. It would accomplish nothing to go after her now. He clenched his teeth against the instinct, which was winding tightly through his insides and fanning the flames in his blood. She would easily escape again so long as she was in the water. Aria was too fast there, and could go under for too long.

He'd have to wait until she went as far inland as she dared, and then pounce. From there he would...he would figure it out. He wanted to hate her, wanted to rage at her, to make her suffer. Wanted to use her to vent all the frustrations and fury he'd amassed in the last week.

But he wanted to coax a smile to her face and taste the sea on her lips far more.

She swam to the shore and walked onto the beach, leaving dark footprints behind her that were soon erased by the surf. As she hurried across the sand, he glided back to the ground, a hand on the bulging water skin at his belt to keep it from making any noise that would alert her.

Wherever it was that she hid all the time, she had to return to this area for supplies quite regularly. Fresh water, in particular, if the bladder tied at her own waist was any indication.

Aria slowed when she came to the forest, and Morthanion followed her silently, making sure to keep back while she cautiously navigated the boughs, twisted roots, and thick undergrowth. He couldn't suppress a bit of admiration for her; she had come ashore in a different place, and was walking a completely different path through the trees than she had the other night. Though evidence of her passing might later be found, there would be no indication that she came through here regularly.

She stopped at the edge of the stream and dropped to her knees. Morthanion halted ten paces behind her. Around them, insects made their strange calls, and the canopy sighed in the breeze. Immediately, she cupped her hands and filled them with water. She drank deeply, having to catch her breath between each mouthful.

He watched with interest, noting the way she drank. Had she been without since their last meeting? She behaved more like she'd just crossed a desert than come ashore from a swim.

After several more handfuls of water, she removed the water skin from her waist and dunked it in the stream, remaining still while it filled. He waited until she was tying it back in place before he took the other into his hand.

"I believe this is yours," he said.

She jumped and spun, and his lips tilted in a half smile. There was something amusing about the situation.

Her eyes were wide, their whites standing out starkly against the dark hair that hung about her face. All humor fled him. He liked the look of fear upon her face less and less every time he saw it. Hated how familiar it was becoming.

She glanced quickly to either side, as though searching for an escape, and then looked to the water skin in his hand. He tossed it to her, and her slender-fingered hands darted up to catch it. Quick reflexes, even with that fear clear in her eyes. He could admire that.

"You played a dirty trick on me," he said, and forced the lopsided smile back into place.

"Did you poison this to get back at me?" she asked, her hands still raised with the water skin between them. Her eyes narrowed as she regarded him warily.

"Why bother with poison?" he replied, casually, though it had been one of his more immediate ideas after what she'd done. It had been followed by a sudden, jarring repulsion that he could not explain. "I don't need to do anything so subtle or underhanded if I want to exact revenge upon you, do I?"

She didn't say anything, didn't pry her gaze from his. But he saw her hands tighten infinitesimally on the container.

"We each have our own problems, Aria," he said, trying to sound warm and friendly. "I need a safe place to rest my head. You are constantly risking yourself to gather the supplies you need to survive. I think we're in a unique position to help one another, don't you?"

"And once I show you the place I hide, you will not need my help anymore."

"Come, now. I'm a man of my word." He smiled again, but this time it actually touched his eyes. His gaze roamed up and down her lithe form, drinking it in like she had the water – thirstily, insatiably. "When I need to be."

Aria shrank back from him. Morthanion's smile plunged and his brows furrowed. Why was she so on-edge, so frightened around him? He was playing nice. At least, as nicely as he knew how. He hadn't yet done anything to harm her, wasn't that enough to start building some trust?

"I won't hurt you," he said.

"Because you are waiting. You have yet to discover where my safe place is."

"It's only a matter of time. I'm offering you something in return for the inevitable. I doubt any of your other neighbors would do the same."

She studied him for a time, her brow knit with thought. He was making some progress. He had to be. How could this girl resist? Resist again, anyway. For a moment, her eyes shifted away, toward the jungle around them.

"It's a lot to think over, I know." Some distant part of his mind said that he was supposed to be angry with her, but he found himself having trouble remembering why. He was more proud of her than anything. Impressed, even. Perhaps he'd played into an obvious ruse – one that he would have seen through easily, had he not been so distracted by her – but she'd pulled it off, one way or another.

"Consider the alternatives," he continued. "You're out one night, looking for food, and as you cross into the woods a group of men set upon you. While you're all alone. They have spears, knives, and...appetites." A ball of fire sparked in his gut at the thought of that. Men like the spearman finding her and sating their lusts.

The demon's claws extended, and he balled his hands into fists to hide them from her. *Don't frighten her anymore.*

"I have your word that you will not harm me?" she asked carefully.

Morthanion dipped his head in a nod. "Yes." His heart skipped. She was seriously considering it.

Her gaze was strangely weighty, and the silence that stretched between them felt thick. For millennia, he'd faced down enemies on battlefields and in alleyways, on rooftops and in dank caves. But never had their assessing stares fallen upon him with so much force as hers did in that moment.

Finally, she nodded, and dropped her attention to her waist. She tied the second water skin beside the first. That done, she started walking, glancing at him for a fleeting moment before she passed, heading back toward the beach. He watched her progress as she went, and then fell into step behind her.

She carefully picked her way through the undergrowth, the demon crossing the same terrain with little effort.

"You said you've been here all your life," he said when they were about halfway to the beach. "How long is that?"

Aria paused, pressing a hand to the trunk of a tree and peering around it. He thought he heard her counting under her breath, but it could easily have been the wind, or some as-yet unidentified wildlife.

"Twenty-two years," she finally replied.

The demon's mouth fell open, and a moment later a disbelieving laugh spilled out. Twenty-two years old? He'd thought her young, but she was a child!

She twisted to look at him, her brows low over her eyes. "Why do you laugh?"

"There's a bit of an age gap between the two of us, is all," he replied, after he'd managed to cease his laughter. Twenty-two years was impressive for a girl alone on an island to have remained hidden. But it was nothing in the grand scheme of life. To him, it was the space between heartbeats.

Her eyes narrowed, and he wondered if she was already reconsidering. A moment later, she started walking again, and he followed. When they reached the edge of the trees, she fell into a crouch, and he followed her gaze to a point of light down the beach. She watched it, a concerned look on her face.

"Two men at a camp fire," he said. "They're too preoccupied to notice us."

"How do you know this?" she asked, incredulous.

"Because I can see them passing around a jug."

"You can see that?"

"You can't?"

"All I see is the light from the fire," she replied.

He'd guessed at the way she had moved through the forest that her vision at night was poor, as was that of most mortals. But that didn't mean she was one, necessarily.

She opened her mouth as though she were about to ask him more, but pressed her lips together instead. He trailed her as she crossed the sand to the cover of the rocks, shielding them from the distant fire. His muscles tensed as they neared the surf. As much as the smell of the ocean was starting to remind him of her, he hadn't forgotten how easily she could escape here.

"You will be flying?" she asked.

Morthanion turned his head, scanning the curving beach that stretched away from the campfire to the north. There was no other sign of life. With a faint rustle of feathers, he brought forth his wings in answer to her question. It was dark enough tonight that he'd be effectively invisible to most onlookers.

He watched her eyes flicker to the wings for an instant before she turned and walked into the sea. She waded out, seemingly unaffected by the tide, and dove in when the water reached her waist. Her head popped up several yards ahead a few moments later, and she began to swim away from the shore.

The demon took to the air and followed. Every time she dipped beneath the surface, his breath caught in his throat and his muscles tensed. Would she come up, or would she vanish again? That tingling had begun at the back of his neck once more, and he found his eyes tracing her progress instinctually, even when she was out of his sight. She wouldn't be able to flee him any longer.

She was *his*.

Aria swam northwest, disappearing under waves when she neared the various rocks that jutted from the sea like the abandoned spines of a massive dragon. Each time, she'd reemerge well clear of them, pushing onward as though the water offered her no resistance.

They were approaching a rocky cape whose cliffs dropped from its peak sharply into the water some forty feet below. Shaggy grass and low, thick bushes clung to the top of the promontory, moving ceaselessly in the wind. Farther back stood a single tree, towering over the smaller vegetation.

He circled the tip of the rock formation as she made her way around it. On the west face, she swam toward the cliffs. He saw her pull herself up, and then she vanished into the rock.

Morthanion flew clear of the cliffs, shifting his wings to turn wide over the sea. Once he was facing the rock again, he sped forward, arms at his sides as he dropped steadily lower. He didn't notice the cave in the cliff side until he was ten or fifteen feet over the water. It had been hidden from above by a bulge in the rock that overhung the opening, and the cliff ran out just a little further into the ocean to either side of it. One would have to be facing it head-on — be out in open water — to see it at all.

Keeping low, he angled toward the cave, waves flitting by below him with exhilarating speed. When he neared the entrance, he spread his wings, tilting back to angle himself vertically. He caught hold of the rock overhead, claws scraping against it, and swung his legs up to fully halt his momentum with his feet on the bottom of the opening.

Beneath the strong smell of sea and stone, the place was sweet with her fragrance. He inhaled it deeply and then looked over his shoulder. Gray water stretched as far as he could see, darkening as it raced toward the horizon. What rocks rose above the surface were jagged and unwelcoming. She was indeed well hidden here.

He released his grip on the rock with one hand, shielding his eyes from the light of the small fire she'd started as he ducked his head to enter the cave. Moments later, vision adjusted to the relative brightness, he swept his gaze around the chamber.

"Marvelous," he said. "Home, sweet home." He favored her with a grin before he started to move about the cave, examining the eclectic collection of items she had within it.

There were dozens of treasures from the sea – agates and shells of all types, driftwood worn gray by time and salty waters, a few rust-laden tools, milky-glassed bottles and bits of fraying rope and netting. There were cruder instruments as well, most consisting of stones chipped sharp and tied to wooden handles. A few precious bits of flint, sparkling now in the fire's light, and a scrap of steel. Even some simple baskets and mats woven of what appeared to be the same sort of grass that clung to the cape so desperately.

"You still haven't told me what you are," he said, lifting one of the trinkets. Seemingly delicate netting strung together a number of pearls in a loop, perfect for a dainty wrist like Aria's. Their colors shifted and swirled slightly as his hand moved, white to pink to blue-green.

"Laudine said that was my mother's," Aria said. "Please be careful with it."

Chapter Five

Aria watched him replace the bracelet as though it would shatter if he moved too quickly, and she breathed out a relieved sigh. It touched her that he could care for something she treasured. Would so dangerous a man bother being gentle with something so frivolous?

She possessed few of her parent's belongings, things that Laudine had rescued when Aria had been just a babe. The rest were objects they had found washed up on the beach. All that remained of Xani and Jasper were Laudine's stories and a few trinkets the older woman had believed to be crafted by Xani's people.

"And what was your mother, Aria?"

"Why is it so important that you know what I am?" she asked.

She met his eyes as he looked at her over his shoulder. Even in the light of the fire, they seemed to dance with their own heat.

"It's not. I am simply curious."

Aria tilted her head and narrowed her eyes. She didn't entirely believe him, but decided not to contest it. Moving to her supplies, she untied the water skins from her waist and added them to the dwindling stock. She glanced at him again; he was still studying her belongings. It was strange having him here. A man. No, a *demon*...but what was the difference?

The light played upon his golden skin, giving him a subtle, warm glow. His hair was thick, lush and dark, hanging nearly to his waist. He was at least half a foot taller than her, with broad shoulders that tapered to narrow hips. Sharply angled eyebrows tilted down toward the bridge of his nose, and the shadow of a beard on his cheeks accentuated his high cheekbones.

Above all, it was his wings that drew her attention. Out in the night, they had been little more than vague, black shapes, but in the light she could make out individual feathers. Each of them reflected a little bit of the fire's glow, giving back sheens of blue and green. It reminded her of the shifting colors on the inside of a seashell. Shadows danced along their surface, through the tiny spaces between them, even to drift off into the air, where they soon dissipated.

"Do you even *know* what you are?" Morthanion asked. He faced her fully, his curiosity unmasked.

"Of course," she said, a small frown touching her lips. She knew well enough, she thought, though she didn't know what it meant. Most of what she could do, she'd discovered by accident, and that only recently.

"Sometimes," he began, resuming his slow trip around the chamber and regarding each item as though they were priceless treasures, "there are young demons – and I imagine it happens to angels, too – who grow up never really knowing what they are. Having strange feelings, discovering terrible powers. Usually, it is because their parents are slain by hunters. Is your situation similar?"

Aria remained silent, watching him pick up a bottle whose glass was clouded by untold years at sea. He turned it in his hand, and when it was clear she wasn't going to answer, he glanced up at her.

"I suppose it likely is. I can understand if you don't want to share. I am, after all, a stranger. Quite a dangerous one, really – at least to others. But I like you." He flashed his white teeth.

"You do not know me." How could he pretend to like her after what she'd done? That fruit could have been far more dangerous for all he'd known, and he could have been killed while he was paralyzed and vulnerable in the jungle. When he'd come up behind her by the stream tonight, she'd been sure he was going to kill her.

"Do you plan on making me dislike you?"

"Considering you now know where I live, it would be a mistake to do so."

"So why worry, then? I like you even knowing so little of you. I don't say that about many people, as I'm sure you can imagine."

Aria stepped toward the driftwood bench set near the fire, water still dripping from her wet clothes down her bare legs. She brushed her fingers over the rough wood. "My father was a prisoner here."

"But not your mother?" he said, looking at her fingertips.

"No." She stepped around the bench and sat down.

"And how could you possibly think that you are not a person of interest?" he said, folding his arms casually across his chest and leaning back against the wall. "Rather than subject you to the depravity of civilization, your parents chose to stay here."

"You can only leave if you are not marked."

Darkness flickered over his face, his eyes dipping to the back of his hand, before he grinned again. "We must be a thousand miles from the mainland out here. A long way to swim, anyway."

Aria lowered her gaze and nodded, fiddling with the array of items stacked beside her on the bench. Scraps of cloth and fur, mostly. Clothing that hadn't been finished.

Silence stretched between them, and she chanced a look at him again. His head was tilted to the side, an odd expression on his face. While he still made her nervous, he intrigued her. She'd managed to keep hidden from all the other islanders for her entire life, but Morthanion kept finding her, and even after her deception, he hadn't harmed her.

"Where are you from?" she asked.

"It is called Argosia by the humans, but it had many other names before that. There are cities of stone and tens of thousands of people, and most can get by without foraging or hunting to eat."

"Cities made of stone?" She tried to picture that, putting it together with the stories Laudine had told her. "Giant buildings that people called homes?"

"Yes, where most mortals have the misfortune of living with their immediate relatives. In small spaces. For most of them, it doesn't seem terribly comfortable."

"Stone is not comfortable," she agreed, her toe brushing against the floor of the cave. If not for the furs, she would likely get little sleep.

Aria's gaze returned to Morthanion when he chuckled, a deep, rich sound full of humor, and her mouth quirked.

His squared jaw belied the soft fullness of his lips. Aria had never stood so close to anyone apart from Laudine, and Morthanion was so strikingly different from her, both in form and face, that she was captivated. He was...beautiful.

"They sleep in beds, usually, stuffed with straw. Somewhat softer than stone, but not any cleaner. Really, cities are filthy places. I don't know how they manage to get more dirt into them than there is out in the wilds, but they do. And the smell..."

His attention wavered, his eyes on the fire, his expression distant.

"The smell?" she nudged, wanting to hear more. Laudine had always described cities as wondrous places with something new to inspire awe around every turn. Morthanion's description was bleak, but somehow only made the pictures Aria already had in her head more real.

Her voice seemed to break him out of his reverie. "Not really a smell you want described to you, I can assure you."

"Is it terrible then?"

"In Delimas, it is human waste, rotting fish, sweat, a thousand different spices that should never be blended together, rancid meat and rotten vegetables, tepid water, and stale ale. Amongst other things. The humans don't seem to notice much."

Aria tilted her head as she listened, detecting the disgust in his voice. She knew the stench of rotting fish and rancid meat, but not of stale ale or spices.

She gathered enough courage to finally ask him the one question that she was most curious about. The one she dreaded. "Why are you here?"

"Because I have many enemies."

"What did you *do* to be sent here?"

"If I tell you that, you might not like me anymore."

"I never said that I did," Aria blurted and bit down on the inside of her lip, fearful that she'd anger him. All he did was frown, and the expression somehow told her that he didn't like her answer for another reason all together.

He was quiet for a time before he finally spoke. "Most recently, I burned down a village in the countryside."

Aria stared at him, his words slow to register. She'd never seen a village, and had to search her memory to recall what Laudine had said. "Why?" she asked, the question spilling out with her exhalation.

Morthanion sighed softly, letting his gaze drift to the jagged roof of the cavern. "Ah, why? That is a question my kind is always asked. Why must an angel seek justice and goodness? Why is a fire hot? Why does a goblin devour the flesh of anything that moves? Things are as they are, and what more can be said about the world? The people of the village didn't want me there. They summoned hunters. I retaliated, as was my nature."

Aria listened, though his response only raised more questions. His answer, essentially, was *because*, and that didn't make it right. "They feared you. So in turn, you killed them. If you are so easily moved to violence, why *would* they want you there? You killed their families. Innocents. Were not their reasons just?"

"I am what I am, Aria. Demons are spawned of the shadow, just as angels are of the light." He brought his hand up and waved it through the air as if brushing the matter aside. "I've long since lost count of the lives taken by my hands."

This only made Aria warier of him, of having shown him her home, her safe place. She wondered if she had judged poorly. He'd killed more people than she'd ever even seen, and waved it off like none of it mattered?

"What is shadow?" She raised her hand, looking to the shadow of it on the cave wall. "That which light does not touch? That does not make it evil. It is cast by light, which you claim is a force of good. But that claim is just as ignorant." Bending her fingers, she turned the shadow into a long-eared rabbit. "The light of this fire can sustain life or consume it, just as shadow can provide fear, or joy. You choose what you are, you are not born to it."

"Mmm, I could say that your own statement is naïve, and very much the words of a young mortal." Head tilted, brow furrowed, he glanced at her shadow. Then he pushed himself away from the wall. "Part of you, I suspect, is driven by needs and desires that are not necessarily your own, yet sometimes you are compelled to follow them. Have you ever simply needed to…swim? To feel the water around you? To see how deep or how long you could go under?"

"I do not feel compelled to kill. That is a choice, and feeling the urge to do it does not make it right."

"You didn't answer my question," he chided. "Does that urge ever overcome you? To get into the water?"

"You seek answers about what I am, and I am not ready to give them."

"No, I seek to make a point to you. Everyone — even humans — is controlled by internal needs that they cannot change. Instinct. In some beings, instinct and nature are amplified, are even more in control."

Aria rose from the bench, her movements casual as she stepped toward the cave's mouth. Water lapped against the cliff below. "When you kill, what do you feel?"

"Most recently? Pride." His shoulders went back and his chin lifted. "Because killing him meant he couldn't hurt you again."

"What did you feel when you burned that village? Full of women and children, people who committed no wrong save being afraid?"

"It reminded me of days long past. The thrill of battle, of the power we once had and should still."

"That does not answer my question."

"Maybe not," he smiled lopsidedly.

"You felt joy then? In the screams as they burned?"

"Do you feel joy when you are swimming?"

Aria could tell he wasn't guessing about what she was anymore. He was seeking confirmation of what he already knew. She'd been right – she had judged poorly. He had enjoyed killing innocents, displaying no remorse, no guilt. What was to stop him from hurting her? He was the same as the other prisoners on the island, the ones who'd killed her parents. The ones who would have killed her, if not for Laudine. She had thought, even hoped, he was like her father. Laudine had always spoken of how Jasper's bitterness and hatred had melted away in his love for Xani.

She cast him one more glance, and she saw the flicker of realization in his eyes. He started toward her right before she stepped off the edge, dropping into the water. She maneuvered around the jagged rocks easily, pushing off with her feet and swimming straight out into the sea. Aria remained beneath for as long as she could before coming up. She just had to make it to the rocks farther out.

When a large wave moved toward her, she dove back under, kicking hard. She knew he followed, knew his anger would be great. That fear of him propelled her, pushed her further and faster. This time, she didn't emerge until she reached her goal, taking hold of the stone to anchor herself in the bobbing water. She turned. Even in the black of night, she could see the darker shadow moving quickly toward her.

Morthanion told himself she wasn't edging toward the opening in order to flee. She'd brought him to her sanctuary, after all. Why would she run now? He doubted she had anywhere as secure as this place to go. He'd won. All that remained was to claim his prize, as the instincts raging within him demanded.

But that look in her eyes said that he was wrong. He hadn't won her over yet, hadn't earned her trust. Fast as he was, she had already hit the water before he even reached the edge of the cave. Fires roared inside of him. How dare she run again? Back out there, where she was constantly in danger, where others might attempt to take her.

His shroud fell away completely as he dove into the water, shadows roiling around him like black flames. Kicking up to the surface, he growled. She was below again. He turned, swimming back to the cliff face, and slammed his claws into the stone. Dragging himself up several feet over the waterline, he twisted, scanning the waves. That tingling sensation was back at the base of his neck, retreating a little more with each lost moment.

It was not a matter of her not trusting him. *He'd* trusted *her* too much, given her too much space. Rather than studying her trinkets, he should have kept himself between Aria and the exit. He should have watched her more closely.

Finally, the demon caught a fleeting glimpse of her as she broke the surface, diving back beneath a rising wave an instant later. She was already a hundred yards out, at least, moving toward a group of rocks.

Morthanion pushed off the cliff side with all his strength, fangs bared, and flew straight toward her. She reached her destination, her head and shoulders rising from the water as she placed a hand on the stone and turned to face him. Did she think that she'd be safe there? That a rock would somehow protect her? Maybe she'd finally admitted to herself what she must already have known – there would be no escape from him.

This time, he wouldn't deny the need to claim her. She was his, by all the gods, and he would have her! No more games, no more opportunity for her to flee. He'd bind her to him right there on her little rock.

Aria didn't move as the distance between them dwindled, save for with the gentle rise and fall of the water.

"You cannot run from me!" he shouted.

Her expression remained calm, startlingly so. Where was the fear she so often wore when he came for her? Something was wrong.

The demon drew his wings in, diving directly toward her. She simply watched, eyes meeting his without wavering.

The world lurched, everything around him blurring and warping. His stomach twisted and sank, and pain flared on his hand. Suddenly, sand was in his face and beneath his prone body.

He pushed his chest off the ground, gritting his teeth against the wave of dizziness and nausea that threatened to overcome him. Looking down, he could see the mark on the back of his hand glowing as though it had just been burned there.

Wiping grit from his cheek, he got to his feet, stumbling in the shifting sand. He turned around fully. Dark water lapped at the beach, thick trees rustled in the breeze a few dozen yards away. But there was no craggy promontory, no rocky teeth jutting up from the water off the shoreline.

No tingling at the base of his skull.

His chest swelled as he drew in breath. He'd been bested by her again. Denied what was his. Now, his mate – she could be nothing else to him – was unprotected, somewhere else on the island. Unable to hold it in any longer, he released an animalistic howl of rage that echoed through the heavens.

Chapter Six

Morthanion watched the water from his cliff top perch, wrapped in shadow. He'd been watching for hours. The moon had risen some time after nightfall, and was past its zenith now. His teeth were clenched tightly enough that they might shatter, and his claws were scraping deep grooves in the rock below. He'd not seen or felt any sign of Aria in two days, and his patience was beyond its limits.

His fury had carried him into the invisible barrier nearly a dozen more times after the first. No matter where he tried, he hit that wall approximately a hundred yards from the shore. Every time, the containment magic plucked him forcibly through space to a random point on the island – he'd seen enough of it now to know there was only water on all sides, stretching endlessly to every horizon.

That the place might have been a thousand miles from his homeland in Argosia – and from the plains where the mages had taken him, from the whole damned continent of Talikar – was frustrating enough. But distance would not contain him. The magical field was another matter entirely. It was no mere containment spell, no – that would have been too simple, too mundane for the mages.

Instead, they'd woven magic he'd not even known possible around the island. It usually took the collective effort of several mages to teleport a single person just once, and often left the casters drained. He could not imagine how they'd managed to wrap an entire island in that sort of power.

He had an idea of what this place was. He'd heard of it, at some point in his long life, and tucked the information away in the recesses of his memory as unimportant. They'd have to catch him to send him there, and that would never happen.

He snorted in disgust and his claws gouged deeper into the rock.

The Isle of the Forgotten.

That's what most people called it. A magical prison crafted by the Mage Councils as their power and dominance began to wither. An inescapable holding cell for the most dangerous beings that walked the world. There were only rumors, some whispered in fear, others with laughter. Surely, it was a foolish jest. It was impossible.

They'd sent him here, to the Isle of the Forgotten, as though he were no better than the humans and elves and other mortal filth that infested the place like rats. They'd sent him here, stripped of his power, and he was being made fool of by a girl not yet a quarter of a century old.

The brand on his hand had been smoking after his last attempt to pass the barrier, the flesh audibly sizzling, the pain an irritant. Still, it had been the rising sun that made him stop. The growing light on the horizon only irritated him further.

It was simply a matter of time before he found a way through the barrier. Finding Aria had delayed his escape, not stopped it. Had given him enough of a distraction to let his anger settle, to clear his head. Once he had her, he could turn his focus to finding a way back to the mainland.

He'd searched the next night for Aria, finally discovering familiar landmarks that guided him back to the section of the island where she lived. Near her cave, there'd only been her lingering scent to tease him and remind him of his failures.

Now, there were no animal calls, no insect night-songs. There was only the soft hiss of grass blades in the breeze and the airy sighing of the ocean, taunting him. *I have her always*, it said to him, *and you never will.*

The demon had gone into the cave only once since he returned to the promontory, and stood in its darkness, letting shadows slide over his skin. Even that was tainted, however. The air was thick and stifling in her absence, too, as though the place missed the woman who had called it home. He allowed himself a cursory search and left.

"She's not going to come back here," he said aloud as his eyes scanned the waves. "Aria is too cunning for that."

There was no choice but to find her. No matter how long it took, he would scour the island until he did. She was in too much danger now, was too vulnerable. And there were more prisoners here than he'd thought.

No, he would find her because he was angry at her. He had to be. She'd duped him. Worse, she had told him she wouldn't run, and then done so at the first opportunity. Finding her was necessary to punish her for betraying his trust.

Morthanion leapt off the cliff, spreading his wings to catch the wind.

He couldn't lie to himself for much longer. The thought of her duplicity was not what made the fires ignite in his chest. No, the only fires she lit were at the thought of her soft, pale skin, and her long, dark hair. The sweet caress of her voice drifting on the salty breeze. The flare of her hips, and the allure of her thighs.

She was unprotected, and that knowledge had hardened into a ball of molten lead inside him, leaving his breath short and his heartbeat rapid. He pushed himself higher, surveying as much of the island he could see. There were probably other caves along the shore, but he guessed that if she'd known of them, she wouldn't have had so much in the one she'd led him to. He'd never had a home, but he knew instinctively that cave had been hers.

Far off on a twilit strand of sand he could make out the flicker of a fire. He knew she was skilled at remaining out of sight, but there was still a chance that someone had seen her. Morthanion had always possessed a talent for persuasion, and he would gladly put it to use if it meant finding her more quickly.

Aria couldn't go back. How naïve she had been. How weak-willed and desperate to have trusted such a dangerous man and brought him to her sanctuary. Her home. Because of her poor judgment, she had been forced to abandon the only piece of the island that had been hers.

She drifted along what she thought was the invisible barrier that Laudine had once explained to her, coming ashore for brief periods of rest. She was thirsty and hungry despite the few clams she'd found, but she didn't dare go inland.

As she got farther from home, she began to see more signs of other inhabitants. There were charred remains of camp fires here and there on the beach, and she even saw a group of three men walking from the sand toward the jungle. She remained as low in the water as she could. When she did sleep, it was fitful. Morthanion was looking for her, she knew, but he wasn't the only person she was trying to avoid.

On the second day, the landscape was different from anything she'd seen before. The beach gave way not to jungle, but to grassy hills that blocked her view of anything beyond them, and the trees were scattered. The vegetation shimmered as it swayed in the wind. Tired and hungry, she was dismayed that there was no shelter in sight. She pressed on.

It wasn't until the moon was high that the coast began to grow rockier, resembling the area around her home. Her body had protested for hours, and she knew she had to find food and fresh water soon. Here, at least, she would have some cover as she went searching.

Aria swam toward the shore, riding the tide to conserve energy. Reluctant to leave the sea, she remained in it until she was almost crawling on her belly in the sand.

She'd always felt heavier, slower, when she got out of the water, but now it felt like there were stones tied to her limbs, dragging her down. As she moved along the rocks, she kept a hand on their irregular surface to steady herself.

An orange glow illuminated the sand ahead of her, bright and alluring.

But it was the smell that moved her closer. She walked slowly, peering around the rock formation.

A fire flickered and crackled in a neat ring on the sand, and the mouth-watering aroma was coming from fish sizzling on spits. Her stomach growled. She covered it with her hand as though that would silence it.

Her eyes drifted away from the fish – reluctantly – toward the two men seated nearby. Their clothes were in a fashion she'd never seen. Dried hides covered their torsos, leaving their arms bare. The garments had laces in the front, but these were loose enough to expose their chests, one of which was covered with dark hair. On one of the men's shoulders was the same mark she'd seen on Laudine and Morthanion. Their leggings were of similar material to their tops, and each had knives on their belts made from either stone or bone.

The men were speaking to each other, their voices too low for her to make out. The larger of the two, the one with the hairy chest, gestured sharply, his voice rising. The thinner one smirked before he replied.

Aria moved closer to the edge of her cover, wanting a better look at them. Apart from Morthanion, she'd never seen any of the other prisoners up close. They were males, like the demon, but there were few other similarities. The larger of these two had a thick chest and burly arms. She knew Morthanion was strong, but there was a leanness to him that made his power surprising. This man's build hid nothing.

The other man, while not much shorter, was lithe and willowy. His ears were not rounded like Aria's, but tapered up to a point. She leaned forward, taking one more step to study them closer.

Suddenly, the big man twisted toward her, his arm moving in a blur. A knife clattered against the rock just beside her head. Aria flinched with a gasp, her heart pounding. She looked down to the knife, which had fallen to the sand, and then back to the men. They were both standing now, staring at her. She pressed against the rock, and its uneven surface dug into her back and shoulders uncomfortably.

"Well, look at this!" the large one exclaimed. "Forgive the slight," he began, flashing her a grin and curling his fingers to beckon her closer, "but you must understand the risks. I am quite glad that I missed."

Aria looked at the human and his smile. It was…welcoming. His companion also smiled, though it was stranger, like he was keeping an amusing secret. Aria hesitated and her eyes flickered toward the water. She was about to run when the larger man spoke.

"Hungry? Or maybe a little thirsty?"

Aria looked back at him to see him lift a clay jug.

"Come, have a drink with us!" He again gestured for her to join them.

She stared at the jug and licked her dry lips with a tongue thickened by thirst.

"We've plenty of food," the slimmer man said, his words oddly accented.

Against her judgment – not that it had been doing her much good lately, anyway – she stepped toward them. Laudine's warnings faded into the background, her thoughts clouded by hunger and thirst.

"Here," the larger man approached, offering her the jug.

Aria stiffened. Her instinct still told her to run for the ocean, but her feet remained where they were. Exhaustion and the gnawing emptiness inside her belly had taken their toll. She took the jug, smiled timidly, and drank.

The liquid sputtered out of her mouth and fell to the ground.

"What is it?" she asked, the overpowering taste lingering on her tongue. It was nothing like water at all.

The man laughed and shook his head. "Have you never had a proper draught before? Try again. Drink deeply this time." He placed a hand on her back and tilted the jug against her lips. "That's it, as much as you want."

Aria swallowed as much as she could stand before she pushed it away, coughing against the burn in the back of her throat. Her eyes watered and inhaled deeply. "What is it?" she asked again.

"The closest thing to a good, strong drink you can find on this island. What is your name, little one?"

"Aria," she said without hesitation, licking her lips and considering another sip. It set her throat on fire, and she'd never had anything like it, but she was acquiring a taste for it. Anything was better than the thirst she'd been suffering. "And yours?"

"Mikel Thatcher, at your service," he took her hand kissed her knuckles. "And my companion, Ithoriel." He gestured to the other man with a flourish that was almost comical, given his size.

"Ithoriel," Aria said and tilted her head. "Your ears are different."

The slimmer man — Ithoriel — chuckled low. "You have never seen an elf before?"

"No, never," she said, and then mumbled, "I find myself meeting a lot of new people recently."

Mikel and Ithoriel exchanged a brief glance.

"Drink," Mikel urged, again tilting the container. His eyes drifted over her. "Are you new to the island?"

"I have lived here my whole life," Aria said, wiping her mouth with the back of her hand.

"Really?" Mikel asked. One of Ithoriel's thin brows arched sharply.

"Yes," Aria said, nodding. "This is very good." She tilted the jug to peer into the opening, though it was too dark to see anything inside.

Mikel snickered. "How do you feel, Aria?"

How did she feel? Her skin was warm, and there was a gentle tingling over its surface. She felt relaxed. She smiled when she looked back up at them. "Very well."

The human placed his hand upon her shoulder and then slowly ran it down her arm to take hers. He raised it over her head, and guided her into a spin.

Aria couldn't hold in her laughter. The world blurred around her, her stomach fluttered, and the soft sand underfoot tickled her toes. It reminded her of when she was a child, twirling on the beach, so carefree, so young.

"It has been some time since I've enjoyed the company of a beautiful woman, especially one with such a musical voice. Do you sing?"

Aria nodded, her smile widening. "I love to sing! Would you like to hear?"

"We would," Ithoriel replied as he stepped back to sit by the fire.

"Take another sip to help your throat and sing away, lass!"

She took a long drink, loving the way it made her body feel so light. Hadn't she barely been able to drag herself out of the water not long ago? She passed the jug back to Mikel, who in turn gave it to the elf. Then she began to sing.

It was a ditty she had learned from Laudine, one that steadily increased tempo, growing more and more energetic with each verse. Soon, her body began to move, her feet prancing upon the sand as she spun and swayed and kicked with the song.

Mikel joined her. She grinned up at him, and he returned it as he stepped closer. They moved together, his hands occasionally touching — fingers brushing her hips, gliding over her lower back — but her movement prevented him from placing them anywhere else. Was this how a man danced with a woman? She had no idea there'd be so much contact, that he'd be so near to her.

"Keep going," Mikel urged. He brushed his knuckles against her cheeks, following the column of her neck to her collarbone. "Such beauty," She continued to sing, but even through the giddy fog in her mind, the sensation of his touch made her skin crawl. It was only a dance. Wasn't it?

She cast him a smile and moved out of his reach. He followed, stepping behind her and placing his hands on her hips, rocking them as he pressed himself against her back.

Aria sucked in a breath, her song faltering. His body swayed behind her, and she could feel something hard pressing against the cleft of her bottom. Her voice died on her lips, the joy of it suddenly gone. Surely this wasn't the way to dance. This was...this was a position she had seen animals in when they mated. This couldn't be right.

What was it Laudine had told her years ago, after Aria succumbed to curiosity and attempted to sneak out to find other people? Something about how people came together like animals to mate. Something about how unpleasant it would be if one of these men forced themselves on her. Laudine explained it all, though it had only been words, many of them devoid of any weight. The concern in the older woman's voice was what had stopped Aria and kept her from taking up that search again.

Gods, Aria, if you were caught...

Uneasy, she shook her head, her thoughts fuzzy.

"I feel strange," she confessed, squeezing her eyes shut.

The elf approached and brushed her hair aside. He ran a wet finger along the side of her neck, causing her eyes to open. "You will enjoy it."

Aria stared at the elf in front of her, unable to comprehend what she was seeing. Firelight danced upon his tanned skin, blood glistening on his chest. He raised a hand, pressing the blade of his knife into his flesh and adding a fresh cut to the others that were already weeping crimson. He shuddered, eyes rolling back in pleasure.

Aria jerked back, only to slam against the large body behind her. Her heart was pounding, drowning out the once comforting sound of the ocean. The way her vision was blurring around the edges only added to her rapidly mounting fear.

"Were it not so long since I last had a woman, your little perversion would certainly kill the mood, elf."

"You should try it yourself, Mikel. It is exhilarating. Especially the way they squirm."

"Don't fight it, lass," the human said, his breath hot against her neck. He ran his palms down her sides toward her outer thighs, hooking the hem of her skirt and slowly sliding it up. Ithoriel traced a bloodied finger from the hollow of her throat to her cleavage, a wicked gleam in his eyes.

No, no this isn't right, she thought, trying in vain to push Mikel's hands away. She felt dizzy and weak. "No," she mumbled. He laughed, bunching her dress in one fist and pulling it upward despite her struggles. His other hand cupped her breast, pinching her nipple through the fabric with rough fingers.

"No!" Aria cried out, forcing all her weight down on his thick arm, trying to free herself. Nauseating panic churned her stomach.

"Oh, yes," Mikel purred against her ear, his finger brushing the crease between her legs.

Aria screamed.

Chapter Seven

The demon rode the air high above the beach, banking slowly to follow the shoreline's lazy curves. The fire was closer now, and he kept careful watch on the ground below, desperate for any sign of Aria. He could feel her again. The sensation had been growing steadily stronger, and he would not risk losing it. He had to be close.

A voice came to him on the wind, high and sweet and joyous. He knew it immediately, without doubt. Aria. It was a voice that reached directly into him and coiled around his heart. He closed his eyes, coasting on air currents, and let it wash over him. He was powerless but to be drawn to her.

Her song faltered and then ended abruptly. A few moments later, her scream sounded through the night sky, and for the first time in Morthanion's life, icy dread spread through his veins. Eyes snapping open, he looked to the firelight. There were three figures there, the smallest caged between the others, and even from this distance he recognized her.

He angled himself directly for them, pushing harder than he ever had.

Sand exploded upward when Morthanion hit the ground, spraying into the fire and making it hiss and waver. The base of his skull was thrumming with the feel of her, and a crimson haze settled over his vision.

The human and the elf looked to him with bulging eyes, but there was something closer to relief in Aria's red, glossy gaze.

"Away from her," he growled. Shadows enveloped him, coursing along his skin like fog over open water.

"Fuck," the human said. The elf's face went a pale, stony gray, but his eyes narrowed.

The large man released his hold on Aria, and she stumbled to the ground, barely catching herself with an extended arm. There were red splotches on her cheeks, but the rest of her skin was bone-white. Morthanion curled his splayed fingers.

These men had been touching her. Taking advantage of her. Aria belonged only to Morthanion, was his alone to touch, his alone to move with in any intimate fashion. They'd drugged her, or poisoned her, or plied her with drink, and that was the most minor of their offenses. Though he had not his magic, a firestorm raged inside the demon.

"Run, mortals," he said through bared fangs, and released the tentative hold he had on himself.

Neither man hesitated to comply, though the elf was a little faster. They ran in different directions, the human hastily tugging weapons from his belt without so much as a glance backward. Morthanion had seen him with his arms around Aria, groping her from behind. He'd die first.

The demon broke into a run of his own, using his wings to catapult himself forward when he drew close to the human. He continued a few feet past his prey as the human hit the sand and rolled onto his back. The burly man swung a knife edged with chipped stone, scrambling back in the giving sand.

Morthanion caught the weapon with his palm. He wrapped his fingers around it, not feeling the gash it opened, and wrenched it from his prey's hold. It landed on the beach with a dull thump. There was no room for thought. The demon gave in to the instincts that coursed so powerfully through him. This man had laid hands upon Aria. Would have done worse, given a bit more time. There was no sympathy to be had.

Morthanion's claws sought yielding flesh, the human's attempts to defend himself flagging as his skin was torn to ribbons. Growled curses quickly turned to pained screams, until the only sound the man could make was a choking, gurgling sputter as blood welled in his throat.

Leaving the human to his fate, the demon leapt skyward, flying in the direction the elf had gone. The instinct demanded that he eliminate the ones who had wronged Aria, to ensure that she would be safe from them forever. He would not defy it, could not. Only blood would sate his need.

A break in the canopy granted him a glimpse of the elf, and he plunged through branches and leaves to land immediately ahead of the mortal. The elf's eyes widened in shock, and he stumbled to a stop just shy of colliding with the demon.

"Fighting for a woman. A piece of flesh. Pathetic!" the elf spat. One of his hands darted out, the end of his crude blade opening a shallow cut on Morthanion's arm.

The demon didn't flinch. He flashed his fangs in a broad grin.

"This isn't a fight. It's a slaughter," he replied, and surged forward, shoving the mortal with one of his clawed hands.

The elf was thrown backwards, his feet working rapidly to try and maintain his balance. His heel caught a root, but he twisted as he fell, catching himself on an arm. The shift in momentum was enough to get him up and running once more, this time back toward the beach.

Morthanion pursued, dodging between trunks and batting aside branches. The elf was quick, but the demon was faster, and by the time the jungle was giving way to the sandy strand, he had caught up to his quarry.

Hooking the back of the elf's vest with his claws, Morthanion heaved, this time lifting the mortal off the ground completely and sending him hurtling through the air. The elf landed on his back, kicking up a puff of sand, and coughed.

What this mortal had been before getting sent to the island was all too clear to the demon. The superficial wounds on the elf's chest, the blood smeared all over it, the crimson stains on his fingertips – here was a mortal who'd been blood-bound to a demon. A sniveling, subservient piece of filth who had latched onto a superior being in the hope of obtaining power.

Morthanion stood over him before the elf could even regain his feet, and wrapped his fingers around the mortal's neck, dragging him up. There was no fear in this one's eyes. Only a smoldering hatred, slow-burning and deep-running.

He raised his free hand, claws pointed toward the elf's face.

A whimper, so soft that he should not have even heard it, shattered the haze that had settled over him. He shifted his attention aside.

Aria had pushed herself up on her arms. Her gaze locked on Morthanion, flickering to his upraised hand. Despite her unshed tears, despite the fear gleaming in her eyes, her voice was strong when she spoke.

"No."

Confusion doused the fires within him. No? What did she mean? He looked again to the elf, who was red-faced, hands digging into the demon's forearm. No, don't kill the mortal? That couldn't be what she meant. It didn't make any sense. After what this elf had been doing to her, with what he would have done to her, why would she want his life spared?

"Morthanion, do not."

His name coming from her lips, spoken in that voice, sent a pleasing shiver down his spine. The red fog began to recede, albeit slowly, as the instinct that had dominated him subtly changed. Gore coated his claws, and for once, he saw what she did. There was no question why she feared him.

There would be no end to her running if he continued down this path. A time would come when she ran to a place he could never reach her. He had to protect her. Had to make her *feel* that she was safe. Not only from others, but from himself. How could she not look upon him and be frightened for her own life?

He had to show her he could deal with this threat without succumbing to savagery and rage.

The demon squeezed his free hand, forcing more blood to ooze from the open wound on his palm, and then pressed it to the cuts on the elf's chest. Though the mortal's face was turning blue and his eyes were bulging, he grit his teeth in defiant fury.

"You live at my whim," Morthanion said, and tossed his foe to the sand. "In thanks, you will make yourself useful and provide me with whatever information I seek, whenever I choose to have it."

The elf coughed hoarsely, pushing himself up on an arm and spitting bloody foam to the ground. Face red, one hand at his throat, he rasped brokenly. "You are superior, immortal."

"Remember that before you let pride lead you to further poor decisions. Go. I will find you when I require you." He could already feel it, a thin, ethereal tether that linked him to the elf. His blood was inside the mortal, now. Fortunately, the brand on his hand hadn't nullified the magic inherent in his demonic blood, just as it couldn't rob him of the shadows. It wasn't a full binding, not in the old way, but the exchange of blood was a useful thing. For him, anyway.

Turning away from the elf, Morthanion looked down at his hands. He was splattered with wet blood from the tips of his claws up to his elbows. Not once had he paused to consider what it must look like to others, to those not of his kind. Outside perspectives had never mattered.

He walked into the tide, letting it sweep around his legs, and crouched. Ignoring the sting of salt on his hand, he scrubbed the blood from his skin. Aria had experienced enough terrors this night. A crimson-drenched demon would no longer be one of them.

When he'd washed as best he could, he walked back to her, not sparing another glance to the elf staggering toward the trees. Drawing close, he tilted his head to study Aria. She had managed to make it ten feet, perhaps, closer to the water before she had fallen again. Now, she was struggling back to her hands and knees to continue her unsteady crawl.

For a moment, he wished the human was alive again, just so he could take him apart one more time.

Morthanion knelt beside Aria. Sliding his arms beneath her, he lifted her up and cradled her to his chest. Her eyes were closed, and her body trembled against him. He didn't know if it was from fear or exhaustion, or some combination of the two. When she opened her eyes, he saw her glance at his clawed hands, and the tremors subsided.

She turned against him, resting her head on his shoulder and inhaling deeply as her eyelids drifted shut. There was a strange feeling in his chest.

"You'll not run from me again," he said, the soft words spoken as a vow. He'd give her no more reason to flee.

She didn't respond, and he guessed by her slow, even breathing that she had fallen asleep. Holding her close, he spread his wings and leapt, doing his best not to jar her. Instinct guided him to her cave, her home, the only safe place for her on the island.

Though the breeze was cool, his skin was hot with her against it, his heart thumping. She was in his arms, holding on to him, her fragrance so sweet it made his head light. Why had he ever let himself scare her away? After all these millennia, how could he still be such a fool?

Entering the cave while holding her was challenging, but he managed to grab the rocky overhang with one hand and swing them inside. Careful as he tried to be, she curled further against him at the change in motion, her weak groan muffled by his shoulder. He carried her to the pallet of furs and gently placed her down.

He frowned at the lines of dried blood on her face and chest, left by the elf. Fury rose inside of him like bile, but he swallowed it despite its heat. She was here now. She was safe. That was enough.

Stepping away, he crouched over the little pile of wood arranged in the center of the chamber, extending his hands toward it. When nothing happened, he frowned, anger sparking. He splayed his fingers further, stretching them almost painfully. It was only then that he caught a glimpse of the symbol seared onto his hand, and remembered that his magic was gone. The fires inside of him, save for those of rage, had been snuffed.

It took several moments, but he found the chip of flint and bit of steel he'd seen the first time he'd come to the cave with her, and set to using it. The process was slow, agonizing, infuriating. Every time he thought the kindling had caught, it would extinguish before he was able to coax it to flame. Just as he was about to throw the flint across the cave, a glowing spark settled on the dried grass. Leaning forward on his hands, he blew on it, his breath shaky with the care he was taking. Gradually, it grew into tiny flames that crept steadily over the surface of the wood. The strength of the pride that flooded him was absurd.

Once the fire was healthy, he took one of her water skins and a scrap of cloth, and draped a loose fur over his arm as he returned to her side. He knelt beside her, laying the fur blanket over her legs. Uncorking the water skin, he wet the fabric and brushed her hair out of her face. He didn't believe she had come to any real harm, but this was likely her first time being drunk.

She stirred and turned her face into his hand, placing one of her own on her stomach. "Water," she rasped. Her expression was tight with discomfort. "Am I dying?"

"No," he replied, and held the skin to her lips to help her drink. "Much as it might feel that way, you'll be fine by tomorrow afternoon." He withdrew the water skin after allowing her a deep drink and corked it.

Aria opened her eyes briefly, glancing at the water. Before he could react, one of her hands darted out and grabbed it from him, clutching it to her chest. She turned onto her side and clung to it as though it were a precious treasure.

Caught off-guard by the speed with which she moved, Morthanion curled the fingers of his now empty hand into a loose fist. How long had she gone without water? Had he come even closer than he'd thought to losing her forever?

He stepped over her to face her again and used the wet cloth to wipe the blood away from her face and chest. She made no move to stop him, nor did she ease her grip on the water.

"Why have you not killed me?"

His eyebrows rose over his red-orange eyes at her question. "When have I ever said I wanted to kill you?"

"You are violent." A pause. "You frighten me."

Somehow, hearing her say it was worse than seeing it in her face all those times. His mouth immediately went dry, his throat tight. He pressed his lips together, forcing himself to reclaim his calm.

"When was the last time you drank water?" he asked, not allowing himself to explain to her why she shouldn't be afraid of him anymore. Simply saying it would avail him nothing.

She frowned at him incredulously, brow furrowing as she finally released her death-grip on the water skin to wag it at him.

"Before a few moments ago," he said, unable to keep a smirk off his face. Apparently whatever the mortals had given her to drink had emboldened her.

She drew the water back against her chest, curling up beneath the fur, and looked away from him again. For a time, she was quiet, and he could see her eyes shifting as though she was in deep thought.

"At the stream...that day," she finally replied.

That answer knotted his insides, a most unpleasant sensation that was unfortunately growing increasingly familiar since he'd met this woman. Aria had gone two days without water because he'd frightened her again, because he'd left her no choice but to flee for her own safety.

He could have been the cause of her death.

"Why are you acting so different now?" she asked, scrutinizing him with clarity that shouldn't be possible after her ordeal.

"I'm not acting any differently now than I have since we met," he says. "Perhaps it's simply because you've finally deigned to give me a fair chance."

"You are being awfully nice."

He scoffed. "Nice? How quaint a word. In all my years, I don't think I've ever been called nice." Now he studied her, the amusement slowly fading from his expression. What was it about Aria that drew him so irresistibly toward her? "You are the most compelling creature I've ever encountered."

"Have you known many people?"

"More than I care to count," he replied, waving it off with a flick of his wrist. A lot of those people had died shortly after, but she was better off without that information.

She frowned, looking away again, seeming to sink deeper into the furs. "I knew Laudine. She was all. Then you...and *them*."

"Well, now it's only *him*. And probably not for long, at that." He watched her closely, gauging her reaction. She shuddered, but her expression didn't change.

"I know you don't approve of what I am or the things I do, but the offer I made you was sincere. You've shown me a secure place, offered me shelter. I will uphold my word, providing you protection and the supplies you need to survive." He turned his head, looking around the cave, everything bathed in the soft orange glow of the fire. "Of course, that will require you to refrain from running away from me."

"Then do not scare me," she mumbled, as though all of it was his fault.

Perhaps it was. Most of it, anyway. He could safely admit to himself that at least half of it was his fault.

"I would like you to know that I am aware of the problem, and I'm currently working to correct it."

Though he was turned away from her, he could feel her eyes on him, searching.

"Why?" she finally asked. "Why me? You could have killed me and taken this place for your own, and saved yourself the burden of aiding me."

"Why not?" he replied, jaw clenching. There was no reason for her question to make him feel so uncomfortable. She just enticed him like no other ever had, made him feel things he'd never experienced before. "At any rate, I'm starting to realize that it's easier to try not to scare you than it is to chase you for days at a time. I'm getting much too old for the constant exertion."

"You are not scary like this," she said, drawing his attention back to her. Aria looked at him with heavy eyes, the corners of her mouth turning up in a quirky little smile. "And you cannot be that old."

She turned her head away, snuggling her cheek into the fur beneath her. "My demon has beautiful eyes," she sighed absently. Then she began humming, the same soft, simple tune she'd been singing the first time he'd found her.

The muscles of Morthanion's jaw worked furiously. Why should that smile, so small and insignificant, cause that fluttery feeling in his chest? Why should those words strike him like a blow? She'd seen him primarily in his true form, without any shroud. He knew his gaze was like fire, red-orange and hungry. There was no beauty to be found in it.

My demon...

All the same, he could not deny the satisfaction of her having shown interest in him. The more at ease she became around him, the more time he would be able to spend with her.

"I am very much older than you think," he said, walking to the worn bench and easing himself down onto it. From time to time, he felt every day of his four-thousand-plus years, and more. It was a crushing weight, an inescapable tide that threatened madness. He hadn't noticed it since finding her.

There was a stack of thin, dry pieces of bark set on the bench, and he tilted his head to the side as he lifted them. They were drawings, made with what appeared to be charcoal. The oldest, which were faded and curling at the edges, were the simple, unsteady scribbles of a child, but they increased in quality steadily as he progressed. The more confident but slightly-off proportions of an adolescent followed, and then finally graduated into the detailed, stunningly realistic sketches of a mature artist.

There were drawings of birds and rocks and the ocean, of the moon and stars and trees, of the cave itself. Throughout was a decidedly maternal figure, identifiable at first by her hair. By the end, he knew who he was looking at. The final sketch of Laudine was lifelike enough that he wouldn't have been surprised if it spoke to him. She was a plain woman, her features worn by years and worry, but there was strength in the set of her jaw, the angle of her brow. Moreover, there was something in her eyes that he thought he was beginning to recognize. It was the same thing that was causing that unpleasant tightness in his chest.

"You drew all of these yourself?" he asked. Long moments passed with no reply. He only then realized that her humming had faded to slow, steady breathing.

He crossed the chamber, stopping to watch her. There was peace on her features, serenity, security. For the first time, he knew what those things felt like. He would ensure that she continued to know them, too.

Turning away, he exited the chamber, the tips of his wings dipping into the water for a few moments as he gained height. He would head inland and prove to her that she'd made the right choice. His woman would want for nothing from this point on.

Chapter Eight

Aria knew she was going to die.

With a groan, she rolled onto her back and slapped her hands over her face. Her head throbbed like the waves crashing against the cliff side, and her entire body ached, muscles stiff. She was pretty sure the moisture on her cheek was drool.

She'd never felt so miserable in her life.

What had happened? Surely she hadn't struck the rocks on her way back to her cave. She would never be as careless as that.

Events of the prior night returned in a flood; the human and elf with their sly smiles and foul drink, luring her in before she realized their true intentions. It had only been Morthanion's appearance that stopped them. If he hadn't arrived when he did…

Aria's eyes snapped open and she scrambled on hands and knees to the mouth of the cave. She bent over the edge, fingers clawing at the rock as her stomach revolted. There was little to be forced out of her, empty as her stomach was. That only made it more agonizing.

When Aria was sure her stomach had settled, she sat back. Closing her eyes against the bright light, she pressed her fingers to her aching temples. Her mouth felt full of sand, dry and gritty, tongue feeling ten times its usual size.

Morthanion.

He'd brought her home. He hadn't harmed her, or shouted at her, or threatened her. Instead of seeking revenge for her trickery, for running away and forcing him into the barrier, he'd talked to her.

He had…cared for her. She recalled him offering her water, and could vaguely remember him wiping blood away from her skin.

But where was he now?

Aria opened her eyes, more slowly this time. It took several moments for them to adjust to the light, but when they did, they widened in surprise. What breath she had escaped in a rush, her mouth agape.

There were mounds of food – a variety of fruit, nuts, and dried meat – much of it piled in the various hand-made bowls she'd had about the cave. And water! She dove for that first, uncorking a water skin and guzzling it in bliss. Tiny streams ran down her jaw and along her neck, but she didn't care. Nothing could have tasted better in that moment. It moistened her mouth, soothed her throat, was deliciously cool. Lowering the water, she looked to the food again. She was starved, but she wasn't sure how her stomach would handle it. It was already uneasy with nothing but water.

Giving her nausea time to settle, Aria decided to use some of the water to wash. She rose on unsteady legs, quickly regaining her balance. Walking to the back of the cave, she passed through the canvas curtain and emptied a water skin into the wash bowl.

Unsure of when Morthanion would return, she made quick work of it. She peeled off her clothing, which was stiff with sea salt and dried sand. Dipping a rag into the water, she used it to scrub her body and wash the filth away. Her hair was a tangled mess, but she managed, yanking her fingers through until it offered no more resistance. Finally, she splashed some of the water on her face.

When she emerged clean, dry, and clothed, Aria again marveled at the amount of food Morthanion had gathered. He had done all this overnight? It was more than Laudine and Aria could have gathered in a month's time, and he had done it in a few hours!

Sitting back on the furs, she plucked a prickly fruit from the pile. Pinching two of its rigid spikes between forefinger and thumb, she pulled apart its shell to reveal its softer yellow insides. She nearly moaned the moment the juice hit her tongue, filling her mouth with its crisp, sweet taste. One bite led to another until she had devoured it with a ravenousness she had never known.

Aria waited a moment to see if her stomach might revolt against the food, and when she felt nothing beyond lingering hunger, she grabbed another piece and peeled it.

She had just bitten into the second fruit when the light dimmed. Her gaze rose to see Morthanion swing himself into the cave. His sudden appearance startled her, and she went still as he straightened to his full height. His eyes immediately settled on her, and his lips parted in a grin.

"Feeling any better?" he asked casually, looking first to the fruit in her hand and then to the peelings scattered on her lap.

She swallowed and brushed the back of her hand over her chin to wipe away the stickiness. Without thinking, her tongue followed, sliding over her lips. The action drew his attention to her mouth and his grin broadened.

"My head aches, but I am fine."

Aria couldn't take her eyes off him. She'd never seen him in the day before. He'd been something to behold by firelight, the shadows dancing over his skin unaffected by the glow. But by sunlight, she could clearly see there was beauty in his demonic features. She no longer feared the differences that made him what he was.

What she had experienced the night before, at the hands of a normal-looking man, had proved that appearances didn't matter. Without that drink clouding her mind, she could remember all of Laudine's warnings – warnings she'd always taken on faith. Now she knew firsthand.

You cannot sneak away like that, Aria! It is too dangerous!

I was curious, Laudine. Besides, you do it all the time. I just...wanted to see people.

I know. And I know I have kept much from you. But those people, they are not like you and I. They are not like your parents. I have told you about sex, but what those men would do would tear you apart from within. It is called rape, child. It is what they did to your mother, to ensure her suffering was as strong as possible before they killed her.

Mikel and Ithoriel had meant to *take* from the moment they saw her. But Morthanion, despite ample opportunities, had done nothing of the sort.

"I am glad to hear it," he replied, pulling her away from her thoughts. Suddenly, those inhuman parts of him vanished, lingering for a moment like the after-image of a bright light.

Gone were the horns and claws, the red-orange of his eyes replaced by blue. Before her stood a man. A striking man, but still only a man. He leaned his shoulder against the wall and folded his arms over his chest. She realized that he was studying her just as closely as she had been him.

"I'm going to have to put my foot down and say you're restricted to nothing stronger than water for the foreseeable future." There was a playfulness in his voice as his smile tilted to one side.

"I will never touch anything stronger than water again," she promised both of them. She never wanted to experience *that* again, much less the after-effects. The reminder of the prior night was enough to make her nauseous again; she needed to take her mind off of it. "Why do you cover yourself?"

"Hmm?" he replied, distracted.

Aria noticed that his eyes were resting on her bare legs, slowly traveling upwards. She arched a brow, though couldn't help the blush that burned her cheeks.

"Oh. It's instinct. A natural means of blending in with mortals."

He hadn't made any effort to hide himself before, and Aria suspected that he was doing it now for her benefit. So she wouldn't be frightened of him and run again.

"I see." She looked back at the food. "Thank you...for all of this."

"Happy to fulfill my side of the arrangement."

He said this as though it had been no significant task, but there was a prideful glint in his eyes. To Aria, it was an amazing feat. He seemed to enjoy her awe.

"Do you spend all your time in here?" Morthanion asked.

"Not all of it, no." She took another bite of the fruit. She'd rarely eaten this variety. Most of it grew farther inland, and was too dangerous to gather. "When there are things I need to do, I am here. Otherwise, I am out there swimming, enjoying the sunshine when I can, though close to home."

"Have you ever been spotted before?"

"If I have been, they never found me afterwards. This side of the island is rocky and hard to travel on foot, so no one tends to come around. I stay nearby, and when I have to leave I do so at night and on paths with plenty of cover."

"Quite amazing, the way you move through the water. I would imagine that, should anyone see you come to this place, they'd never survive the swim over."

Aria looked down at the pile of supplies, and then glanced up at him through her lashes. "You already know what I am, so I do not think you truly need confirmation."

"I have my guesses. But don't reduce yourself to being simply your race. There is so much more to you. I quite enjoy learning every nuance, bit by bit."

"I do not know anything about my race, only what I have discovered myself and what little Laudine was able to tell me." She stood, picking up one of the bowls of food and carrying it to the area where she normally stored her fresh pickings.

Morthanion didn't move from where he was leaning against the wall, but she felt his gaze following her.

"This Laudine…she was a human who took care of you after your parents were gone?"

"She was a mother to me in every way but blood. She was the only person I ever knew. Until you."

"Well, I can't offer any motherly advice, but I might be able to show you a good time."

Aria could only look at him with question in her eyes, unable to comprehend the meaning of his words. She wasn't even sure she trusted their true meaning.

"How long have you been on your own, Aria?" he asked, the mirth fading from his features.

"Two months," she answered softly, and saying it out loud only made her miss the woman more. Laudine's voice had been absent from the place for all that time, and Aria's heart grew a little heavier each day in the silence. She had always been beside Aria, to provide companionship, to share conversation, laughter, and sorrow. All of that had been taken away so suddenly.

"Two months," Morthanion repeated, his brow furrowed. "I'm…sorry." He appeared uncomfortable, as though the apology was not something he was used to. "Not alone anymore, at any rate."

"No, I suppose not," Aria said with a hint of a smile. She was quiet for a time, taking him in as he remained in his relaxed position across the cave.

Drawn by curiosity, she stepped toward him. It was, perhaps, the first time she had willingly approached him. All the other times, she had been too frightened. Now, she was simply intrigued. Morthanion's breath hitched in his throat. He remained very still, as though any movement might scare her away. Still, he betrayed no other sign of what her approach made him feel.

Tentatively, she reached out and moved her hand over the place his horns had been. It passed through air.

"They are part of me, but it is a part tied directly to the shadow. They only manifest when I will it."

"Oh," Aria said and tilted her head as she lowered her hand. His gazed dipped to her lips. Wanting to keep him distracted, she urged him to continue. "Manifest? You mean appear? So you have to really focus in order to keep them away?"

Her question succeeded in regaining his attention, an enigmatic ghost of a smile touching his lips. "No, I don't have to focus, but it can be a delicate balance. Younger demons sometimes have trouble maintaining it, but I scarce have to think about it at my age."

"You speak as if you were ancient."

"What does *ancient* mean to you?" There was a mischievous twinkle in his eyes.

"Old. Laudine used to tell me how ancient she felt."

"And she was what? Forty years? Fifty?"

"She was forty-seven."

"Ancient, perhaps, to a young human. I've at least four thousand years on her."

Aria stared at him, searching his face for a sign that he was jesting. But, despite that playful light, he appeared serious. He looked like he couldn't be more than ten years her elder, his face devoid of the age lines Laudine had developed.

"That's being forty-seven nearly a hundred times over," he added.

"I know; I am simply wondering if what you say is an untruth."

Morthanion chuckled, a dark, rich sound of genuine amusement that sent a flutter down through her belly. "Demons lie all the time, Aria. We're made for it. But everybody else lies just as much, and usually better. This is the truth."

"What other lies have you told me?"

"Only the ones that make me seem more intriguing than I actually am," he said, that spark of playfulness still in his eyes.

Aria eyed him, a smirk on her lips. Finally, she turned back to the items he'd gathered, and crouched to pick up one of the folded fabrics she hadn't noticed earlier. It unfurled when she lifted it, and she turned it back and forth to inspect it. It was a tunic with lacing down the front. The next one was shorter, made of stiffer material, and was laced from top to bottom on one side. She'd never seen anything like it.

"This is all new to you, isn't it?"

Aria glanced up at him. "What is?"

"The clothing."

"Laudine had one similar to this," she lifted the tunic piece higher, "but I have never seen this," she said, giving the stiffer article a little shake. "I don't imagine it covers much."

"That goes on over the tunic," he said, sounding distracted again as he stared at the clothing.

Setting them both down, Aria went through the other garments, wondering how he had obtained them. She guessed he'd taken them from someone else. Did it matter? Whoever he had gotten them from had probably stolen them to begin with.

"Have you ever seen any female prisoners, besides Laudine, in all the time you've been here?"

"Like I said, the others do not come here. Laudine always told me that it was very important that I stayed near home and out of sight. She taught me how to remain hidden. She was very good at it, unlike me," she said, smiling sadly. "She said there were some like her, when she arrived, but that without magic many of the women were left vulnerable. She did not tell me much more, only that men were stronger and that I must never be caught by one." She'd nearly allowed herself to be caught by two last night.

"A very wise woman," he said with sincerity. "I am going to have to lay down a second decree and say that you should continue to follow that advice."

"Did I not already stray from it? I seem to have been caught by a demon," she grinned.

"There are worse things to be caught by," he replied, his eyes narrowing.

"Nothing could be worse than that drink I had," she shuddered as her stomach clenched.

"It could have been much worse than it turned out," he said, a hint of anger in his tone.

"Yes. If I had taken a few more sips of that, it likely would have killed me," she replied with a forced laugh.

"Aria," he closed the distance between them to take her chin and gently force her to look at him, "you are much too young to understand this, especially having been on your own." He stared at her, intensity clear in his eyes. "There are many things worse than death. Many things."

She frowned at the anger in his voice. "I am not too young to understand, especially if it is something that you are not telling me. What things?" She already knew the drink had been the least of the dangers. Already knew what might have happened to her, though she couldn't imagine the damage it would have wrought.

Morthanion shook his head. "Nothing we need to darken your home with."

He released her chin and stepped away from her. She turned toward him in time to see him snatch up a piece of fruit and bite into it. Her brows drew down. He ate as though he hadn't just given her an ominous warning.

"Would it not be better for me to be informed?" Aria asked him, refusing to be brushed off.

He swallowed a mouthful before he spoke. "No. I don't intend to let any of those things happen to you, so there shouldn't be any worry."

"You will not always be with me, demon," she stated, head tilting.

"Only if you run away again," he said, watching her intently as he chewed.

Aria's eyes narrowed on him. "Not unless you give me reason to. I do not like the idea of you shadowing my every move."

"But we've been over this before," he mock-whined. "I'm a demon. I'm made of shadow. What else am I supposed to do with my time?"

"For someone who claims he is so old, your manners are very childish." The corners of her mouth twitched, but she forced herself not to smile.

"One must maintain a touch of immaturity to weather so many years and stay moderately sane."

Aria studied him silently. He was handsome enough, but somehow not real. She preferred the traits that made him unique from everyone else she'd seen. They suited him better. It made her feel like there were no walls between them, no lies. Only truth.

"Could you...show yourself?" she asked.

Morthanion's brow furrowed at her request before he smiled wickedly and obliged her. His entire image flickered and darkened, wisps of shadow creeping over him. Sparks lit in his eyes, blue consumed by red-orange. His fingers seemed to lengthen, black claws forming at their tips, and the shadow coalesced into the shapes of horns and wings.

It happened so quickly that she would have missed it had she blinked. The effect left her with the sense that this was how he always appeared, and her eyes had somehow deceived her before.

"Could I see your wings?" She hadn't meant to blurt it out, but there it was.

He spread them wide, never looking away from her. She was startled by the suddenness of it, but wasn't frightened. They must have stretched twenty feet, tip to tip, though she would never have guessed it seeing them folded up on his back. The feathers reminded her of a crow's, but thicker, more jagged. In the daylight, their iridescence was amplified.

Aria's gaze traveled along the length of them before she stepped closer to him, looking up at his horns. She raised a hand and lightly touched one. It was hard and solid, though darkness danced around her fingers while she was in contact with it. Morthanion watched her closely, but remained still and silent. Her touch lingered before she lowered her arm.

Again her attention returned to his wings. This close, she could see the detail, the shadows that coursed over their surface and sometimes drifted off into the air. They were fascinating. When she walked around to his back, her fingers itched with the desire to touch them. She reached out with both hands and placed them upon their main arch.

Morthanion stiffened, but didn't move from her grasp. Emboldened, she ran her hands along the length of his wings.

"They are so soft," she mused as she continued to stroke the feathers, "but you would not think they were from the look of them." She watched the shadows lick and swirl around her hands as though they were embracing her.

Then her hands smoothed back toward where the wings connected to his back, feeling strong muscle beneath. Aria heard him suck in a sharp breath, and a powerful shudder wracked his body.

Her touch was so delicate, so intimate and innocent, that he was instantly aroused. When her hands brushed over the part of his wings closest to his back, Morthanion gritted his teeth and clenched his fists against the pleasure that blasted through him. She had no way of knowing the sensitivity of that area, had no idea that he would have let no one else but her even get near them.

And in that moment, he didn't care if she knew or not.

His limbs trembled as a wave of euphoria flooded him, sweeping everything from his mind save for Aria.

"Did I hurt you?" she asked, dropping her hands away.

He turned suddenly, shadowy feathers rustling, her hair blowing to the side with the speed of his movement. Startled, she stepped back, and he followed.

The instinct in him demanded all of her. It urged him to leave his claim on her irrevocably. But he knew that he'd only begun to earn her trust. He would settle for just a taste.

He reached forward, wrapping an arm around her waist to draw her against him. Heat radiated from her, teasing his senses. His other hand slipped into her hair, which was smoother and softer than he'd imagined.

For a fleeting moment, he simply stared down into her eyes. The fires she ignited inside of him were unlike any he'd ever experienced, and made the old ones seem cold in comparison.

Leaning forward, he pressed his lips to hers. Warmth blossomed across his face, spreading throughout his body, a delightful tingling following in its wake. His eyes closed, leaving only the feel of her, of their bodies pressed together. The air between them, perfumed with her scent, intoxicated him.

Her hands shot up to his shoulders, pushing for an instant before she stilled. That tension remained in her for a time, and then she yielded. The tips of her fingers squeezed his arms gently, and she pressed her body more firmly against his. Surrendering.

When her soft lips parted, his tongue delved into her mouth, sampling, exploring. She tasted ambrosial. How could a kiss make his whole body crackle with an undefined energy? It was only further proof of what she was to him. His fated mate. The only other being who could complete his soul.

She slid her hands up, wrapping them around his neck, kissing him back. Her lips were hesitant, unsure, and more arousing than anything Morthanion had ever experienced. That this could be her first kiss, that he was the one to share it with her, sparked a savage possessiveness within him.

Slowly, without conscious thought, his wings wrapped around the two of them, enfolding them in darkness and leaving only touch. His feathers brushed against her bare skin and he felt a shiver run through her body. He released a low, primal groan at the feel of her soft stomach against his hard groin. He was lost in ecstasy, surrounded by her scent, her taste, by *her*. The fires within him burned so hot that he didn't know how they could ever be extinguished, didn't think he'd ever want them to be.

This was where she belonged; in his arms, body nestled against his. That was what all this meant. She truly belonged to him. His to use, his to enjoy, his to keep. His alone.

Morthanion pulled his mouth from hers and lowered his head to the tender place where her shoulder and neck met. He licked and kissed, her responses communicating her growing need. Unable to resist, he bit at her skin, a nip of possession. She tensed in his arms and gasped.

Aria shifted her hands to his chest, the heat of her palms exciting him further. It took him a few moments to realize that she was trying to push away from him again. He brushed his lips against hers, but didn't release her from the strong embrace of his arms, or the shadowy one of his wings.

"There's nothing to fight," he rumbled. He opened his eyes. She was disheveled, her cheeks flushed and lips swollen. Desire shined bright in her gaze, but there was something else there now. He recognized it immediately, having seen it far too often. She was afraid.

"No," Aria breathed and gave his chest another push. He didn't relinquish his hold on her, and she only succeeded in brushing against his throbbing cock.

Morthanion tilted his head back and groaned. Everything within him screamed to take her now, to tear off the flimsy dress and bury himself deep, to pound into her until she screamed his name in pleasure, until she screamed it for mercy. But somewhere inside was a small voice that said *no*. If he wanted her – not just her body, but her mind, heart, and soul – that was not the way to do it. If he took her now, she would be lost to him forever.

Still, he held her against him, his body reacting to her struggles. It would be so easy.

In that instant, the entire scene played out in his mind's eye. The aftermath of it had his insides twisting in disgust.

He released her, immediately raising the shroud. Aria stumbled back. Keeping his features masked took a considerable amount of effort.

Her gaze trailed downward, and he knew she saw what had been hard against her stomach a moment before.

"I—I need—" she breathed, moving toward the mouth of the cave.

He needed, too, and he was sure his expression burned with it.

"I need time to think," she finally said, and before he guessed her intent, she stepped off the edge.

Morthanion surged forward, unable to hold back the nauseating sense that he'd done this already, that he had experienced this same thing more times than he could ever bear. He reached out to grab her, but was fast enough only to snag her empty dress from the air as her form shimmered and turned to mist before his eyes, mixing with the sea below. The same thing she'd done that first night.

Claws digging into the stone, he leaned forward on his knees, scanning the waves for any sign of her. His heart was pounding for an entirely new reason now. She had fled again, even after the agreement they'd made, even after the words they'd exchanged. He closed his eyes, reaching into himself to call upon the new sense that was solely focused on locating her. Unlikely as it was – neither blood nor magic connected them – he knew it was real, knew it was accurate.

Yet the tingling at the base of his skull was muted and uncertain now.

Was it the form she had taken? How long could she maintain it, how fast could she move like that? The instinct roared that he should be airborne already, searching for her, allowing himself no rest until he found her and brought her back here where she would be safe. Damn the daylight, and damn anyone that might see him flying. Laying his claim on her was more important, having her back here with him was all that mattered.

But that little voice spoke again. She'd asked for time. She hadn't run from him, she was simply seeking space to collect her thoughts. How could either of them have thought clearly in such close proximity to one another?

Find her now, claim her now, the instinct growled, the force of it tensing every muscle in his body. Every moment she spent without being bound to him was a moment of complete vulnerability for her.

Grant her this, and she will come back.

Yes. And if she didn't, then he would find her. He would always find her.

Chapter Nine

Baltherus reclined on the central dais of the great hall. Directly ahead, a spitted boar roasted over a pit of coals, filling the hall with its aroma. The men gathered around – and the handful of women serving them – wore sheens of sweat. No perspiration beaded on Baltherus's skin. The broad-shouldered demon didn't even notice the heat of the flames.

He surveyed the chamber with a smug smile, still taking pride in what he'd accomplished here. Like everyone else, he'd been stripped of his magic before banishment, but he hadn't let that stop him. A demon was still faster, stronger, and more cunning than any mortal. Truly fit to rule.

In his earliest days here, he had brought fear and pain and death, driven by his own fury. Now, he ensured the other prisoners' survival. More than that, he allowed them prosperity.

One of the heavy doors at the main entrance swung open, and the surly, bronze-skinned human Rogar walked inside. Baltherus had catalogued all the prisoners in his camp. Rogar was one of many who'd entered into a pact with a demon to obtain more power. Such matters were frowned upon by the Mage Councils of the mainland. Strangely, many of the mortals who had made such pacts – warlocks, they had been called – were eager servants here, even without the potential for magical power.

It was probably just an inherent desire for mortals to seek out things greater than themselves and serve.

"Got an elf requesting audience, boss," Rogar said. "Name's Ithnorian, or some kinda elfish nonsense."

The demon shifted on his cushions and smiled. The air was sweet with the scent of sizzling meat and fresh fruit, promising a satisfying feast in the evening. His people would enjoy themselves, and share in the spoils of their mutual labor. They would look to him, grateful for his leadership, for his guidance, for his benevolence, and know that without him they'd be out in the jungle, starving, if they hadn't already been killed by their neighbors.

"Ithoriel. Is he not supposed to be scouting the south shore with Mikel?"

"Said they run into some trouble, boss. Wouldn't tell me what."

"Send him in, then."

Rogar nodded, and made his exit with long strides. Shortly after, a tall elf with tanned skin entered the great hall. Baltherus watched the elf's eyes shift from side to side, glancing at the others, but never directly looking at anyone.

Ithoriel stopped a few feet away from the dais and knelt, head bowed. It was entertaining the way so many of these warlocks had never emerged from the relationship they'd had with demons in their old lives. The mortals received power they couldn't have imagined. The demons gained willing pawns.

The elf was just one of many who had eagerly gone through the blood-binding ritual with Baltherus. Blood was a powerful thing, and even the brand given by the mages couldn't nullify its potency.

"Ithoriel, welcome. Have you eaten? We shall dine well this night, and there is always a place for you at my table."

"Thank you for your hospitality, master," the elf said.

Baltherus widened his grin. *Yes*, he thought, *avert your gaze. Treat me like the god I ought to be.*

"I come bearing news from the south that might be of importance to you."

The demon leaned back, spreading his thick arms to either side. "I am intrigued, my friend. You and your companion were not due back for some days. This news must be important, indeed."

"There is another demon, master. Very old, very strong. He tore Mikel to pieces with his bare hands, and nearly had me. He attempted to bind me to him."

Baltherus tensed. There'd never been another of his kind sent to this place. The only other being of significance was Gaelin, but the angel had never openly challenged Baltherus's rule, and hadn't emerged from hiding in decades. Would that change, if there really was another demon on the island?

"Did he make any indication that he knew you were already bound?

"No, sire." The elf looked up, dark circles beneath his eyes. "I can feel his blood in me now. The only reason I'm able to fight it is because I've been bound to you for so long."

"Did this demon have a name?"

"The girl called him Morthanion."

Baltherus felt his blood chill, despite the stifling heat from the fire. All demons knew of their forebears, the Betrayers of Light. But there were others of their kind who had become infamous in their day. Morthanion Ulthander, Keeper of Flame. Nearly as well-known as Morgalien the Incinerator.

He swallowed, the sound thicker than he hoped it would be, and regained his composure.

"What girl?" he asked. Women were almost as precious a commodity as food and water; many of the rougher islanders had given in to their hungers early on, and females had often taken the worst of it. At least until Baltherus had imposed control.

"She came from the sea, master. I didn't see a mark upon her, and she was near starved and withered from thirst."

"I've not been informed of any shipwrecks, but I suppose it is possible she washed up on shore separate of the wreckage," the demon mused, though opportunity was beginning to make itself clear in the back of his mind.

"I cannot say if she was a prisoner or not, master," Ithoriel said. "We were…being charitable, and sharing our provisions with her, when the other demon arrived. The way he looked at her…I think she is his mate."

Baltherus studied the elf closely. There was something being omitted from the story, the demon knew. Likely about the nature of their interaction with the girl; the cuts crisscrossed on Ithoriel's chest were not from a demon's claws, and there had been just enough hesitation. Still, the elf had taken in some of Morthanion's blood…which could prove useful.

"That is a bold conclusion to draw, Ithoriel. What do you know of such matters?" the demon asked, his voice low.

The elf dropped his gaze again. "Enough, master, to suspect it to be the case when a being of his strength and savagery has me by the throat but stays his hand at the command of a girl."

That broad grin split Baltherus's lips again. He laughed, loud and heartily, and slapped his thigh. He was powerful on his own, but with a demon like Morthanion as an ally? They would control the entire island. And the girl could prove the key to the elder demon's cooperation. "You, Ithoriel, have made a good day all the better. Tonight, you'll dine at my right hand. We've plans to lay, you and I, and a promising future to reach for."

*****

Aria sat upon the sand, knees drawn up, the incoming tide lapping around her. The moon was high in the clear sky, its reflection broken into countless points of light that sparkled upon the waves. Her voice was soft as she sang. Head bowed, she absently braided a lock of hair, the rest flowing freely around her in the breeze.

The night was peaceful, which she desperately needed. After her time in Morthanion's company, Aria had sought a way to calm her turbulent thoughts, to cool her hypersensitive body. The things that he made her feel, and the utter loss of control he provoked bewildered her.

She felt something while she touched him. It had been mere fascination when she first ran her hands over his feathers, but that changed quickly. There was a longing beneath her curiosity that she hadn't known she harbored. When he pulled her against him and kissed her, she became fully aware of it. Her innocent exploration had turned into something so...so stimulating!

He was a demon. A killer. And he had enjoyed taking life. Shouldn't she be repulsed? To know the hands that had held her had slain so many? Had turned men, women, and children to ash?

A shudder ran through her, and Aria tried to push those thoughts away. She just wanted to find that peaceful place in her soul again.

Morthanion had never said he'd enjoyed killing, though. He'd spoken with pride of protecting her, and had turned her questions around on her, but he'd never actually admitted to enjoying the spilling of blood.

And he had stopped when she asked him to.

She'd seen his rage when he'd killed Mikel, and knew that he had done so to protect her. His demeanor hadn't changed when he had grabbed Ithoriel. Not until she called out to him, asking him to spare the elf's life.

Perhaps he wasn't as terrible as he made himself out to be. Perhaps he was changing. For her? Surely not. He wanted her company, nothing more.

Or was there more?

Aria released the braid and brushed her fingers over her bottom lip, then the spot he'd grazed with his teeth. It left no mark, but it had shot such pleasure through her that she'd barely been able to hold in a cry.

Jasper had changed because of Xani. She had gentled his soul, given him peace and happiness, if only for a short time. Could Aria do the same for Morthanion? Was that possible?

Recalling his kiss, his touch, and the way his heat had felt against her, Aria was sorely tempted to take the chance. Her body had ached fiercely, her breasts heavy and sensitive as they pressed to his hard chest, her pearled nipples brushing against the fabric of her dress. Held in the circle of his arms, she had experienced a restlessness that was foreign to her.

The sensations had been so powerful that she panicked. Laudine's descriptions hadn't prepared Aria for how good his touch felt or how deeply his kiss affected her.

A tumbling stone jarred her from her thoughts, and Aria could sense him near. She hadn't gone far from the cave, the prior day's events too fresh in her mind. All she needed was space, time alone to think and clear her head. He'd granted it, but she knew it wouldn't be long before he sought her out.

Aria pretended to ignore his presence, though every part of her came to life with the knowledge that he was so close. She continued to sing, grasping for tranquility that she knew now would not come.

She held the final note of the song, letting it drift away on the salty-sweet air to become part of the ocean's music. Finally, she turned her head. All she could see of him were two points of light amidst the darkness, the shadows that clung to him even darker than the sky above.

Morthanion. The name was like a sigh in her mind.

He slid off the rock and began to approach her. Almost as though he'd heard her calling his name.

"That is close enough," she commanded when he was but a few feet from her. She wrapped her arms around her legs, pulling them tighter against her chest.

Morthanion stopped and came no closer. He tossed her dress, the white cloth fluttering on its short trip to land over her shoulder. For long moments, they stared at one another, until finally he turned away with a barely audible scoff.

Keeping her back to him, she pulled the dress over her head as another gentle wave washed over the sand.

Aria rose quickly, water streaming in rivulets down her legs. The material of her garment clung to her thighs and hips. He was already facing her when she turned. His gaze dropped, and smoldered.

"What is it you want?" Aria asked, her brows lowering as she narrowed her eyes. "You have kept your part of the bargain. There is food and supplies, and I am fine. I do not need you with me always." Still, she found comfort in his presence. He made her feel safe, when she wasn't overwhelmed by all the other emotions he sparked inside her.

"What I want should be obvious. You."

Aria inhaled sharply.

"I could've taken you a dozen times, at least, before today. But I enjoy your company rather too much to do that to you."

Aria was stunned by his admission, making thought and speech difficult. Surely he meant just her company, someone to talk to. She could relate to that kind of loneliness.

"Taken...me?" The way he had before? Kissing her, his arms around her, his wings enfolding them, every little touch consuming her body in flames until they melded into one?

"So you will not do *that* anymore, then?" she asked slowly. "Because you enjoy my company."

"You are confused," he said, and started to move closer. "Conflicted. You enjoyed what we shared, but you do not understand it."

Aria took several steps back. "No. I said no closer."

"Do you fear me?" he asked and slowed to a stop, that red-orange gaze heating her skin. "Or do you fear what I make you feel?

"You...scare me a little," she admitted. How could he not when a single touch could make her heart pound so fiercely?

"I don't think I could harm you."

"But there is a possibility you could," she returned. She had seen him fight, his speed, his strength. He could crush her.

"And there is a possibility you could hurt me," he said and tilted his head slightly. "I am not invincible, Aria"

"Demon, how would I be able to hurt you?" she asked, disbelieving.

"I am not without my vulnerabilities. I bleed when cut. I feel pain. I can be killed, just as any other living thing can be."

Aria didn't like hearing that. He carried himself with such surety, such confidence, that it seemed as though no one could hurt him, that no one would even dare to try. The thought that he could be brought down like anyone else made her stomach turn.

She frowned, confused. She didn't understand these emotions. Didn't understand whatever it was he was making her feel. She had been close to Laudine all her life, had loved the woman as a mother. It was the closest comparison she had to her relationship with the demon, but all of her emotions regarding him were more intense and more confusing. He drew her like a moth to a flame, even though she knew how easily he could burn her. The pull he had on her kept growing.

The shadows around Morthanion dissipated and he stood before her as a man, save for his glowing eyes. She watched as he eased himself down onto the sand and sat looking out over the glittering, churning ocean water. He inhaled deeply and closed his eyes for several moments before looking up at her.

"Sit with me awhile," he invited, patting the sand beside him.

Aria bit her lip as her gaze roamed over his features, now highlighted in the moon's glow. He was beautiful like this, but strangely, she preferred him the other way. Shadows and horns and black wings. Still, his relaxed posture and soothing tone put her at ease.

She stepped toward him and lowered herself down where he had suggested.

"I am not frightened of your true form," Aria admitted to him. If she was honest with herself, it enthralled her. It was almost as thrilling to look at him as it had been to touch him.

"Then what *are* you frightened of?" he asked her, his attention drifting back to the moon, the stars, the gray smudges of cloud. It seemed to be an effort on his part to allow her to feel comfortable in his presence, to not unsettle her. "The things I have done? What I am capable of doing?"

"Yes."

"Most of us here were not sent because we've done good deeds." His face was serious when he turned to her again. "Even Laudine, and your father, committed some crime that saw them banished to this place. I have done terrible things to many people. Some of those people were bad, some of them good, though it's rarely so simple. But I've done nothing to harm you."

"They changed," she said. Laudine had spoken of her own mistakes, her own regrets. She'd even told Aria about some of the things Jasper had done before his banishment. "Many here deserve what might come to them, because they *are* cruel. But it's the thought that you...enjoy killing. That you are just like them, that if you could, you would burn another village, and another, without remorse." She shook her head. "I just cannot agree with that. You help me, but for what purpose?"

"Purely selfish reasons," he said, without hesitation. "Because something about you intrigues me, attracts me, like nothing else in four thousand years. Fire has always been a part of me, and that was taken away when I was sent here. It seems," he paused, his eyes burning into her own, "that water may fill that void, too."

Aria stared at him, still unable to understand exactly what he wanted from her. "You enjoy my company? Talking with me?"

"Talking. Looking. Listening." He brought his hand up and brushed it across the hanging strands of her hair. "Touching."

His mouth tilted into a lopsided grin. A thrill coursed through her that was strong enough to make her breath hitch.

"Were you angry with me?" she asked in a rush of breath.

"When?"

"When I was touching your wings. You shuddered, so I thought perhaps I hurt you, and then you turned on me and looked...angry." It had been anger, hadn't it? His eyes had been so heated, features set, jaw clenched before he had pulled her to him to kiss her.

Morthanion chuckled, and his fingers caressed the skin of her cheek. "No, Aria, I was not angry with you."

"You did not appear happy," she managed to say, perplexed. With him touching her again, her cheeks flushed.

"You have much to learn, Aria. You just have to overcome your fear of being taught."

"Taught what?" Laudine had shown her so much, and yet Aria was discovering she knew so little of the world.

"You may find out, over time. It's nothing you need to rush into it. I was happier than I've been in a long, long while. Trust that."

Aria was surprised to hear that from him. Was there no joy in his life, for his only happiness to come at her touch?

"So it did not hurt? Touching your wings?" she asked.

"No, it did not. Did the kiss I gave you hurt?"

Her face flamed as she recalled it. "No. I...liked the feel of your feathers...and the kiss."

"And why would I have done that if I was angry or unhappy?" he asked, gently. "I much enjoyed it, myself."

How could she expect to understand her own feelings when his were so intense and easily misread? He confused her almost as much as she was attracted to him...but her fascination was still intact. "Would you remain still if I asked you to?"

"I can promise to try." Morthanion smiled at her with genuine charm.

Aria returned it, albeit shyly. "And show me your true form?"

She delighted in his appearance the moment he shed his human guise. Leaning forward, she shifted onto her knees. Unsure, but determined, she dropped her gaze to his lips. When her face was inches from his, she brought a hand to his cheek. She slid it down to cup his jaw with her palm, and brought her other hand up to cradle his face. Then she leaned forward and softly brushed her mouth against his.

Even that faint contact had her body reacting in a way she didn't believe possible. It was stirring. She felt a shudder flow through him, and it spurred her on. She kissed him a few more times before she nipped lightly at his lower lip, and was rewarded by his groan. *That* affected her even more than the kiss had. The sound of it vibrated straight down between her legs, creating a rush of heat.

She enjoyed this tremendously now that she knew what to expect. It had been his ferocity and the unfamiliar contact that had startled her. She was beginning to understand that kissing was a prelude to something more, something that she wanted to revel in and discover. With him.

That thought in mind, she flicked her tongue against his lip to taste him. Morthanion's control shattered.

His arms wrapped around her and she felt herself falling back into the soft sand. He eased his weight atop her and nipped at her lips, swiftly taking control. Aria gasped, and as if of their own accord, her hands left his cheeks and moved to grasp his horns.

Morthanion growled, his hips jerking forward. One of his hands slipped beneath her to cup her bottom, and he lifted her to him as he nestled deeper between her legs.

A shock burst through her as he ground against her, feeling his hardness snug against her exposed mound, between her nether lips. Aria's thighs fell open wider and her mouth tore away from his to inhale sharply as her back arched.

He took advantage of her exposed throat and pressed his mouth to it, running his lips and fangs over the delicate skin. He continued to stroke against her silken folds and Aria was powerless but to meet him. Pleasure blossomed within her, taking over all reason.

"Aria," Morthanion groaned huskily, one of his hands sliding up her body to tangle his claws in her hair. "You smell so damned sweet."

His voice washed over her like the waters of the sea, yet she was burning. Hot, so hot. Her hands tightened on his horns, an anchor to keep her grounded as her body tensed and she whimpered. Like fire, he consumed her. Her breasts swelled, warmth flooded her, and she craved something she had no knowledge of.

Then he slanted his mouth over hers and devoured her.

Aria had no control over the sensations that were overpowering her. She'd never known anything like them. The desire was overwhelming. She forced her eyes open, looking up into his to seek reassurance.

Chapter Ten

Morthanion was dominated by his lust for Aria. His body demanded hers, energy crackling like lightning over the surface of his skin with each bit of friction between them. His blood was liquid fire, and he could feel that same heat roiling off of her, from her very core, carrying the delicious scent of her arousal. Instinct was flooding his mind, driving him onward toward new heights of pleasure he'd never dreamed were possible until Aria.

He drew back from her, looking down to his prize, his mate, his woman, and she opened her eyes to look up at him. Her cheeks were flushed, lips swollen and parted, but the set of her eyebrows didn't speak of desire or passion. She was still afraid.

The realization hit him like a blow, constricting his throat in the coils of a foreign emotion. It took several moments for him to identify it as shame. This was all new to her. She was afraid of him, afraid of what he was doing to her, of what he was making her feel.

He'd be a fool not to acknowledge that it was largely new to him, too.

Leaning down, he pressed his forehead and nose to hers, shrinking their mutual world to nothing more than each other.

"Nothing to fear," he whispered, stroking her hair, "not from me."

She was tense beneath him, her limbs taut as though she were on the verge of flight.

He felt the change in her immediately. Her body softened. She wrapped her arms around him, hands sliding along the muscles of his back. Groaning deeply, he resumed the motion of his hips, driven steadily faster by the little sounds she made. Her breaths were short and fast, and he knew she was on the verge of coming, likely for the first time. A primal satisfaction welled in him.

"Thanion," she half-whispered, half-groaned. "I—"

She tensed again, her back arching, creating more sweet pressure between them. She was close, and he knew that once she shattered he would be helpless but to claim her. Gazing at him through her thick lashes, she opened her mouth as though to release a soundless cry.

Then her eyes went wide, and she stilled beneath him, all that passion gone. He heard the sound a fraction of an instant later – the soft beat of wings, barely audible with the din of the ocean.

In the space of a heartbeat, Morthanion had shoved up to his feet, spreading his dark wings wide to shield Aria from view. The being that was flying down to them must have seemed little more than a moving shadow to Aria, but Morthanion could see it for what it was. Another demon.

He had been so taken by Aria that he'd forgotten he might have to deal with others of his kind on this island. He'd forgotten, briefly, that he might have to deal with *anyone* apart from her. It was a less than ideal situation, with his mate potentially exposed to harm. Already the instinct was shifting, moving from the need to claim her to the need to protect her by any means necessary.

The other demon stretched his wings, rolled his shoulders, and smiled. He was broad-framed and more heavily muscled than Morthanion, wearing a plain vest and loose-fitting pants.

"You must be our newest addition," he said, his voice smooth and amiable.

Morthanion felt Aria get to her feet behind him, pressing one shaky hand to his back to steady herself. He shifted his wings to better conceal her.

"It would appear you have the advantage," he replied, the calm in his voice belying the raging instincts inside of him. There was no greater threat on this island to Aria than another demon.

"You don't remember me at all, do you?" the other demon asked, his smile widening. He started to walk slowly, circling Morthanion without getting any closer.

Morthanion shifted to keep himself between the newcomer and Aria, tearing through the annals of his memory. There were so many faces, so many battles, so many years, all in a jumbled heap. Yes. He recognized that smile, so warm and charming. From the time before demons were forced into hiding, when immortal armies marched and made war freely.

"Baltherus."

"Yes, Morthanion. Welcome to my island. It is rare for us to have so...distinguished a guest."

"Your island?" Morthanion asked, and laughed. "King of the prisoners, I suppose? Lording over all the little mortals?"

The expression on the larger demon's face wavered for a fleeting moment. "Something like that." He moved a little closer, trying to mask his cautious approach with his easy tone. "I never thought I'd see the likes of you captured. I thought they'd surely kill you, given the chance."

"They certainly tried," Morthanion could feel the fear and uncertainty radiating from Aria behind him just as surely as he could feel the ocean breeze on his skin. "Ultimately, they settled for exile. It cost them less blood."

"They expect us to destroy ourselves here," Baltherus said, coming to a stop. "They figure us capable only of chaos and death. But my group has instilled order. And we live well. Better than we ever could have in hiding. Here, no one can dispute our right to rule."

"That's good for you and yours."

The larger demon stood on his toes, tilting his head to the side to peer around Morthanion's wings.

"Aren't you going to introduce me to the woman?"

Fury bubbled inside of Morthanion at that request. This was Baltherus finally getting to the heart of the matter. Both of them knew that if Aria was the elder demon's mate, she was a potentially powerful bargaining tool.

"I don't much care for sharing what I've taken," Morthanion replied, keeping his tone even. The demon before him was younger, but had always been ambitious. Weren't they all?

"Everything on this island belongs to me, Morthanion. Whether it's paid in tribute or I take it, it's *all* mine. Join me, and you can have as much as you want. As large a share as you desire."

"I'll have to disagree with you, Baltherus. I've no interest in these games."

"Direct, as always, I see." Baltherus shook his head. "Just imagine the things we could accomplish together, Morthanion. There isn't anything here that we couldn't have. We would crush any enemy, and bend everyone else to our will. Blood and fire, like in ages past.

"I know you yearn for those times. I remember just as clearly as you when we could walk in the open and take whatever, *who*ever we wanted. When we made rivers run red and the night skies bright with fire. Here, you can fill the air with the screams of the women you rape. Here, we can be kings again."

"I'm sure you'll manage well enough on your own," Morthanion replied. He felt Aria's arm stiffen before her hand dropped away from his back, leaving the place it had been oddly cold.

"I have been, and will continue to do so." Baltherus shifted again, looking past Morthanion's shoulder, and the sharp intake of breath from Aria told him that she'd been seen. The big demon smiled, his teeth white and straight and his manner nonchalant.

"Mind yourself, Morthanion. There are many people here who will stop at nothing to have a go with any woman. Especially the one you've managed to obtain."

Rage erupted anew within Morthanion, and he bared his fangs, body tensing to strike.

"Good evening," Baltherus said with a chuckle, still looking at Aria, and leapt into the air.

Morthanion shifted forward to give chase, but caught himself. He knew Baltherus had allies, knew the other demon hadn't lied about that. Leaving Aria alone meant leaving her exposed, vulnerable. And that would mean he was vulnerable, too. Clenching his jaw, he watched Baltherus shrink into the distance and folded his wings against his back.

He turned to face her, still bristling. "I'll not let him lay a hand on you," he said, voice a low growl as he shed the last semblance of calm and control. It had taken more than four thousand years to find the one woman that belonged to him completely, and he would not allow her to be taken.

Aria met his gaze, her face pale, brow furrowed with uncertainty. "You know him."

He nodded.

"You...killed together?"

"We burned and pillaged. Waged war on the light for centuries, without mercy. They showed none to us, either."

Confusion was plain on her face. To her, this island was the entire world, the handful of people she'd seen its entire population. How could she fathom hundreds, thousands of beings locked in bloody battle?

"And raped?" He'd never seen her eyes so cold as they went in that moment, and somehow, her skin paled further. She was already frightened of him, had already seen what he was capable of. This wouldn't help her opinion of him.

Aria stepped back from him, and his insides knotted. "You did this?" she breathed. Emotions were warring on her face, sparkling in her eyes.

"I've had women," he said, jaw muscles tensing. What reason would she have to believe him if he told her he hadn't forced any of them? That his thrill in battle had been in the flames and not the flesh? "All of them came to me by their own accord."

"And what of me?"

"What we've shared is different."

"Because I was willing?" she asked flatly.

"And aren't you?" he demanded, stepping forward as anger clutched him. He could not avoid it. For her — the one person whose trust he craved — to think of him in that manner was unbearable. "I've done nothing that you haven't wanted!"

"It's what you have done that frightens me." She backed away from him further.

"What I have done is in the past! It cannot be undone, it cannot be taken back. Can you not—"

"But you feel no guilt!"

His mouth snapped shut, and he could feel heat flare in his eyes. Frustration ran through his body in little tremors. "And what guilt should I feel, having done what I was made to do?" he asked in a low voice and pressed his lips tightly together.

"The only ones who have tried to do me harm were not demons! So if you were made to do those things, why have you not just *taken* me as you claimed you could have?" she shouted, her fear finally cracking to let her own anger break through. "Raped me? Slit my throat? Burned me while there is still breath in my body and laughed in delight?"

"Have I not said it is different with you?" he said, his gaze upon the sand. The images that her words conjured in his mind were enough to make his stomach churn, to make him tremble with a jumble of emotions he could not begin to understand. He knew only that he could not succumb to them, could not allow them to seize control and drive him to violence. "That I've done none of those things to you should be proof of that."

"Why? What makes me so special? Is it because I am the only female you have come across here?"

"Because you are the first woman that *I* have sought for myself!" he bellowed, his chest burning. It was a burst of rage, but so unlike the sort he'd always known. For once, it was directed inward. The words made his mouth dry, and he had to swallow the lump in his throat.

Her eyes widened for a moment before she pressed her lips into a tight line, visibly withdrawing. Just when he'd finally gotten her to open up to him.

"I am part of your life now," he said. "You can accept it, or you can reject it. If you choose the latter, things may be very hard on you."

Outrage was still strong in her eyes, but it was tempered by hurt. "We have our bargain. Nothing more," she said softly. She turned away and began to walk along the beach.

He opened his mouth to retort sharply, to inflict more pain. But the damage had already been done, hadn't it? Anything more was just cruelty, and despite his anger, there was already ice creeping through his veins at the realization of what had just happened. Of what she'd said to him, of what she must think of him.

The only regret he could muster in regards to his past deeds was that they had made her think so poorly of him. The road behind him had been drenched in blood, but how could he be sorry for it when it was the path that had led him to her? One small change, one small mercy shown, might have completely changed where he wound up, and he may never have found her. That was unacceptable. Inconceivable.

He began to follow, closing the distance between them to nine or ten yards. She needed space again? This is all he would give, now that the island had proven more dangerous than he'd guessed.

She walked slowly, arms wrapped around herself, head angled down. The ocean's song seemed more sorrowful now, somehow heavy as it washed over Morthanion.

When Aria stopped, he did too, and watched as she turned her head to look out to the waves. He traced her gaze over rolling waters. She knew that if she went far enough – not far at all, really – she could be out of his reach. He wondered if she was weighing the unknown of the open sea against the monster that had latched onto her. For the first time in his life, he wasn't fully confident that he'd win.

He knew that Talikar was out there, somewhere to the northeast or northwest. Talikar, where he'd been Morthanion the Flame Keeper, and had done things to make mortals quake in fear and angels take up their swords in the name of righteousness. Where he'd been a disciple of Morgalien the Incinerator. Where he had burned and killed without regard for anything save the joy of dealing death. But here…

Here, there was a chance for him to be something different. To be *someone* different. Just Morthanion…just Thanion. But it all depended upon her, and her willingness to accept him despite of what he had done, and help him work toward a different future. The island was his chance to treat someone – this one person in all the world – like she was the most important thing in existence.

"I will find a way," he said, raising his voice over the sea song.

"There is no way."

"There isn't anything that will stop me from finding you." In that, at least, he was certain.

"Not while you remain marked," she said. He wondered if Laudine had tried. How else would she have known what crossing the barrier would do to him?

"You don't understand." His words were not spoken unkindly. "But some day, you will. Going past that barrier may keep you from me for a few days. A few weeks. Maybe a few years. But I will break it eventually, and then there is nowhere in all the world that you would be able to hide."

Aria was silent, dropping her gaze from the horizon. He could see her fingers rubbing her arms, lost in thought.

"Now, more than ever, we need each other," he said.

She turned to him, the thoughtfulness on her face replaced by incredulousness.

"I can understand how you would think that I might need you, but I am not so foolish as to believe you need me. Protect you? Against another demon? I cannot even get away from you!" She flinched at her own words.

His lips twitched in the ghost of a smile. "The best sort of protection is the kind that avoids fighting all together, isn't it? You know these waters, the rocks in them, better than anyone. Surely there are more caves along the shore. And you know the land on this part of the island well. You've gone twenty years without being spotted."

"Because I had Laudine!" she cried, her face crumpling. He could see moisture glistening in her eyes, and understood how alone she felt in that moment. "She left me, and I have no one else. I just want her back."

Morthanion moved to her, acting on instinct. He put his hands on her shoulders. "You had her, yes, and nothing can bring her back," he said, ignoring the spark that her skin produced on his own, "and you have her still. Everything that she taught you. *You* are the one with that knowledge now. *You* are the one with that skill. And you are the one that I will need to help me. To help me keep you safe. Both of us safe."

She didn't move away from him, didn't so much as flinch at his touch. She nodded curtly, her eyes still glossy with unshed tears.

"I want to go home now," she said.

He could see the strength and resolve in her, and knew that she was a woman to be admired and cherished. She had amazed him at every turn, intrigued him when she should have been welcoming only his wrath.

"By air or by sea?" he asked.

"I cannot fly. So both."

Morthanion nodded, a sinking feeling in his belly. She'd let him close only to reclaim the distance. "I will keep watch from on high." Reluctantly, he dropped his hands away, his gaze lingering on her for a breath's space before he took to the air with a beat of his black wings.

Chapter Eleven

Aria watched Morthanion rise into the sky until he was nothing more than a speck of darkness moving between the stars. She turned to the sea and walked into the water, finding comfort as it rose up around her legs and to her waist. Easing down into it, she let the current carry her out further before swimming.

She wished she had known her father. What had he been like before Xani? Had he done terrible things in his past? He must have, to be sent to this island. Yet Xani had looked beyond all that. He had changed, had become a better man. Laudine had told her that she had seen the regret and shame in his eyes. But Jasper had been human. He had a few decades to commit his crimes. What could they have been, compared to four thousand years of the demon's wrongdoing?

He blamed it all on what he was. Aria didn't want to believe that. Many of the prisoners on the island had committed similar crimes, but demon blood did not run through their veins. Her father had a choice. Wasn't it possible Morthanion had one, too?

Aria reached the landing of her cliff side cave and pulled herself up. Her dress clung, and water ran off her body as she sat on the edge of the opening. She wrung her hair out before entering and lighting the fire.

Morthanion arrived shortly after. His wings faded away, their shadowy forms lingering in her vision for several seconds afterwards. She was still awed by this. He stood beside her, scanning the cave entrance.

"We need to find something to hang in here to hide the rear of the cave from view."

"What do you mean?" she asked, tilting her head as she followed his gaze.

"Baltherus can fly. When the tide is low, there's a chance he might be able to see right into this place. The fire at night will make it even easier to spot. And there's no telling if he has anyone else in his group that can fly like me or swim like you." He looked down at her. "We can't take any risks now. I don't want you to come to harm because of me."

"It would not be because of you," she said, turning and walking toward the back of the cave, where she and Laudine had stored various items they'd found over the years.

He followed close behind her. "Everything that's happened to you in the last week has been because of me."

"Someone would have seen me eventually. You did. It was only a matter of time." She picked up item after item, shifting them aside as Baltherus's words echoed in her mind.

There are many people here who will stop at nothing to have a go with any woman. Especially the one you've managed to obtain.

What she had experienced at the hands of Mikel and Ithoriel was only a hint of what could happen to her. The thought made her frown as she lifted a large, folded canvas that had been part of a sail.

"Would this work?"

Morthanion took it from her and hauled it out to spread over the floor. "Couldn't be more perfect. The sea is indeed bountiful."

He looked at her as he said this, smiling, and Aria felt her cheeks heat with the intensity in his bright eyes. She glanced away, ignoring that twinge deep inside her chest. She left him to the sail and gathered some fresh water and clean clothing before disappearing behind the curtain hung in the back of the cave.

When she emerged, she took her comb and sat on the bench. As she ran it through her hair, she watched Morthanion work at hanging the sail. It took him some time to improvise a means of fastening it in place, but when he was done, canvas stretched across the entire opening. It fluttered slightly with the breeze, dulling the sound of the ocean.

The demon stepped back to survey his work, leaning from side to side and bending down to check for any gaps that might allow light through. When he seemed satisfied, he lowered himself onto the furs just across from her. She looked elsewhere, pretending to be in deep thought, not ready to be reminded of what his presence made her feel.

Morthanion was quiet, but she could feel him watching her as she worked the tangles out of her hair. Finally, she gave in and met his eyes, if only to stop the prickle they caused on her skin.

"You were happy here? With Laudine?" he asked, his voice stilted, as though the question were uncomfortable for him to voice.

Was he genuinely curious? Did he really wish to know about her past, to know if she'd been happy?

"Yes," she answered, dropping her attention to the fire. She took a thick clump of hair and worked the comb through. Laudine had always done it for her when she was young. "She was a mother to me, and despite the dangers, we were happy. She taught me many things that she had learned beyond the sea. And told me stories...so many stories. But I always had one favorite."

"Which was your favorite?"

Aria glanced up again and saw his soft smile, an expression she hadn't seen him wear before. She set her comb down and tilted her head. "You truly want to know this?"

Morthanion nodded, features solemn.

"Laudine told me she had been a spy," she said as she rose from the bench, moving around the fire to sit beside him. "It was how she survived on this island for so long. She knew how to hide, to notice details that others would not ever think about and piece the information together."

"A spy, was she?" He leaned back against the wall.

Aria nodded. "She spied on my parents. They never realized she was there. She told me that she felt as if she knew everything about them, that she was part of their lives, though they never even knew she existed. It had been my mother's laughter that drew her." She smiled fondly. "She came upon Xani sitting in the tall grasses near the shore, and there was a man on his hand and knees, offering a flower.

"She told me 'All I had ever known was cruelty and betrayal. But the light I saw in his eyes when he gazed upon the woman lounging in the grass is something I shall never forget. Hope. Love. A future.' Xani, my mother, had reached out to take the flower, but was startled when Jasper grabbed her hand. He brought it up to his face, pressing her palm to his cheek, and closed his eyes with a look of bliss."

"Did she ever tell you why your father had been sent here?" Morthanion asked.

"He told Xani that he had betrayed his order, using the skill and magic they had taught him against them. He was a battle mage, she said, but he sold his skills and delved into dark magic against his foes, had even killed some of the people who trained him."

"But he put that behind him for your mother?" he asked.

"Yes. Just as she stayed behind when her people left the island, so she could be with him."

"There were others of your kind here? That recently?"

"A few. Laudine overheard Xani saying that there had been many. They were peaceful, but when the prisoners began to appear, they had been driven into hiding until they could no longer stay for fear of their lives. So they fled."

"Leave it to the Council of Mages to drive off an entire people to establish an island where anyone they deem a threat can kill one another off," Morthanion said.

Aria cocked her head as she looked at him, hearing his bitterness. It didn't surprise her. He had been stripped of his magic and placed here, unable to leave like all the others. "Why would they do this?"

"The mage councils were once one, a singular group powerful enough that they acted as their own law when it came to magic and its practices. That's what The Order of the Justicars did, upheld the law of the Council and carried out their will. Your father was one of them, once.

"They did as they pleased where they pleased, without regard for kings or their realms. But when they battled the warlocks in Foronon, they suffered great loses. After that, they didn't have as much sway, and they fragmented.

"Over time, kings and queens began to question the right of the councils to execute their subjects. The compromise was this place; it made the monarchs and the mages look merciful, all while neatly sweeping away those who were considered a sufficient enough threat."

"That does not seem much better than killing those people themselves," she said.

"It's essentially the same. Just prevents them from bloodying their hands." She saw the muscles in his jaw tick, but he regained his composure quickly. "You were saying your mother remained here for your father? Please, continue."

"Yes, and Laudine remained close, very rarely leaving them alone unless they were doing something...personal." Aria's skin flushed. She now knew what that meant. "She said that she was enthralled by them, unable to miss a moment of their happiness, had to witness everything she could despite feeling like a voyeur. She watched people all of her life. But she allowed them privacy when needed."

"Why did she never reveal herself to them? It seems she might have been able to help them survive this place."

"That was her biggest regret. She kept hidden out of fear. They had become the family she never had, and she was afraid that she would lose that if she approached them."

"It sounds like your parents were very happy together. Despite everything they must have seen and been through." There was a hint of hope in his voice.

"They were."

She proceeded to tell him the story, narrating it as Laudine had, repeating it word for word. When she closed her eyes, she could almost feel Laudine with her, could almost hear her voice. Aria told him how her parents had made a small place to call home, how they'd conversed about things both joyful and sorrowful, and had dared to be hopeful for their shared future.

She spoke of the night when the two had stood in the lapping waves of the sea beneath a full moon and spoken the binding vows of Xani's people. They had bound not only their hearts, but their souls, and Laudine had never seen a more passionate kiss. Then she told him about the joy and fear they had both experienced when Xani discovered herself with child, and Jasper's worry as he begged her to leave.

"He was frightened for her. For his unborn child," she said, and felt her father's love even then.

"As any parent should be in a place like this," Morthanion replied, his voice soft. All the things he'd done in his life seemed so terrible, so wasteful, after listening to her tell her story of love in a place so devoid of hope and compassion. Had his parents ever really cared about him?

He'd never thought about it before, not once that he could recall in over four thousand years.

He still longed for fire, but couldn't passion fill that void in him, too? Wasn't that just another sort of flame?

"She couldn't leave him. He asked her to, many times, and she refused because she loved him too much." Aria looked down to the furs, running the tips of her fingers over their soft surface. "Time passed, and my mother began to grow with her pregnancy. Laudine was amazed, completely taken by the changes, longing to experience what Xani was feeling. To have another life inside of her, to feel its flutter of movement, to nurture it as it grew."

The demon could not fathom the thought. He was male, but he'd spent so long wading through blood and death that the idea of a new life growing inside of a woman was almost too foreign to him to be possible. All he'd known was how to destroy, not how to create. How to hate in the absence of love.

For Aria to have been conceived in such a place was a miracle. The relationship between her parents should never have taken root, should never have blossomed amidst the harshness of the island. She was born out of pure love, and he'd never understood until now how powerful a thing that could be. It made her all the more special to him.

She continued her story, shifting to lie down and stare up at the ceiling of the cave. She described the way Jasper had fretted over Xani as her belly swelled, insisting on doing everything for her, and the way Xani would smile at his efforts. Her story ended with her mother very close to giving birth, sharing in the happiness of the family she was creating with her husband.

"I don't know that I've ever been told a better story," he said. Everything about her was new to him, so genuine and pure and innocent. He had existed too long in a world filled with darkness and corruption and greed and hatred, a world of shadowy dealings and frequent betrayals. He'd thought that he had enjoyed every moment of it. But for all his centuries of life, he had experienced so small a range of emotions. He knew so little.

Looking back, how could he deny that emptiness had been the most prevalent sensation for hundreds of years?

"Laudine would tell me that story each and every night, sometimes more than once if I asked her to. She did not want my parents to be strangers to me. Even though I never knew them, I have memories of them thanks to her."

"I have the vaguest memories of my parents," he said, after a long silence. "Sometimes, I think I can almost remember what their names were...but never quite." It was the closest he could come to relating to her. Still, his own statement stirred less emotion in him than did her tale. She had Laudine, kind and patient and nurturing, and he'd had Morgalien, one of The Six Betrayers of Light, who had taught him to control the fires that roiled within him and use them to burn everyone and everything in their way.

She turned her head and frowned at him. "Because of how old you are?"

"You haven't believed me when I've told you that the things I've done have been because of what I am. I'll grant you that it's a severe over-simplification of it...what do you know of demons? Of angels? Did Laudine ever tell you any of those stories?"

"I had names and vague warnings, but no stories. It was why I did not know what you were when I first saw you."

"Well, what we are – you and I – is not quite so different as it might seem. When life was first created, the tales say, many of the gods were jealous. They wanted their own people, their own servants and followers. Wanted their vanity fulfilled. So, many of them created beings from the very elements they commanded. From water came your mother's people, and there are others formed of fire and earth and wind. There are beings, they say, that walk between life and death. Ones that dwell outside of time. Angels, above all, were the fairest. Radiant and beautiful, with wings both white and a dozen other opalescent colors.

"They were born of light, and it was they, in their supposed perfection, who enslaved themselves. They fought to defend weaker races. Helped to heal them, and guide them, and show them the beauty of Aura's light. The more aid they offered, the more was demanded of them. Some grew dissatisfied with that. Some realized that, in their power, angels should rule. When these rebels were shunned by their own kind, they turned to the Borgeln, the God of Shadow, and he was all too eager to help them.

"He used his power to warp and twist the angels – those first six, and soon after, their followers – into demons. And the demons rose up and fought to take the place they should have held, lording over all life.

"My parents were not of the original six, but they were angels, once. They were changed by the shadow. I was amongst the first generation born into it. Amongst the first to be born a demon, instead of made into one. My only purpose was to fight the war against the light, to work toward overthrowing it and claim our right to rule over all we could see."

His eyes had been upon her as he spoke, and he watched the emotions shift in her face; wonder, distress, sorrow. He guessed that, just as he couldn't imagine what it'd be like to harbor a babe in one's own body, she couldn't begin to picture the scale and ferocity of the battles, or even the diversity of the many peoples who walked the world.

"What happened to your parents?" she asked.

"I don't know. Probably killed, like so many of us have been over the millennia. I was very young when they gave me to Morgalien. I shared his affinity for infernal fire, and he taught me to use it for war. I never saw either of my parents again after that."

He wasn't certain, but he thought there were tears starting to well in her eyes. Was she sad because of what he'd been through? After the things he'd done to her, the fear that he'd instilled in her, the way he had forced himself into her life, she had tears to spill *for* him?

"Do you have at least one happy memory, demon?"

One corner of his mouth lifted. "Yes. I do. Several."

"What are they?"

"The times I've spent with you."

Aria looked away from him, seeming startled by his answer. She cleared her throat, and then he saw her lips twitch into a little smile of her own.

"I hardly see how my tricking you into eating the sleeping fruit would be a happy moment."

"Angry as I was," he said, "I was also quite proud of you. Your acting was rather convincing. It's rarely easy to trick a demon who's seen four millennia."

She was silent for a time. "You *are* old."

He couldn't help but chuckle at that. "I've told you that I am. Your mother may have been as old, or even older. And you may very well get there, too." If he had anything to do with it, she would. "It seems unfathomable, I know. I felt the same in my youth. But…after a while, the years start to roll by, faster and faster. Time takes on a different meaning."

"Perhaps with my father's human blood, I will not get to be so old." She punctuated this with a yawn, as though twenty-two years was already too much to bear.

"From what I've seen of similar unions, the immortal blood seems to be dominant. I've known half-demons who were centuries old. And your mother was a water elemental. Immortal, just as I am."

He hoped he was right. He had a feeling that he could spend another four thousand years with her and still be surprised by her.

Aria's smile softened, her eyelids drooping until they finally closed. It had been another long night for her.

"Maybe. But then I would have to explore beyond this island…" she said, her words turning to mumbling as she drifted.

"I'll take you beyond, some day," he promised. Because she deserved the world, even if he did not – and there was no way in all the hells that he'd let her go out there without his protection.

Chapter Twelve

Aria awoke to the faraway cries of gulls mingled with the sea lapping against the cliff side. When she opened her eyes, it was dimmer than she was accustomed to, and she recalled Morthanion hanging the canvas across the entrance. She lifted her head, searching the chamber. There was no sign of him.

As she lay there, watching the sail gently fluttering in the breeze, she recalled their conversation from the night before. Despite beginning with Baltherus's visit, it ended well. They had talked for hours, and he had listened to her raptly. She was surprised with how much he'd opened up to her. What he'd revealed was disheartening.

How sad that he had never known any joy in his life.

A sudden thought came to her, and she rose from her pallet. She quickly combed her hair, scrubbed her teeth with sweet-smelling leaves, and then moved to the small clay bowls where she kept some of her little treasures. Digging through them, she plucked out some shells and placed them into a small pouch. She added several thin strips of rawhide and a handful of beads before tying the pouch around her waist, and then moved to the back of the chamber.

She hadn't shown Morthanion yet, but she would. Aria rarely used the small tunnel; the sea was faster and safer for her. According to Laudine, it was very unlikely that anyone on the island would be able to survive the swim if they tried to follow Aria through the rocky waters and back to the cave. The tunnel had been more useful for the elder woman.

Moving aside the large planks, she slipped through the narrow gap and covered it behind her. The only light in the tunnel came through the small gaps in the planks, but it was easy enough to follow in the dark.

She made her way down the slanted path, keeping her hands before her to avoid walking into the damp rock walls. Slowly, the path curved to a natural incline, and when she reached the end, she shifted the boards and vegetation blocking it. She parted the grass just enough to peer out, making sure it was clear before she climbed into the open.

The mouth of the tunnel was near the only tree that stood upon the promontory, and its leaves rustled gently behind her. Laudine had once told her that its prodding roots, combined with rain water, had probably helped to open the tunnel enough for a person to fit through.

Aria replaced the covering and started on the rocky path that led down to the shore. It had been here that Laudine had taken her fall. It was steep and narrow, the footing often uneven, so she was cautious with each step.

The stone merged into the sand at the bottom, where the rock opened up to a wedge of beach that was enclosed on two sides by the cliffs. It was where Laudine and Aria had spent much of their time when they left the cave — bathing in the sun, fishing, dancing. It was away from prying eyes, the only place besides her home where she could let her guard down.

Aria had come for a specific reason this time, and began her search immediately. She wasn't sure when Morthanion would return, and she wanted to surprise him.

Not long after, her pouch was full of new shells. She found a relatively flat rock and sat down, excitedly spreading her haul out on its surface. As an image formed in her mind, she arranged them, using their shapes and colors to create a pattern. She inspected each one closely, setting aside those she wasn't satisfied with.

Aria hummed to herself with a soft smile as she assembled it, tying knots in a leather thong to keep the beads and shells spaced evenly. Occasionally, she paused to glance up, searching the sky. She knew Morthanion often appeared without warning, and she didn't want the surprise spoiled.

He always found her. That wasn't as unsettling to her now as it had been.

If she let herself dwell on it, she couldn't hide from the truth. She wanted him to find her. The way he had touched and kissed her had been exhilarating. Now that she better understood the things he made her feel, she craved more of it.

Holding it delicately between two fingers, she studied the center piece. It had been amongst her treasures for some time, and she finally had a reason put it to use. The clam shell was simple, white and coral, with a little hole at its narrow end. Many of the other shells she found had holes burrowed through them, but this one was positioned just right.

As she continued to tie her knots and arrange the adornments, uncertainty wound through her. Would Morthanion like it? He came from a distant land filled with wonders. The thing she held in her hands was so simple, so plain. There were thousands of shells littering the shore. Why would he think any of these were worth a second glance?

She wanted to do something for him, to give him a happy memory. Aria wondered if he had ever received a gift before. Surely, he would remember it fondly, wouldn't he?

Tying the ends together, she cut off the excess leather. She bit her lip as she stared down at the finished necklace. *Morthanion will like it*, she told herself before tucking the rest of the shells away in her pouch and wrapping the thick necklace around her wrist.

Rising, Aria brushed away the sand and made her way back up the cliff, climbing the steep rock steps. As she came closer to the top, she slowed and surveyed the land. Below, she was utterly hidden, but up here, she was far too exposed.

When she reached the hidden tunnel, she cast one last look around her, trying to keep low in the grass. When she was sure it was clear, Aria shifted the board and slipped into the tunnel, covering it once more so that no one would find it.

All she had to do now was await Morthanion's return. Absently, she touched her wrist and smiled at the thought she was giving him something that might bring him joy.

*****

Morthanion moved slowly and silently through the thick jungle undergrowth, sticking to the scant shadows the trees offered. Prowling in daylight was never something he enjoyed, but he'd been compelled to do so. The instinct was driving him again, and he had to protect her. That meant gathering enough supplies to keep them comfortable. It also meant knowing what moves, if any, Baltherus was making in the area.

By the voices he'd heard nearby, he knew there were at least two people in the area, but not if they were affiliated with the rival demon. Baltherus undoubtedly wielded power upon the island, but it wasn't absolute. Otherwise, he wouldn't have tried to persuade Morthanion into joining him.

Regardless of their allegiances, he planned to have choice selection of their supplies. He led them on a convoluted chase through the jungle, leaving just enough of a path for them to follow with a little effort. A broken branch here, some torn leaves there, a crushed fern and a boot print in the mud. It wasn't so long ago that he'd just have killed them and taken everything they had.

What would Aria have thought of that, though? How would she have looked at him, at the items he brought back, if she knew he'd bloodied his hands again to obtain them?

Despite not having the cover of darkness, he felt oddly energized, carried forward with cautious zeal thanks to his newfound purpose. He was protecting and providing, all at once. It helped that he'd actually slept the night before, for the first time in a long while. He hadn't done so *with* Aria, but he'd been *near* her. As a result, his sleep had been restful and deep.

He halted as he came to the edge of the clearing in which the men had set up camp. Crouching low, he peered through thick, fragrant leaves. Food, water, tools – it was all there, exposed. How could he not take it?

From somewhere behind him came the snapping of branches and rustling of vegetation. He sank lower, masking himself completely in the brush, and listened.

"Probably was him," said a man entering the campsite. Another human, a dark-skinned drow, and an orc entered close behind him. Apparently, Morthanion had misjudged their numbers. They moved to the center of the clearing, backs to him.

"Don't matter," said the orc. "Boss said not to split up, that it were too dangerous. No sense in us runnin' round in circles all day long."

"I've already said he was likely leading us away to raid our supplies." The accent marked that one as the drow.

"Well, our supplies're still here, aren't they?"

"Because we returned here with haste. If he truly is a demon, he can be patient. He could sit and watch us until we all grow old and crumble to dust if he wanted to."

"Orders are simple, boys. Whatever this guy can do, you think it'll be any worse'n what the boss'll do to us if we screw up?"

The group settled in, the four taking more comfortable postures, though they scanned their surroundings frequently. With great care, Morthanion shifted his position to get a better view of their provisions.

"He's dangerous," the orc said in a deep, rumbling voice. He'd produced a worn axe, and was running a stone along its blade. His bare torso was covered with intricate black tattoos. Morthanion had seen such markings among many of the roaming orc tribes. "But boss wants him. Boss *needs* him. Don't bode well for the rest of us."

"All I know is that it's been a while since I had a woman apart from the same ones we've had all along. Don't know if I'll be able to stop myself…"

Morthanion nearly burst from the jungle, his muscles coiling to spring. It was only an immense expenditure of willpower that kept him in place, seething. There were four of them. He'd stood against greater numbers before, but he hadn't lied to Aria; he could be killed. If he was killed, he would not be able to get back to her. Would not be able to keep her safe.

Clenching his jaw and fists, he eased back, remaining low in the undergrowth as he retreated from the camp. The men had adequate supplies to remain out here for some time. Were they just advance scouts, or were they watchmen? How many more such men did Baltherus have under his influence?

He'd found only a few pieces of fruit and a musty blanket, but it would have to be enough for the day. If Baltherus already had so many men on this part of the island – where Aria said others rarely ventured – Morthanion may have underestimated him. That notion had him moving through the jungle rapidly. It meant there was a chance she had already been found, already been taken.

Before long, he was sprinting between trees, holding back the growing urge to fly. It was too risky with the sun approaching its zenith. If they hadn't found her, he'd lead them straight to her by taking to the sky. He had to trust that the cave was safe enough. He couldn't give in to his fears.

Fluttering heat spread from the base of his skull, as it always seemed to when she was near, but in his panic the sensations seemed confused. Their home was drawing near, but it didn't feel like she was there. Was she being dragged away even now? He followed it, telling himself it was wrong, that it was simply anxiety leading him astray, pretending that his heart wasn't as loud as crackling thunder on a stormy night.

As he emerged from the trees, the terrain grew rapidly rocky. It was the start of the cliffs that led to the promontory which held their cave. He scrambled over the stone, climbing to the crest. He should feel her presence more to the west, yet its lingering traces told him it was somewhere just east.

He leaned forward on hands and knees and searched the beach below. There were footprints in the sand, tracing a meandering path. Were they hers, or had someone else left them? If Baltherus had come, he may not have even set foot on the ground.

The water lapped at the shore lazily, caring nothing for his plight, and it felt for a moment as though his heart was trying to claw up to his throat. Had she simply decided to wait for him to leave so she could slip away into the ocean, to escape his grasp forever?

Digging his claws into the rock beneath them, he swallowed thickly. He had to go find her. His skull was throbbing, telling him she was somewhere, but he couldn't even pinpoint a direction. Couldn't waste more time trying to decipher it. Cursing the daylight under his breath, he spread his wings and thrust off the top of the cliff.

He caught the wind current and used it to propel himself out past the outcropping, wheeling back around to aim himself directly at the cave. Against his better judgment, he'd left her there earlier. They couldn't have taken her from it without leaving some sign. She couldn't have abandoned him, not now.

But she has run so many times already, he reminded himself.

Blood racing, he let his wings dissipate just before he reached the mouth of the cave, his momentum carrying him into the small opening. He burst through the canvas, nearly tearing it down, and stopped himself by raking his claws over the hard floor. The fire was out, and the place was utterly still and too quiet. Rising, he searched the chamber, every corner and crevice – not that there were many – and found nothing out of the ordinary.

Except that she wasn't there. No sign of a struggle, none of the supplies depleted. Just a cold, empty cave. Her scent still lingered.

If she'd gone beyond the barrier, would she even need any of these things? She was a water elemental. Surely the sea was all she required. Why had he ever thought she might need him? They hadn't been bound yet, and she could pursue anyone in the world if she chose to. For him, Aria was it. There could be no one else.

That old, familiar fury started to churn in him. It quickly reached a boil, igniting from a spark to a full flame. Things had just begun to get better between them. For the first time in his existence, he'd felt like he wasn't alone, like he could trust another person. And she'd left to go out *there*? Directly into danger?

There were so many ways he could lose her forever. It had taken four thousand years to find her, and he was only just beginning to identify the new feelings she stirred within him. How could he bear to lose that after scant few days?

How could he ever bear losing her?

There was a faint rustle of movement at the rear of the cave. He snapped his eyes up. Aria was standing there, replacing a panel he'd not noticed before.

She'd gone out. Put herself in danger, knowing full well there were powerful forces against them.

Aria turned to him, her eyes widening.

Morthanion's vision darkened, shadows encroaching upon it. He should have given in to the instinct. He should have claimed her, bound her to him. That way he could be sure to protect her. That way he wouldn't have to feel so helpless. He wouldn't have to feel his gut twisting, acidic with fear.

He surged forward, his speed leaving her no time to react. Seizing her by her upper arms, he lifted her off her feet and pressed her back to the wall.

"Why would you go out?" he demanded, voice distorted and harsh. "In broad daylight, when there are people looking for you? Did you mean to flee again? Did you mean to leave me?"

The thought wrenched his insides further. He tightened his grip and shook her once.

Her eyes, perfect circles, stared down into his with unmasked fear.

"What were you thinking?" he roared.

She flinched, her face paling.

"There is nowhere else to go! No one else who can have you!"

She bit back a sound of pain, her features tightening with his grip. Her skin was hot beneath his palms, her fragrance enveloped him. Blood hot, cock stiff, every instinct in him demanded he take her. That he bind her to him irrevocably.

In the red mist he'd plunged into, that was the only course of action. He had to put his mark on her. He had to claim her, so she and everyone else would know she was his. Had to forever solidify his possession of her.

He spun, laying her on the furs, and straddled her thighs. Hooking the fabric of her dress with his claws, he tore it down the front, catching a glimpse of the supple flesh beneath.

"No!" she cried, pushing with her hands and scratching with her nails.

He caught her wrists and pinned them over her head. Something bit into his palm, but he ignored it. There was no room for pain, now. With his free hand, he tore away the remainder of her garment, and tossed it aside. Her body writhed, back arching, and he looked down to see her bared breasts straining toward him.

He cupped one, stroking her nipple with his thumb, and then leaned down to twirl his tongue around it. Her skin was sweeter than honey. He sucked it into his mouth and nipped at it with his fangs.

She gasped. He could smell her arousal; it would not be unpleasant for her. She'd learn quickly.

"No! No no no no no! Not like this!" she yelled, twisting beneath him, brushing her body against his and creating a delightful friction.

He reached up and clamped a hand over her mouth. Her breath was warm against his skin. Fate had chosen them for each other, and they would share that fate no matter what. Aria would appreciate it soon enough. All he needed to do was enter her, to tear off his pants and bury himself deep in her sex, to spill his scorching seed inside of her and burn himself forever into her soul.

Sliding up, he traced her collarbone to the line of her neck with the tip of a fang. She was tugging at her arms, straining to pull away. A sharp jerk of her head broke his hold on her mouth.

"Stop, Thanion! Please! Not like this," she sobbed.

He lifted his head and looked down at her face. Tears streamed from her eyes, leaving wet trails down her cheeks. There weren't supposed to be tears in those eyes, not in Aria's. Never. Where was her desire? The need he had once seen brightening her gaze?

His insides clenched suddenly, savagely, as he realized what he was doing. His stomach heaved and revolted against him, and there was no more room for breath in his lungs.

What had he done? They had finally been on the path to something real, something more, and what had he done?

Was this how he was going to take his mate for the first time? With terror and tears in her eyes?

He leapt back from her, stumbling away. She sat up, drawing her knees in front of her and scrambled back to the wall. Wrapping her arms around her legs, she stared at him with round, wounded eyes. He could see red marks on her arms where his claws had broken her skin.

Morthanion looked down to his shaking hands, and could see the faint glistening of blood on the tips of his claws.

What have I done?

Though he'd never really known it before, shame crashed over him with the force of a tidal wave. In that moment, he knew what it meant to hate himself, to be disgusted by his own actions. He'd almost done that to her – to his Aria – after he had told her he didn't think himself capable of harming her.

He stepped toward her, reaching out. He had to comfort her, had to tell her he was sorry, that he wouldn't do it again. But her face was wet with tears, his hands stained with her blood.

She had been right to fear him. And he'd been a fool to think she shouldn't.

Aria met his gaze just as more moisture welled at the corner of her eyes, riding her lashes to tumble down her cheeks. An icy fist closed around his heart, and he fled.

Batting aside the sail, he leapt from the ledge.

"Thanion!" he thought he heard her call, but it might have just been the sound of the ocean. The water seemed to say *I knew you would do this.*

Could she have been more wrong about him? There was no choice, there was no overcoming his nature. He was fated to have her. And he was born a demon. What capacity did he have for gentleness, for kindness? His every thought, emotion, and action had always been and would always be corrupted, tainted, twisted. Getting her to believe otherwise was only proof of it.

He flew, pumping his wings faster and faster, turning from the sorrowfully mocking sea to soar over sand and rock, and crashed into the jungle.

Aria stood, staring at the sail, chest heaving after her attempt to call Morthanion back. There were so many conflicting emotions warring inside her; fear, want, confusion, worry.

She had seen so much in his eyes, so much torment and anguish. He had looked disgusted and ashamed. Completely shocked by what he had been doing to her. And now he was gone. Surely he would be fine. He was an old demon, strong and capable.

Aria wiped her eyes with the heels of her hands, but the tears kept coming, blinding her.

Why had he reacted the way he had? Why had he been so furious with her?

Why would you go out? In broad daylight, when there are people looking for you? Did you mean to flee again? Did you mean to leave me?

He thought she had left him. Again. Run away as she had so many times before.

He had worried for her.

Morthanion had reached some sort of breaking point and utterly snapped in fear for her.

Weary, confused, she shakily grabbed a tunic from the pile of clothing he'd gathered and pulled it over her head. It was longer than her dresses, the hem falling to her knees. She had to roll up the sleeves to keep them from covering her hands.

That's when she remembered the necklace wrapped around her wrist. Unraveling it, she could see the dark imprints the shells had made in her skin when he'd held her arms down. She squeezed it to her chest, choking back a sob, and sunk down on the furs. Her head fell into her hands and she closed her eyes.

Chapter Thirteen

During Morthanion's absence, Aria did what she could to pass the time, returning the items that had been scattered on the floor to their proper places. When she found her dress, she held it out in front of her, its now tattered fabric swaying in her trembling hands. She released a shaky breath, tears stinging her eyes at the memory of being held beneath him.

She had run from him so many times, had tricked and misled him, but he'd never hurt her. The force he'd used against her, the anger, had not been from the man she'd come to know. There had been something unsettling in his eyes – they were devoid of any recognition, like he somehow looked through her. Something had taken him over from within.

Unwilling to waste the cloth, she tore it into strips to use as bandages and put them away. A soft clattering made her pause. She looked to her wrist, around which she'd once more wrapped the necklace. Her throat constricted and her eyes burned; it was supposed to have been a happy memory.

It didn't take long to clean up, and the rest of the day passed slowly.

She fretted, she paced, she peered past the canvas many times, scouring the sky for sign of him. Would he come back? Loneliness had almost consumed her once, and she didn't want to go back to that. Talking to Morthanion had been a comfort. He listened to her intently, and she enjoyed his stories of the world beyond the island.

She took pleasure in his company. Even when silence fell between them, it was relaxing. Familiar.

For a time, she sat with a piece of bark and sketched. Every movement of the charcoal built a little more of him, shaping his strong jaw, his angled, defiant brows, his crooked smile. It was easy to create his likeness, which surprised her – it had taken years to get Laudine right – but she knew the charcoal, no matter her skill, could not capture the burning intensity of his gaze.

Finally setting the drawing with all her others, she returned to the canvas and pulled it aside. The sky was red-orange, so similar to his eyes, as the sun sank on the western horizon. Thick, dark clouds were rolling toward the sunset, threatening to swallow the remaining light. Turning away, she crouched to start a fire, and then sat on the furs to wait.

Despite how tired she felt, she knew sleep would not come. Images of what had happened kept swirling through her mind, sparking little flares of emotion. Above that, however, was her concern for Morthanion. Absently, she braided her hair and stared at the fire as the sail flapped in the building wind.

She looked up as lightning flashed in the darkened sky, and knew the silhouette cast through the canvas was his. He brushed the flap aside and stepped into the chamber.

"You are back," she said, sagging in relief. He had masked his true form again. He was hiding from her behind the human visage, and Aria knew he was trying to make himself appear as unthreatening as possible.

He hesitated before he moved further into the cave. It brought a pang to her chest to see him like this, lacking the confidence he normally displayed. He placed a cloth-wrapped bundle on the floor in front of her. She glanced at it only briefly before lifting her eyes back to him.

His face was guarded, gaze averted from her.

"What is it?"

"Meat. Fruit. Water."

"From people? Close by?"

"From some of them, yes," he answered, tension clear in his stiff posture.

Aria studied him, searching his face. Even though his eyes were bright blue instead of the fiery red she loved so much, he was beautiful to her. But he was withdrawn, shielding whatever was going on inside by masking his real features.

"Thanion," she coaxed softly. *Please look at me.*

Morthanion turned his head away sharply, as if he'd been slapped.

Aria frowned. "You prefer I call you Morthanion?"

"You may call me what you wish," he replied, and still didn't look at her.

"Demon…" she sighed.

His gaze fell on her then, lured by the yearning in her voice. There was confusion in his furrowed brow, but longing on his parted lips.

"After what I've done, you speak to me that way?"

"Are you still angry with me?"

Morthanion laughed bitterly. It was something she had never heard from him. He had always made light of everything, a grin upon his face. She frowned, wondering if she'd read him wrong.

"You are still?" she asked hesitantly.

"No. But you should be, with me."

Aria knew why he would think that. She had seen the anguish, shame, and disgust in his eyes before he had left. Saw it even now in his expression and stance. He hadn't felt remorse for the things he'd done in his past, but he felt it for what he had nearly done to her.

"I was not. I am not," she answered softly.

Some of the tension eased from Morthanion, but he still appeared conflicted.

"Why did you leave?" he finally asked.

Aria rose from the furs, hesitating before she approached him. As she closed the small distance between then, she unraveled the necklace from her wrist, and raised the trinket in offering.

"A gift. For you."

The necklace was made of rawhide strips braided together with small shells woven in. The dark beads she and Laudine had discovered on the beach one day years ago were perfect contrast to the pale shells. At the center was the larger clam shell. It was simply crafted, and she feared that he might reject it as pointless.

Instead, Morthanion took it from her carefully and examined it as though it were the most delicate thing in the world. He ran his fingers over the pieces reverently, following the ridges and grooves on the shells.

"I wanted to give you another happy memory," she said. Warmth spread through her at sight of the wonder on his face. It melted away her anxiety.

"Beginning to lose count of those, these days," he murmured.

"I did not mean to worry you. I was careful."

"I know you were." He took hold of the rawhide, spreading it, and pulled it over his head.

Aria watched him, her lips lifting into a smile.

"There are at least two groups in the area, looking for us. Sent by Baltherus, undoubtedly."

Her smile faded as quickly as it had come. For so long, this part of the island had been mostly deserted. Now, it seemed to be filling with prisoners. It was only a matter of time before the cave was discovered. Before she lost her home.

"The way you entered earlier...it is well hidden?" he asked, glancing at the back of the cave.

"It is."

"Good. I—" He stiffened, his eyes dropping to her neck.

Aria saw his remorse immediately and knew he'd noticed the angry line his fangs had left on her collarbone. She raised her hand to cover it. Morthanion's mouth snapped shut.

"I never meant to hurt you," he said gruffly. It was likely the closest he had ever come to apologizing to anyone.

"I know." She adjusted the tunic to cover the small wound. "And I forgive you."

Morthanion's tense muscles eased visibly, and he drew her into his arms. He used none of the superhuman speed that had frightened her earlier, though he held her like a drowning man would a floating scrap of wood. She accepted his embrace, pressing her hands to his chest, curling her fingers slightly at the feel of his heartbeat.

Aria's eyes drifted closed when he pressed his lips against her forehead. He inhaled deeply, his body shuddering, and she could feel the turmoil within him. It was like being in his arms opened her to the conflicting emotions that roiled in his heart. Had he ever known kindness, or a comforting embrace?

Still, she was surprised – and pleased – by his gentleness. Despite what had transpired earlier, she knew he would protect her until his last breath.

"What happened?" she asked, recalling the mad gleam in his eyes, as if he had been driven by something unseen.

"I lost myself." He held her just a little tighter, like he feared she'd slip away.

When he didn't say more, she asked, "What made you stop?"

"I looked into your eyes and saw your tears."

Aria lifted her head, her searching gaze meeting his. What she saw made her heart skip a beat. Even behind the false blue of his eyes, she could see the flickering of his inner fires, and knew they burned for her. Concern and guilt had his eyebrows low, his jaw clamped, but it did not diminish the longing in his expression.

Despite everything he had told her of his past, she trusted him. His anger had been motivated by worry. It had been anger at her placing herself in danger, at exposing herself when she could have been found and taken. Morthanion was old, and strong, and his fear had consumed him. While he'd left superficial marks on her, he hadn't truly harmed her. He had stopped.

Aria stepped back and took one of his rough, beautiful hands. She ran her finger along the tips of his, which seemed strange without his dark claws. Lifting his hand, she placed a light kiss upon the pads of his fingers. She felt a ripple of pleasure flow through him, and looked up to see the heat in his eyes. He reclaimed his hand and stepped close, scooping her up into his arms.

Aria giggled as he held her against him. Then he eased down onto the furs, shifting her to his side, and wrapped her in his arms. Their bodies fit together perfectly.

"I like that sound," he said.

"What sound?"

"Your laughter."

There was another flash of lightning outside, followed closely by booming thunder. The sail hiding their little cave fluttered and whipped. Aria lay silently and listened to the storm, absorbing the warmth radiating from him, surrounded by his scent. She was afraid to move. Afraid that the peaceful moment would end. Her eyes caught the shell resting on his skin and she smiled. She placed her palm on his chest, feeling the beating of his heart, happy.

He settled his hand atop hers, absently tracing the little bumps and ridges of the shells on the necklace she'd made for him. Not once in his life had he been given anything out of kindness, not once had he been given something so simple, yet so meaningful. Now, he could look at all of it – at what she was giving him, at her – and know that he didn't deserve any of it. Not too long ago, he'd been a lord of everything he could see, superior and entitled. He had taken anything he'd desired.

All he wanted now was Aria, and he knew that she wasn't a thing to be taken. She was a person to be earned. Whether or not he claimed her, she would — or would not — be his of her own accord. And now he was learning that there could be great enjoyment in winning her. This would not be another quick, empty conquest. He'd come dangerously close to that, but he would not falter again.

He'd almost thrown it all away. Almost denied himself the only chance at happiness he would ever get.

Crashing through the overgrown jungle, he had tried to flee from himself, tried to flee from her, tried to escape the things he had done and had almost done. The emotions inside of him had never been so thick, so powerful, so full of self-disgust that they'd made him ill.

But he could not outrun his desire for her. His *need* for her. Each step farther away brought more pain. Inside, his very soul had shuddered and writhed, clawing at him to return to her side, to keep her safe, seemingly oblivious to the harm he had just caused her.

She was his mate. If he had doubted before, he couldn't deny it now. Even after what had passed between them, he still wanted her. He didn't know how she would react to the information. Would she understand what a mate was, what it meant? Would she accept it, or rail against it as a violation of her free will, her right to choose?

No. Much as he loathed himself for what he'd nearly done to her, he knew there was no choice. She was *his*. They were made for one another, and there'd be no controlling himself if someone else tried to have her.

Even now, it was a struggle to keep from sliding atop her again. Every bit of contact was like magic, crackling over his skin with delicious, tantalizing heat. It was *better* than magic. He would choose these new fires over the old without hesitation.

The storm raged outside, building intensity, but the two of them were oblivious to everything save their embrace. Before he was sent here, he would never have imagined lying like this with a woman. Now, he wanted nothing more than to lie in contentment by her side.

"Can you remove it?" she asked, her breath tickling the skin on his chest.

It took him a few moments to realize what she meant, but once he did, he obliged. He dropped the shroud away, releasing it from that mostly-subconscious part of his mind that had controlled it for most of his life, exposing all but his wings. Was she really so fascinated by his true appearance? To most, it was monstrous. His face remained the same – handsome, chiseled features that many found irresistible – but his mien was perverted by the shadow, by horns and fangs and claws and eyes that burned like twin fires.

She sat up and looked at him, brushing a hand over his cheek.

"I want to see you," she said, as though he'd voiced his doubts aloud.

Her eyes dipped away from his face. She watched her own fingers as she ran them over his claws, slowly, and took her lower lip between her teeth.

"I want to see…all…of you."

Liquid fire surged through his veins. Had he heard her correctly? Surely not after…

"Oh?" He raised one of his dark brows, one side of his mouth tilting up.

She flushed at that, and it felt like the warmth coming from her intensified.

"I enjoyed what we shared on the beach. And today…I…I did not want it to be like that. I want it to be like *this*." She pressed her palms to his chest and leaned forward, kissing the upturned corner of his lips. Before he could return it, she pulled away. "Let me see you."

Gently, he guided her aside so he could get onto his knees. He allowed himself to run his fingertips over the soft skin of her neck, marveling at the way her cheeks had darkened to a rosy hue.

His shaft, which seemed to always remain half-rigid these days, stiffened instantly. Aria's delectable aroma was making his head foggy in the best of ways. With reluctance, he broke contact with her and stood, gathering the hem of his shirt in his hands and drawing it over his head. He tossed it aside without looking where it went. It was unimportant. Everything was, save the woman before him, whose eyes were upon him, darkening with desire.

Firelight and shadow danced over his sculpted torso, allowing glimpses of old scars and tattoos. As his wings coalesced, he stretched them to either side, the tips of his feathers brushing the ceiling of the cave.

He dropped his hands to the waistline of his pants, lowering them to expose dark, thick hair. Pausing, he searched her gaze. Even in the headiness of his longing, he understood this was a threshold from which there was no returning.

Aria's lips were parted, her attention rapt upon the little he'd bared. It was all the confirmation he needed from her.

He slid his trousers over his hips, cock springing free, and let them fall to the floor. She gasped, hands covering her eyes. Her fingers parted for another tentative glance before she averted her gaze fully, letting her hands drop to her lap. She caught her lower lip between her teeth again, and he had the sudden urge to nip at it himself.

Somehow, her cheeks had reddened further. His smile broadened with each new expression that flitted over her face. He couldn't deny a surge of pride at her reaction, knowing now that he was indeed the first man she'd ever beheld. He eagerly anticipated removing her clothing to see her fully, to see her pale skin flushed with desire.

She had been right. This was how he wanted it, too, without the fear, without the drive of mindless instinct. Aria was his, and he would treat her well. He'd teach her more of life's pleasures than she could imagine, and would ensure they were mutual.

This time when she looked back at him, she seemed to have bolstered her resolve. She stared him with a mixture of curiosity and awe. He wasn't sure if it was possible, but he hardened further, throbbing painfully with need for her.

Aria stood up. He extended his arms to wrap around her, to draw her body against his, but she stopped him with a shake of her head. "I want to you explore you."

He regarded her with slitted eyes. Then he spread his arms to either side and dipped into a shallow bow. "As you like," he said.

Slowly, her eyes roamed over him, heating his skin and making him hunger for her touch. She avoided looking directly at his erection, instead focusing on the sculpted muscles of his abdomen, the various scars, the broad expanse of his chest. His fingers twitched, rebelling against his restraint, but he held against the urge to reach for her. This was new to him. Allowing her control only seemed to make the situation more arousing.

She stepped behind him, and a shudder ran up his spine in anticipation, his wings stretching. He could feel her breath against his feathers, more gentle and caressing than a summer breeze. He'd never trusted anyone else to touch them. Like some joke from the gods, they were amongst the most sensitive parts on a demon's body, and could bring one to his knees in pleasure or pain with equal ease.

His lips parted when her hand settled on the arch of a wing. She followed it down, sending ripples of ecstasy throughout him, until her palm rested on the place where it emerged from his back. He sucked in a shaky breath, shoulders quaking, and dipped his head. Sweet tension coursed through his limbs, curling his fingers and toes.

When she pressed her body against his back, he swayed, warmth radiating from her. He could feel the softness of her breasts even through her tunic. Delicately, she ran her fingers over his feathers, sending electric pulses through him that made his cock leap in response.

"Your wings are beautiful," she said, pulling away. A moment later, he could feel her lips against the skin between them.

"Not nearly as beautiful as you," he replied huskily.

Hesitantly, her fingers brushed over his buttocks. His chest swelled with another sharp inhalation. When she walked back around to his front, he was smirking.

Her cheeks were bright pink, and though her smile was small, there was a blossoming confidence in it. She pressed her hands to his chest, shifting a few of the necklace's shells with one finger. That widened her smile visibly. Something tightened in his chest, and he felt his own lips lift up a little further.

Aria ran her hands over his chest, up to his shoulders, and then back down over his ribs and the rigid muscles of his stomach. With more gentleness than he thought possible, she leaned forward and kissed every scar she encountered. He had to clench his fists to keep from twining his fingers in her hair and devouring her mouth.

"What do these mean?" she asked, pressing the pads of her fingers to a pair of his tattoos, tracing their intricate designs.

"They are focuses for my magic," he replied, and then corrected himself, "*were* focuses for my magic. Made it stronger." They buzzed with a new energy beneath her touch, a new form of magic that he was finding much more satisfying than the unfathomable power of the old.

She dropped her gaze. His need was close to setting his limbs to trembling. He clenched his jaw, trying to settle himself. Then she reached down, and brushed her fingers over the head of his shaft.

A fire roared in his belly as his erection jumped in reaction, and he barely held in a groan. The cave was gone, forgotten, the island a thing of distant memory. All he was aware of was her, standing in front of him in nothing but an old tunic, looking delectable.

Her wide, innocent eyes rose to his face for a moment, and then she was looking back down again. This time, she took him in hand, wrapping her fingers around his aching length, stroking it with her thumb.

Morthanion bared his teeth and growled, rocking back on his heels. He shifted his arms, clasping his hands behind his back and digging his claws into his own skin to keep from succumbing to his desires. Her touch was fire and ice, pleasure enhanced by a hint of agony. Regardless of his need for her, he had to maintain control. This was for *her*. He would not deny her what she wanted in order to satisfy his own need.

"This pains you?" she asked, frowning, and pulled her hand away.

"Not in the way you think," he said, dipping his head to motion her hand back. "I am yours to explore." He'd never begged anyone for anything in all his life, but if she didn't take hold of him again, he'd drop to the floor and plead for it.

She smiled again, and lowered herself to her knees. Just the sight of it had his cock straining toward her, his breath short and quick through parted lips. Her head tilted as she studied him.

With that light touch, she traced his length from dark hair to crown, circling it with the tips of her fingers. Moisture gathered at the tip. Seeing such fascination on her face, knowing that she was so enthralled, was intoxicating. She had him nearing his climax with little more than a few strokes of her soft little hands, his head tilting back as waves of pleasure roiled through him.

He squeezed his eyes shut as she gripped him again and began to run her hand up and down his shaft with teasing slowness. Every muscle in his body contracted as he fought the thrill of it, as he battled to remain still for her. Bursts of light went off behind his eyelids. His hips bucked, and she paused.

He looked down just in time to see her lean forward and brush the tip of his cock against the soft skin of her cheek, teasingly close to her pink lips.

Morthanion growled, and whatever control he'd maintained shattered.

Chapter Fourteen

In a blur of motion, he had her down on the furs, his body propped over hers. He grabbed her tunic to tear off the final barrier between them. She lightly touched his hand, heat flaring up his arm, and he stilled.

No. Not like this.

He needed to explore her, too. To take time to learn every little part of her.

Claim her, demanded the instinct. *She is yours, and it doesn't matter how.*

"Thanion," she said, reaching up to cup his cheeks.

I am not claiming her. I am winning her.

He exhaled; the worry faded from her expression. Her body eased beneath him, and he knelt between her parted legs.

He cupped her calf with one hand, and slid his palm up, over the soft skin behind her knee, following the outside of her thigh. She shivered, though her skin was aflame. Slowly, he lifted the hem of the tunic higher, revealing more of her creamy flesh.

His attention dipped to the spot between her legs, and he pulled back slightly to get a better view. Her thighs were parted, giving him a glimpse of her glistening sex. He slid his hands to the flare of her hips, thumbs brushing her smooth stomach. Her scent was maddening. He had to taste her.

He leaned down, his tongue slipping between her folds.

"Thanion!" she cried, her entire body jerking.

She tasted sweeter than anything he'd ever known, utterly ambrosial, and her reaction urged him on. He greedily lapped at her, wrapping his arms around her thighs to keep her from squirming away. She was already dripping wet, and each flick of his tongue over her clitoris coaxed more of the soft sounds from her that he longed to hear.

Aria writhed in his hold, her body trembling, back arching as her hips gyrated. Morthanion circled the bud of her desire with his tongue and then closed his lips over it, sucking.

"Demon!" she moaned, her voice husky.

She tensed, grabbing hold of his horns as she cried out her pleasure. Now she was both pulling his mouth closer and thrusting her hips at him. He would never have guessed she'd be so eager and passionate a creature.

His own hips were rocking, sliding his length along the furs beneath him, wishing the ripples of pleasure were as strong as they had been at her touch. *Soon*, he promised himself.

"Come for me, Aria," he growled against her.

Morthanion continued to devour her, her reactions to his attention only pushing him on more ravenously. Shifting his hold on her, he slipped a finger between her tight, dripping folds. He groaned against her sex as her inner walls clamped down, drawing it further in. She was driven as wild by him as he was by her.

He would never have enough of her. Never in all eternity.

She lifted her backside off the floor, her legs falling wider as she gave herself over. Yanking down on his horns, she cried out again. Hot moisture flowed from her, and he drank her nectar greedily.

Rising over her, he hooked the hem of her tunic and drew it up, his hands running over her waistline, her ribs, the swell of her breasts. He slid it over her head, leaving her naked, pale, exquisite in the flickering light. Her dark hair was pooled around her, shimmering like the water she so favored.

The tip of his shaft pressed against her entrance, but he denied himself a little longer. He gazed down at her, committing every detail to memory. His chest constricted when he looked at her arms. Bruises ringed her biceps, broken only by the scabs forming where his claws had punctured her skin. They made the scratch on her collarbone, where he'd raked her with a fang, look minor.

Leaning down, he tenderly pressed his lips to the wounds he'd inflicted. The guilt for what he'd done did nothing to dampen his need. Desire consumed him, driven on by an instinct he could not deny. He looked up to find her watching him, warmth in her half-lidded eyes.

She raised a hand, brushing hair out of his face. Morthanion propped himself up on one arm as she traced a path from cheek to brow, and there was something in her expression that he could not quite read. Something that he didn't fully understand. That look made his chest ache.

It had to be now. There was no guarantee that he'd have such control if he waited any longer.

Taking himself in hand, he rolled his hips and guided himself to her opening. He felt her body stiffen beneath him.

There was uncertainty in her expression now. Lowering himself to an elbow, he gently took her by the chin, forcing her to meet his gaze.

"Look at me, and trust me," he said, wondering how much trust he was about to lose by causing her pain.

She stared at him, searching his eyes. "I do," she replied, and lifted her head to kiss him.

His eyelids shut, those two little words having a profound effect upon him. He thrust forward, breaching that delicate wall, claiming her.

His arms trembled. Something surged through him, and he nearly sagged onto her as his breath escaped him. Her quick exhalation tickled his skin, her inner muscles clamping down on his shaft. He held himself still, battling the need to drive deeper into her.

Something shifted inside of him, something indefinable yet undeniable. Every sense was suddenly more acute when it came to her. Her fragrance stronger and more alluring, permeating the whole chamber, the heat she gave off more intense, the softness of her skin enough to send thrills through him. And her pain…he could feel that, too, like it was his own.

Aria inhaled in surprise at the sudden, sharp flash of pain. Her fingers tangled in his hair and she squeezed her eyes shut.

He filled her, stretched her, and pressed deeper. Above her and within her, Morthanion remained utterly still. She breathed shakily against the inner burn. Slowly, the sting began to fade. She had a vague sense that there was more to this. In the depths of her being, there was a different burning, one that was somehow pleasing. It was a growing sense of need, much as she'd felt before he'd entered her.

She opened her eyes to find him staring down at her, his brow furrowed and lips pressed into a straight line as though he was in pain, too. She felt a more profound connection between them, like he was sharing in the burden of her discomfort. More aware of him than ever before, she relaxed.

As the last bit of tension eased from her, Morthanion began to move. He pulled almost entirely out of her, and Aria found herself nearly protesting the loss. Then he thrust back in and her eyes widened. There was no pain, only exquisite fullness and something potent enough to make her thoughts swim. It was nothing like when he had used his mouth on her. This was a slow build, like gently blowing on embers to bring them back to a full, roaring flame.

His gaze sparkled with wonder, and burned with desire.

As he moved, she found herself matching him, craving more. The next time he pulled back, Aria wrapped her legs around his hips and used the leverage to take him deeper and harder.

He bared his fangs, his wings snapping out and around them, feathers brushing against her flesh. Shadows coalesced on his face, leaving only two fiery orbs that penetrated her very soul.

That slow burn that he ignited within her grew into an inferno. She arched her back, closing her eyes against the overwhelming feel of it. She moved beneath him, breasts rubbing against his chest, nipples tight and overly sensitive. Her moans overpowered the cacophony of the storm outside, echoing off the cave walls to fill the chamber.

She ached, oh gods, she ached. The need was consuming her.

"Demon," she whispered, begging.

"Aria," he growled, clenching his teeth, "you burn like a fire in the darkness."

Her arms slipped around his sides, grasping his wings where they met his back. A blast of pleasure swept through her.

"Fuck!" He pumped his hips in a frenzy, his breath sweetly ragged.

She clung to him, taking everything he gave.

Then it hit her.

Aria came, her body trembling, inner muscles contracting around him, pulling him deeper. She bit his shoulder, muffling her cries as wave after wave crashed over her.

The moment her teeth sunk into his flesh, Morthanion stiffened, releasing a roar as his seed exploded inside her, hot and forceful.

His climax carried her to another peak, and she released his wings to clutch at his back, nails digging into his skin. Her lips parted in a cry made silent by the intensity of what she was feeling. It left her breathless, and for a time she didn't know where she ended and he began.

Morthanion continued to thrust forward and back, each motion drawing out her shuddering climax, until he finally sagged atop her. She kept her arms around him, his breath hot against her sweat-dampened neck, her own chest rising and falling rapidly as she drifted down from the heights to which he'd lifted her. Moving her hand to twine in his hair, she finally opened her eyes.

The cave seemed darker than it had been before, like the fire's light could not penetrate the thickened shadows. Almost solid wisps of darkness drifted around the chamber, swallowing the light and releasing it again at odd angles.

She cradled him against her, more amazed by what they had shared, by the ferocity of it, than she was by the shadows dominating the cave. That was just another part of him. And she felt him. Not just his body upon her, or his length still nestled between her legs, but all of him, imprinted on her heart, on her soul. She was still herself, but she felt…changed. Like she carried a piece of him now.

Her beautiful, beautiful demon.

She kissed his shoulder.

"Aria," he said, breathlessly. He held himself up on one arm and stared down at her, awe glittering in his eyes. Then he groaned and rolled off, lying on his side and wrapping his arms around her to draw her close.

She shut her eyes and sighed, smiling softly in her contentment. Her body was sated, replete, and now cocooned by his. "I wanted it to be like this," she mumbled.

Morthanion held her close, her lithe body fitting perfectly against him. He pressed his chin lightly atop her head, drawing in the scent of her hair with every deep inhalation.

"I'm glad it was," he said. He'd managed to satisfy himself – for a short while, anyway – and bring her great pleasure. It filled him with pride again. He'd provided for her, protected her, and made her happy. Those things were more important than anything had ever been to him.

It was a jarring realization for a being who had lived selfishly for four thousand years. Had he lost a part of himself in this? He knew he had indeed given something up, but there was no hole inside, no void to be filled. His magic had been wrenched away from him, leaving a gaping chasm in its wake, and he had changed in the time since…but now Aria had filled it in with her light and made him whole again.

' *It's not like I'm selfless now,* he thought, the feel of her bare skin against his sending another surge of fire through his veins. He would selfishly enjoy every single moment he had with her.

She was his now, fully. He could feel her, heart and soul, could sense the elation coming from her as easily as he could sense his own. They were bound forever. She would always belong to him, and the opposite seemed to be true, as well. He was hers, irrevocably, without regret.

There'd be nowhere to hide for anyone who dared try to take her from him.

*****

Thunder rumbled through the cave, awakening Aria suddenly. Her eyes opened to darkness, the fire having burned out long ago. The sail whipped in the wind, allowing mist, result of the torrential rain and the waves battering the cliffs, to sweep inside. Everything was illuminated eerily when lightning forked outside, followed closely by another blast of thunder.

Disoriented, Aria began to shift, then went still. There were arms and legs wrapped around her, a warm body nestled against her back.

Morthanion's body, Aria thought with a languid smile.

Her mind drifted back to the intimacy they had shared, the frenzied love making, and she could hardly believe she'd partaken so eagerly. She had been wild, reveling in ecstasy.

A flush rose on her skin remembering how she had begged him, clawed at him, and even bit him! The memory of his skin against hers, of the way he had felt within her, had that heady desire rushing through her again. She squeezed her thighs together to ease the ache between them.

It was then that she felt that hard swell, nestled against her folds. She caught her lower lip with her teeth. Her need grew more potent by the second. Her body was sore, deliciously so, but feeling him against that sensitive spot had heat pooling low in her belly.

He remained still apart from the slow rise and fall of his chest against her back. Was he still asleep? Unable to help herself, she moved her hips, rocking gently against him. She had to press her mouth closed to suppress a soft moan. His throbbing shaft slid along her moist sex, the tip brushing the small place that sent currents of pleasure through her. Closing her eyes, she did it again, and once more before she forced herself to stop, already panting softly against the pent up arousal.

One of Morthanion's hands cupped her breast, stroking her pearled nipple. Aria went still, sucking in a breath as a sharp thrill raced through her.

"So...my little Aria wants more, does she?" he purred, his voice rumbling from his chest, his breath hot on her neck.

She wanted to bury her face in the furs in embarrassment. Like an animal in heat, she had been rubbing against him, panting for him…while he slept!

As if reading her thoughts, an amused chuckle shook his shoulders. "Ah Aria, you need only ask."

His hand moved from her breast, traveling down toward her thighs, and her heart pattered in her chest. His fingers brushed over that swelling, sensitive bud, and Aria's body jerked. She couldn't contain the gasp this time. Her hand moved to his, covering it, but she couldn't guide it away. Instead, she found herself pressing it down more firmly, sighing at the increase in pressure.

Her breath came out in short pants as he stroked her. Her hips moved along his shaft, matching the rhythm of his fingers. She felt the flat of his teeth against her back before he nipped at her neck.

"Thanion!"

He continued his ministrations, causing her hips to buck. That fire inside her began to burn hotter and hotter, and she strained for it. Then he stopped, his hand going still.

"No!" she cried out, nearly sobbing.

"Do you enjoy this?" She could hear the grin in his voice.

"Yes! I want more!"

"More? Are you sure?" His fingers slipped into her.

"Demon!" Aria growled, twisting toward him to wrap her arm around his head. Without his assistance, she gyrated quickly against his hand and shaft, and the moment his blunt tip bumped against her swollen bud, she came. Her body tensed as moisture flooded her.

Morthanion groaned. With unbelievable speed, he grasped her hips, lifted her off the floor, and spun her to face him. Then he lay on his back and held her astride him. His eyes blazed up at her, mirroring her own hunger. He bared his fangs in a wide grin.

"Ravenous for your demon, aren't you?"

Hands at her waist, he lowered her. She felt the head of his shaft at her entrance, parting her. Slowly, inch by inch, her sex drew him in, sensitive and quivering from her last orgasm. He hummed and grunted in pleasure as he buried himself in her completely.

In this position, he seemed to fill her even more than before. She couldn't believe how good it felt, every minute throb and twitch echoing through her with increasing potency. She looked down at him, grasped his cheeks in her hands, and kissed him. He returned it, nipping her lips. His tongue darted into her mouth, in time with a thrust of his hips. He started slow, almost teasingly so, letting the sensation build in both speed and pleasure.

Aria's hands dropped to the floor, clenching fistfuls of fur. He was driving her mad, and she took satisfaction in his ragged breaths and grunts, knowing it was mutual. The way he moved within her left her entire body shivering.

She broke the kiss and pulled herself up, pressing her palms to his chest. Then she used her new leverage to slam down on him, needing him as deep as he could go. Her thighs spread just a little more and...

There!

She gasped, her head falling back, and she rode him hard and fast, teetering on the edge of release.

"Thanion, please," she pleaded, lost in the blossoming ecstasy.

Morthanion laughed aloud; it was fraught with the frenzy and power of their lovemaking, heavy with delight, thick with pleasure and promise. He increased his pace, faster, and faster. Her feel, her scent, the sounds she uttered, it all made his head swim sensuously.

He felt like a volcano on the brink of eruption. It was almost too much, almost painful, but he pressed on.

Her body went rigid, her fingers curling to dig her nails into his flesh as an orgasm rocked her. He listened to her cries of pleasure as it vibrated through her body, passing into his. They swept over him like hurricane winds, triggering his own climax. His seed rushed in a lava flow to fill her. She fell upon his chest, breathing against his neck, her hair spilling around them. They shuddered in unison when she rolled her pelvis. He placed his hands on her ass and guided her to do it again.

Closing his eyes, he traced the line of her spine up to take a fistful of her hair. He forced her head back and kissed her. It was a claiming kiss, a scalding kiss, one that further cemented the eternal link they now shared. And, finally, he allowed her body's weight to settle atop him, combing his fingers gently through her dark tresses to pull them away from her face.

The rise and fall of his chest as he regained his breath moved her like gentle ocean waters. He lay there, content to simply hold her. He could not have asked for a better mate. Whenever he thought he'd figured her out, she surprised him by revealing a new aspect of herself. He settled his other hand on her thigh, giving it a squeeze, his cock pulsing inside of her.

She chuckled sleepily.

"I haven't the words to describe you," he said with a grin, "and it is not often that I am rendered speechless."

Aria laughed again. It was fast becoming his favorite sound in all the world. "I will have to practice inspiring awe in you then, demon."

He knew she would be sore, so he refrained from pursuing his unquenchable thirst for more. He wished this could last forever, having never realized there could be so much satisfaction in the aftermath of something so explosive. How could he have known that simply lying with her, listening to her soft breathing, being surrounded by her scent and feeling her heart beat to the rhythm of his own would be so gratifying?

More thunder cracked outside, and the canvas sail continued to flap. There was a storm raging out there, and he knew their little paradise inside couldn't last forever. Another storm would follow this one, and the cave would not long shelter them from it. If Baltherus had his way, Aria would never be safe again. Morthanion knew it was best to cherish every moment with her, every instant of peace and joy she provided. He knew he'd be up to his elbows in blood and fire again before long, and the stakes would be higher than ever.

Aria slid her hand up his torso, breaking him from his dark thoughts. When she found the necklace, she took hold of the middle shell, pulling it toward the center of his chest. She loosely curled her fingers around it as she rubbed her cheek against his shoulder.

"I fear I might be liking this too much," she said, and he felt her skin heat with the confession.

"You can never like it too much," Morthanion replied.

He felt her lips curve against his skin, and she released a long, heavy, contented sigh. It was strangely comforting to sense what she was feeling. Though temporarily sated, he knew he could continue for hours before experiencing any fatigue. Yet her exhaustion whispered into him, a faint echo of what she felt. She began to drift, her body languid.

She stirred and said in a drowsy, quiet voice, "No, Demon. Love it with you."

Morthanion didn't respond, lying very still as she faded into sleep. Her breathing slowed and evened. He didn't exhale for a very long time.

He thought, for a moment, she had said she loved him, and he didn't know how to respond to that. But she said she loved *it* with him. Sex. He could handle it being purely sexual. Could handle her liking him – he certainly liked her. But...love?

He didn't really know what that meant. Didn't know what it entailed. Didn't know if he was even capable of giving it back to her. But he found, despite those misgivings, that he wanted her love.

Needed it.

That once unfamiliar tightness was back in his chest, making it hard to breath, and his stomach seemed to be whipping around not unlike the sail at the mouth of the cave. If he had to forsake the chance of ever leaving this place, of ever seeing anyone else in all his life, just to keep her safe...he thought he would. Because her love would be worth all the rest of the world and more. To be loved by her would leave everything else forgotten in the shadows that had dominated his life.

He could only hope he was worthy of receiving it, should she choose to give it to him.

Chapter Fifteen

For two days, Aria and Morthanion remained within their sanctuary as the storm raged on.

The morning after that first night, she awoke to find herself lying upon his chest. He was watching her with a strange expression, like she was a puzzle and he was trying to visualize where the pieces fit. She wanted him again, but she was too tender. Instead, Morthanion carefully set her aside and fetched a cloth and water. She was mortified as he cleaned her, gently washing away the dried blood on her thighs, pressing the cold cloth against her center, soothing her. Despite the care he took in his actions, his eyes were aflame with desire.

And gods if she didn't *feel* his want as if it were her own.

Instead, knowing she was too sore, he got them food, and they listened to the storm as they ate.

After that, they talked. Aria told him more about her time with Laudine. She even ventured to speak of the woman's death, and was surprised that her emotions regarding it were no longer so raw. Having Morthanion near, being able to talk to him about it, seemed to ease the pain of Laudine's passing more than she thought possible.

He spoke of his past, too, and she was still amazed at how long a life he'd led.

"When my kind went into hiding, I was lost," he said. "My entire reason for existence had been to battle the light. That was my education as a child, my experience as a man. And then, suddenly, I had to stop and find a place to cower.

"But I had to keep hidden, couldn't draw attention to myself. One of the Betrayers – Fordrell the Flayer – had been killed by Oranius's hunters, and they were still prowling. I couldn't stomach places with so many humans, anyway." He sneered to punctuate the statement.

Aria recalled the night she first met him. There had been a peculiarity to his gestures, in his smile – like he wasn't accustomed to performing them – that had made her uneasy. She was beginning to understand it now. He'd been even more isolated from the human world than she was. She'd at least had Laudine to guide her. Morthanion had no one. He could have gone anywhere in the world, and would always have been an outsider.

"What did you do next?" she asked, encouraging him to continue.

"For a time, I resided in a cave. It was not nearly so nice as this one. My presence scared all the bats off from the start, but the spiders tolerated me. They were pale, hairless things that felt around in the dark with their spindly legs, devouring whatever hapless victims blundered into their domain, running purely on instinct."

He stared off at the wall, his eyes unfocused. Yet there was the hint of a smile at the corner of his mouth.

"With little else to do, I watched them. For days at a stretch, I sat in that dank cave and stared at the spiders, fascinated by the way they navigated the dark, by the way they interacted and fed and lived and died. These creatures didn't have fires burning in them, didn't have a higher purpose to drive them. They didn't have any direction.

"I don't know how long a cave spider lives, but I sat in that cave for generations of them. Named their family lines and chronicled their legacy in my mind. Even ate a few, to get some variety in my meals.

"And when I finally left that cave, I didn't feel any less lost than I did when I went in." There seemed to be more in his expression, and his lips even parted to speak further. But he closed his mouth, offered her a strangely off-balance smile, and asked her to tell him more about her childhood.

Inspired by his story, she recounted the various ways she and Laudine had passed time in their cave, none of which involved spiders. The woman had tried to teach her many things, having only her own memory to work from, but always made everything fun. Lessons had come in the form of little games, leaving Aria hungry for more.

She laughed with her demon when she told him about the time she'd scared Laudine half to death by staying under water past a count of three hundred, after which the woman had finally found her and dragged her to the surface. Laudine's panic had given way to the harshest scolding Aria had ever received, once it was clear the girl was unharmed.

Much later, Aria reached out for Morthanion, and they explored each other's bodies. He took her with his mouth again that night.

Morthanion spent the second day going through her things, studying every object, asking countless questions. He even found some of the objects left behind by her mother's people, most of it saved by Laudine from Jasper and Xani's home before it was stolen, damaged by the elements, or decayed through neglect.

There were sheets of bark with writing in Xani's language; it hadn't been familiar to Laudine, so Aria didn't know what they said. She kept them to feel closer to her mother, trying to imagine the hands that wrote the characters when she traced them with her fingertips.

The few weapons in her possession seemed to catch his interest, though most were heavily worn or rendered useless by too much time in the sea. She watched, enthralled by him and his curiosity. He hadn't bothered to mask himself, knowing she preferred his true form. Every chance she got, she would brush her fingers over his feathers, and the pleasure that rippled through him would echo back into her.

Since their first night together, everything seemed enhanced. She felt more intensely than she ever had before. And it all centered on Morthanion. She had no way of explaining it, but she found no reason to deny it, either.

It was now three nights since they'd come together, and Aria sat upon one of the rocks off the coast and listened to the waves as they flowed around her. She hummed softly, enjoying the fresh night air, while Morthanion scouted the surrounding area. It was the first time either of them had emerged from the cave since the skies had cleared. The first time they'd been apart.

The gale had passed, leaving the water calm once again. Morthanion had remained in the cave most of the day, hesitant to leave her; he had wanted to see if the weather had made any difference in pushing the islanders back or if they remained camped nearby. As much as she enjoyed their time together, their supplies were beginning to dwindle, and they couldn't remain cooped up forever.

She needed the fresh air, needed the sea. He had reluctantly given in, forcing her to promise to stay near. So she used the time to swim, relishing the water.

Aria opened her eyes to stare up at the star-filled sky, only to glimpse a dark shape plummeting toward her. Her heart leapt, sinking as the dark shape grew more clearly into Baltherus. He landed in a crouch only a few feet behind her.

She jerked her head toward him, watching as he rose, unfazed by the force with which he'd hit the stone. He smiled at her. He was taller than Morthanion, and broader, with thick muscles on his torso. His hair was golden, pale in the moonlight.

"So you are the one he tried to hide from me," he said, his tone conversational.

Fear nearly stopped her heart when her eyes met the demon's. His were the green of fresh grown leaves, but there was a cool, inhuman calculation in them. She scrambled to her feet and stepped back from him.

"No need to run," he said, open hands raised. It looked less awkward than when Morthanion had done the same, but she found it more unsettling. "I'm not here to do you any harm. I just wanted to see what he was keeping to himself. You're rather fetching, aren't you?"

"I do not believe you," Aria said, ignoring his compliment. "If that is all you wanted, you saw me. Now go."

"What is your name?" He inched closer. All the while, his warm smile never faded – though it never reflected in his eyes.

Aria retreated, keeping him in view. She didn't trust him.

It was so similar to her first meeting with Morthanion, yet so different. With Morthanion, she had been scared, running because that was what she had been taught to do. Yet, Morthanion hadn't hidden anything, even that first night. When it came down to it, she had never truly been terrified of him. Not like she was with Baltherus standing before her, his amiable air sending chills up her spine.

"A name you will not get."

"That is unfortunate," he said, frowning. Aria was surprised; there seemed to be real disappointment in his gaze.

"All that I want is for the three of us to be good friends. To share the bounty that has come our way." He paused, like he was weighing his next words.

"Morthanion has been stealing from my men. Did you know that's where he's getting his supplies? With all that there is to take on this island, he steals from those less capable than him." Baltherus shook his head, slowly.

"You and yours stole from my mother's people, who lived on this island long before you arrived. You murdered them," Aria snapped, suddenly angry. How dare he act as though Morthanion's actions were any less honorable than his own?

Uncertainty flickered over his face for the briefest of moments before he regained his composure.

"I suppose, then, there can be no friendship between us. I am sorry."

Before Aria could guess his intentions, the demon blasted forward, crushing her in his grasp and knocking the air out of her lungs. She stared in dawning horror as the rock she had been standing on fell away beneath her.

She screamed, hair whipping against her face from the wind as the demon flew higher, carrying her over his shoulder. His claws dug into her thigh and she cried out against the pain, beating her fists against his back, yanking his hair.

"A gift for you," he said, ignoring her attempts to be free, "to share with Morthanion." His hand smeared over her wound.

She thought she heard Morthanion's voice, but the sound of her own heart was too loud in her ears to make out his words.

Aria's fear morphed into fury. Straining against their upward momentum, she reared back and went for his face. He cursed when her nails scratched the corner of his eye, but his grip only tightened. The need to escape grew.

"Fine!" Baltherus snapped. One hand took a fistful of her hair, yanking her head backward. She hung over empty air, anchored only by the claws sunken into her thighs. His yellow eyes bored into hers. "Let him have you—"

She splayed her fingers as power surged through her. It rushed from her center and set her limbs to trembling with its force. A cold jet of water burst from her hands, filling his mouth, cutting off his words. It knocked her out of his hold; its strength thrust him back.

He tumbled away from her, his wings folding.

And Aria fell.

Morthanion crept along the ridge, keeping low among the jagged rocks. He scanned the jungle with keen eyes. Baltherus's men were out there even now, only the faintest glows from their mostly-hidden fires visible through the dense foliage. The cave hadn't been discovered yet, of that he was confident, but there seemed to be a few more mortals in the area with each passing day, and they were steadily spreading their camps to cover more and more territory. The younger demon had his forces mobilized and organized. Baltherus played to win.

The logic couldn't be argued. Morthanion had displayed particular interest in and possessiveness of Aria, and it would have been simple for Baltherus to infer that she was his elder's mate. A mate meant weakness, meant vulnerability. Especially because she was not a demon. She was of inferior breeding, a half-mortal drawn into a world of demigods. Capable as she had proven, how could she possibly defend herself against a demon bent on doing her real harm?

Baltherus wanted an ally, and knew, failing that, Morthanion would prove a formidable rival. That couldn't be permitted. Aria was the key to controlling the situation. The men making camps on this part of the island hadn't come to subdue Morthanion, they'd come to find *her*.

He paused in his movement, letting himself settle into the shadows that filled the crevices between the rocks. She was out swimming not far away, and each moment apart had his anxiety increasing. But, just as he needed the embrace of darkness, he knew she needed the same of the sea, as much as either of them needed food to eat and water to drink.

There had been a burning in his throat when she'd told him she wanted to go for a swim while he scouted, and his first instinct had been to flatly refuse. He knew she needed fresh air, needed to ride the water currents and drift on the tide, but he could not deny his worry, could not dismiss the dangers.

Grudgingly, he'd finally agreed, insisting they remain in the same area. He would scout the land for a short while and return for her. He knew finding her wouldn't be difficult, now that he could sense her so clearly. She was a source of heat, an extension of himself, always alluring, and all he had to do was follow that warmth to find her.

She was safest in the water anyway, he reminded himself. She could swim faster than anyone he'd ever seen, and could remain beneath the surface for at least three or four times longer than it would take most people to drown. But what if she was caught off-guard? He'd done it a few times. Baltherus would be just as capable. How long could he afford to play this waiting game before the rules changed?

Aria abhorred bloodshed, but Morthanion knew there'd be little other way to settle this.

He began toward the forest, so low to the ground that he was nearly crawling. Though he was outnumbered, he had stealth, cunning, and speed. He couldn't fight them all head-on, but he could give them something to fear. A thing unseen, more terrible in their imaginations than in reality.

Ice slithered through his veins, halting his movement abruptly. He twisted, looking back toward the sea. It was…fear. Not an emotion he was accustomed to, but he recognized it. Like a chilled finger, it trailed up his spine, threatening to freeze him completely.

The instinct roared to life, thawing the frost, and his wings burst from his back. Pushing with arms and legs, he catapulted himself into the air, flying toward her with reckless speed. Following the feel of her, he found himself climbing higher, higher…

No! Damned be all the gods, how had Baltherus found her already?

His heart was pounding, as much with his own panic as with her fear. Above, he could see them. Her pale, lithe form was nearly enveloped by the broad, bronze-skinned demon.

"Let go of her!" Morthanion roared.

She kicked and thrashed in Baltherus's clutches, but any words they exchanged were lost to Morthanion on the wind. Helplessness welled in his throat like bile. If Baltherus imprisoned her in his encampment, even Morthanion would have a hard time getting her back.

He watched, still far enough away that the distance was painful, as water sprayed over Baltherus's face, breaking on the large demon like a wave against a cliff. The demon released his hold on her as he tumbled away, and she began to fall.

Morthanion froze. Everything in him was still, his heart stopped, his breath caught. Directly beneath her lay the ocean, yes, and at least a dozen rocks thrusting up from it. How many more were just under the surface?

He dropped into a dive, air rushing by him and filling his ears with its roar. It was not enough to silence the thumping of his heart. He knew she could turn to water, but what if she wasn't able to? What if their combined fear was too much? Every muscle strained to get him below her.

If she couldn't change, and he was just a moment too late…

He swept back his wings and thrust out his arms. The force of her fall dragged him down, but he clutched at her, pulling her tight against his chest. A few of his feather tips dipped into the water as he fought to keep them airborne. Her body trembling, she wrapped her arms around his neck.

Mate safe in his embrace, he landed on one of the larger rocks, his breath like fire in his chest as he placed her on her feet. He could smell Baltherus on her, could smell blood. All the strength in her little body seemed to be engaged in holding on to him; he had to force her hands apart and hold them at her sides to get her at arm's length. Immediately, he searched her for harm.

Nothing was visible, so he turned her around. There were angry scratches on the back of her thigh. Blood oozed from deeper gouges on two of them, where Baltherus's claws had punctured her skin. He could smell her blood, knew its scent from when he'd hurt her. There was something else in it now, something foreign. Rage flared in his gut. He searched the sky for the other demon, but there was no sign of his foe.

"No," he growled, and then turned to the shoreline. "I will drain your blood into the sand, Baltherus! I will drape your entrails from one side of this island to the other!" Part of him urged pursuit, knew that Baltherus ran because he was outmatched and wanted to press that advantage. To finish it once and for all.

He shifted his attention back to Aria, turning her to face him again. Taking her face between his hands, he looked into her eyes, and tried to ignore the sulfurous scent of Baltherus's blood on her. His heart was beating frantically, filling his head with its mad rhythm.

"Aria. Are you all right?" He forced his breath out, slowly, and then drew it back in with equal care. If he didn't calm himself, she wouldn't be able to shake her own panic.

Tremors still ran through her, her eyes round. "I am fine. He said…he said he wanted to see what you were hiding. He is not happy that you are stealing from him."

Morthanion brushed her hair back from her face and pressed his lips to her forehead, trying to will his heart to slow. He focused on the smell of her hair, the salt tang of the ocean mist, on anything but the scent of the blood. It didn't work.

Now, Baltherus knew. Morthanion's attempts to hide Aria from the other demon's sight had been enough to arouse his suspicion. There could be no room left for doubt after what had just happened. Baltherus's blood at her wound could only mean that he'd tried to bind her to him. Whether it was meant as a test, to see if she truly was Morthanion's mate, or simply as an insult, the damage had been done.

He embraced her again. "We need to get that cleaned and bandaged," he said, crouching to scoop her up. As he leapt into the air, she slipped her arms around him and rested her head against his shoulder.

*****

Baltherus paced, dragging his fingers through still damp hair. Ithoriel's eyes followed him, the elf's expression masked. The demon wanted to look at what had happened as a victory, wanted to view it with optimism and use it to plan his next move. But he knew that it hadn't been a victory, and lying to himself would taste too bitter.

It had been the perfect opportunity. The two of them were separated; the girl had been alone and vulnerable. Was Morthanion slipping? To leave his mate unguarded, out in the open, knowing that there would be people looking for her, was either madness or senility.

But, ultimately, it had been Baltherus who'd blundered. He had seized her, held the future in his hands, and then let it sift through his fingers like so much sand.

He halted to slam a fist on the table. Clay bowls and cups rattled. The female was supposed to have been the final game piece, the tool with which he could manipulate Morthanion in any direction he chose. She was the elder demon's mate, that much was without question now. But it was the only question he'd managed to answer. Everything had happened quickly, and he couldn't be sure what she'd done...

That was untrue. He knew it, deep in his bones. He'd felt the power. Felt that familiar hum at his core. He hadn't known magic in decades, but he hadn't forgotten.

A demon and a mage...and who would be able to stand against them on this island, where everyone had been castrated, stripped of the arcane? She was a lovely little creature, but she was more than a mere bargaining tool. The girl was no longer just a piece on the board; she was the end goal.

If he could win her, he'd have magic and a second demon at his side. Hell, between the three of them, they might even be able to find a way off this accursed island! Ithoriel's encounter with the girl and her demon was proving to have been more fortuitous with each passing moment.

"I must have her," he said, twisting his hand to rake claws over the soft wood beneath it.

"She remains the key, master?" asked Ithoriel.

"The key and the treasure both."

"They will only be more careful, now."

Baltherus waved his hand, dismissing the elf's words as obvious. Morthanion had already made mistakes. He would make more. Caution had never been one of the Keeper of Flame's strongest traits. They would simply have to be prepared to capitalize on those mistakes.

"They are hiding in some hole out there." Baltherus was certain of it; they had a sanctuary somewhere on the west shore. All the sightings of them had been reported there, within a span of a few miles.

"Why not just have killed her, and let him come to you?"

The demon laughed, turning to face the elf. "In what way would that further our goals?"

Contempt was writ plain upon Ithoriel's face, smoldering in his eyes. "Because then the both of them would be dead, and your power once more absolute."

"The simpler way, perhaps. But shortsighted. The girl possesses magic. Here, that is invaluable. It may well be the thing that could get us back to the mainland." But, the more he thought about that, the more he doubted his desire to leave.

This island had been his for decades, now. Here, he was master, he was without challenge, he was in control. So what if the place was too big for him to keep fully in his power? His people had high walls and weapons, and were more than a match for the packs of savages that prowled the thicker parts of the jungle. All the others who refused to bend knee to him were few and scattered. They posed little threat. Even the angel, Gaelin, had proven no challenge, choosing to remain hidden. On Talikar, though, Baltherus was just another demon. Forced to hide lest he be hunted, damned simply because of his parentage.

"Or it may well be the thing that gets us all killed," Ithoriel said.

Baltherus clenched his jaw. It was not becoming of him to give in to anger, but the tone of the elf's words was infuriating. There'd be no challenge in breaking the frail creature's neck, or tearing out his innards, or putting out his eyes. There'd also be no gain in it. Ithoriel had proven valuable thus far. There was the resolve of a survivor in the elf.

"Have faith, Ithoriel," the demon said, keeping his voice even and calm, "and know that the advantage is still ours."

"Numbers do us little good if they are spread thin across the entirety of the island."

"You are beginning to try my patience, friend. I've been at this game far longer than you've even existed."

"Yet here we both stand."

The demon felt his claws curl out, hardening from shadow. "You tempt my wrath, Ithoriel."

"I've every interest in survival, *master*. I know you do, as well, which is why you should stay your hand. This Morthanion has already killed two of your best, Mikel and Kralgar. He has eternity to kill off the rest of us, one by one."

"Kralgar?" Baltherus uttered an oath. Of the mortals here, Kralgar had been one of a handful who might have stood a chance against a demon in singles combat. "When did that happen?"

"We found what was left of him, washed up on a beach two days ago. Clawed to pieces. Before the sea creatures got to him, at any rate. A few of his markings were intact."

The demon's nostrils flared. The situation was starting to slip out of his grasp, and he did not appreciate the sour feeling left in his gut. Even his subjects were starting to speak out against him. Meek, submissive Ithoriel foremost among them!

"Does that discovery give you leave to speak to me in such a manner? Have I shown you anything other than kindness in your time here?"

There were still embers burning in the elf's eyes. "That is why I must speak to you so, sire. For loyalty to you, I say the things no one else dares to. This threat is great, and each of us depends upon you and your boundless generosity to survive this place with the peace and comfort we've come to know."

Yes. These words are the truth. I have more than myself to consider in all this, Baltherus thought. Already, his anger was abating. He nodded, slightly, allowing the elf to continue.

"The girl and her demon threaten all of us because they are a threat to you. I've seen firsthand what he is willing to do. He's mad, and can be nothing but a danger. The girl may be young and timid enough to be tamed, but Morthanion must die."

Decades, even centuries, before, Baltherus would have slain any mortal for speaking that way about another demon, even one he personally disliked. Even the most loathsome of them were superior to mortals. But time and circumstance had changed his views, had allowed him to see the value in these short-lived beings.

"Bold as your words are, your counsel bears wisdom." He folded his arms across his chest and resumed pacing, drumming his fingers over the bulge of his bicep. Perhaps his initial imaginings of flying side-by-side with Morthanion, lording over the island, had been foolish. He had wanted to avoid bloodshed, had wanted to avoid unnecessary killing when life was already so unforgiving here, but it was growing increasingly clear that it would be unavoidable.

"All spoken to further your greatness, master."

There had been one thing Baltherus had overlooked, in his despair. An important detail. He knew that Morthanion and the girl had a secluded place they were sheltering, yes, but he also had a way to find them.

It was diluted greatly by the girl's bond with the other demon, but Baltherus had shared blood with her. Blood called to blood, even through the restraints of the brand he'd been given, even though she was bound to her mate. The feel of it was faint, but he had a vague idea of the direction she was in. It might take time, but all they needed was a more specific area. Then he could focus his resources and find her.

"Our greatness, Ithoriel," the demon said, smiling. His next move was increasingly clear, and when it succeeded, Morthanion would have no choice but to bow to Baltherus's whims. "You will share fully in our coming triumph."

Chapter Sixteen

Aria lay on her front, her head turned to watch Morthanion over her shoulder. His eyes were bright, narrowed in concentration as he gently worked. Scowl deepening, he wiped blood away from her wounds. She winced, not for the first time, and his jaw tightened.

When he was done rinsing the gouges, he carefully wrapped a clean scrap of cloth around her thigh.

"Thank you," she said when he finished. Anger radiated beneath his skin and she could feel it hovering in the recesses of her mind. She knew most of it was directed at Baltherus, but wondered if some of it was for her.

"From this point forward," he said tightly, "you will remain in my sight at all times. It is too dangerous for you to venture out alone. Especially now."

She pressed her lips together, sat up, and faced him. "You expect me to be a prisoner in here?"

"We are not going to be here for much longer. It's not safe." His gaze was unwavering. "And I cannot protect you if I am not near. He could have killed you. Could have done things to you…"

His hands, now tipped in claws, clenched; blood dripped slowly from his palms. A flare of rage swept through her.

"But he did not." She had fought Baltherus. Had actually hurt him, even before that power had flowed from her. She was still shocked, unsure if it had been real or just a product of her imagination. But how else could she have gotten free?

"Are you really going to argue that point with me?" His eyebrows fell heavy over his eyes.

"I am only saying that he did not hurt me more that this." She gestured toward her bandaged thigh. "If he wanted me dead, he could have killed me. And we are on an island, Morthanion. One you cannot leave. Where else can we go? There are prisoners everywhere, and they are all watching for us."

"They are looking for us around *here*. There are countless places to hide on this island, miles away from this cave. This place will be discovered, eventually."

Aria's brows snapped down and she turned her face away. Anger like she had never known burned inside of her, steadily growing. This was her *home*. The place held all of her possessions, and so many of her memories. She refused to leave it.

"Are you angry at him, or at me?" Morthanion asked.

"Him for what he is doing, and you for trying to force me from my home."

"Do you think that I want to leave this place?" His words came through clenched teeth, his eyes blazing. "This feels like the only home I've ever had! But it's only a damned cave. What good is it to either of us if you are dead?"

Sudden fury quaked through her, making her prior emotion seem feeble in comparison. She had noticed such things, to a lesser degree, in the time they'd spent together. It had never been strong enough to make her question it, but this time, it was suspiciously in accordance with Morthanion's outburst.

"It would still be shelter for you were I to die," she snapped. Her chest was burning, and she realized that her voice had been rising. She hadn't even been this way during her few childhood spats with Laudine.

"If you were to die, there would be nowhere on this island safe for *anyone*." His voice was low, terribly low, and there was promise in those dark words.

She squeezed her eyes closed, her breath rasping in and out. A maelstrom was tearing up her insides, drawing in all her conscious thought and twisting it toward violence. She didn't know how to control it. It was too much.

"Stop it!" she shouted, hands flying to her ears as though that might block out the anger pouring through her.

Morthanion was silent. She felt his hands on her wrists, gently pulling them from her ears. Immediately the intensity lessened, followed quickly by shame and impotent frustration.

"Arguing with one another will not solve any of our problems," he said, straining for calm.

She looked at him, trembling as exhaustion and confusion overlapped the myriad, now subdued emotions within her. "No, it will not," she agreed, breathing a little easier. "What happened?"

"We are picking up each other's emotions and feeding into them."

"How?"

"We share a deep bond. It was more than our bodies that came together that night. You are mine, Aria. Mine alone. And that means all of you. Even what resides in your heart. Our souls are entwined, irrevocably."

She could feel the weight of his words, the depth of their meaning, and knew that they were true. Her eyes closed.

With a sigh, Morthanion brushed her hair back from her cheek. "I don't want to take you from here, and I understand that you don't want to go. For now, can we just set aside some supplies we can take if we need to leave in a hurry? Just in case?"

It wasn't a command, but a request. He was trying to compromise with her. Aria nodded slowly. The tenderness that flooded her as she looked at him had been steadily growing stronger and stronger each day.

She gazed at the rest of her home. "Just in case."

Taking her chin, Morthanion gently guided her eyes back to his. "But I also want you to seriously consider how safe we are here. If you are comfortable, so be it. I am only concerned that if you did hurt Baltherus badly, he may be vengeful. He may increase his efforts in finding you." He leaned closer. "I know you don't care for the blood on my hands. But I will kill to protect you and I will not feel the slightest remorse for it. I'm not asking you to like that, but you need to accept it. It *will* happen."

Her father fought to protect his wife and newborn child, and Aria could see no wrong in him doing so. But Jasper and Xani had both died, anyway. Why sow more pointless death when even her little world already had so much of it?

"It is the needless killing I do not accept, Thanion. Killing to defend those you care about is different."

As if sensing her melancholy thoughts, Morthanion cupped her cheek.

"Aria," he said softly, his fiery gaze darkening.

Her breath hitched, his fear seeping into her. Fear of losing *her*.

Aria was amazed by how much he had changed in the time she had known him.

His hand shifted to the back of her head, fingers in her hair, and drew her forward into a kiss.

Aria responded immediately. Needing to be closer, she rose up on her knees and slipped her arms around his neck. They kissed deeply, breath mingling, tongues touching and stroking. Her own hands slid into his hair, but she couldn't get close enough.

Her entire life had been spent in calm, quiet isolation. Yet, when it came to Morthanion, something fierce and passionate sparked inside of her. It made her feel alive.

She could have been killed – or worse – tonight. She knew now what Morthanion had tried explaining to her before. Were Baltherus to take her, to force himself upon her, she would die inside. Wither into nothing but a shell.

With that thought, she clung to Morthanion, breaking the kiss to press her forehead against his. What they shared went much deeper than physical connection and the pleasure it brought. Each touch was a bolt of lightning, every exchanged word was the gentle rolling of waves against the shore, unearthing new treasures in the sand and eroding a little more of the barriers remaining between them. His very nearness pulsed with the comforting heat of sunshine, as necessary to her now as eating or drinking.

He had told her their souls were entwined, and she believed him. She *felt* it, felt *him*.

"Thanion," she whispered fervently.

"Shh," he soothed as his hands worked to slowly strip her of her tunic. "We have no need to rush. There's only me and you in this place, and nothing else in all the world right now."

The tunic gathered around her knees and Aria trembled when his fingers ran over the smooth skin of her back. A rush of heat pooled between her legs when he laid a hand on her thigh, pulling her closer. But she needed contact with him, skin to skin, with nothing between them. She needed to feel him all over, to surround herself with his warmth, his scent, with everything that was Morthanion.

They both stood together, clothes divested. As his hands explored her, he worshipped her with his mouth, kissing her tender, sensitive skin all over. She shivered.

Aria wanted to do the same for him.

She felt his length between them, hard against her belly. He was always unselfish in pleasing her. He deserved that, too. Recalling how he pleased her with his mouth, she pulled back, trailing her lips down his chest and stomach. Her hands ran along his sides to settle on his hips. Then she was back on her knees. She touched her tongue to the tip of his shaft, licking up the drop of liquid beaded there.

Morthanion's head reared back, and he groaned in pleasure.

Smiling to herself, she took him into her mouth.

His body stiffened and his hands hovered above her, clenching and unclenching.

She savored his taste, his earthy scent. When she sat back to look at his pulsing length, she stroked it and bit her lip, gazing up only to meet his fiery stare. Need burned within them both, and she took him into her mouth again.

Air brushed against her as his wings snapped out, the feathers rustling. His hands fell into her hair then, taking handfuls, guiding her upon his shaft. He didn't force her, but she could feel his urgency as he strained to hold himself back. Wisps of shadow flickered over his skin, caressing hers. Every part of him beckoned her, even his darkness.

"*Fuck*, Aria," he said breathlessly, her name an impassioned prayer.

Aria took delight in his reaction, even more so when his restraint began to crumble and his hips bucked. She enjoyed the sounds rumbling from him, his ragged breath; she closed her eyes, savoring the sensations that swept through her, knowing that some were his.

Morthanion was losing himself. His eyes rolled back as the pleasure built toward its peak, the pressure near unbearable. She was the boldest woman he'd ever known, considering that only a few days before she had been untouched, with no knowledge of sensuality. Aria displayed willingness to explore, a hunger to experience it all.

Her hand gripped his shaft and her mouth stroked every inch of him. It was sublime. But he didn't want her to finish him like this, amazing as it felt.

He stopped her, pulling her to her feet. She made a sound of protest and his erection throbbed painfully as he stared into the dark pools of her eyes. He took her mouth in a fierce kiss and lifted her body against him, guiding her legs around his waist. Hands on her ass, he entered her hot sex with one deep thrust.

Breaking the kiss, he leaned his forehead against hers, relishing the paradise she offered. When they were like this, he could forget every worry he'd ever had. He didn't have to remember the terrible things he'd done, or how little those things bothered him. She took him to a state of mind he'd never been able to achieve before her, let him be a person he would never have been without her. She completed him, improved him, and with her, he felt whole.

Slowly, he slid in and out of her, the friction running electric tendrils up his spine to fork throughout his body.

"Aria," he rasped, their eyes locking.

It was fire and water coming together to create some impossible, amazing thing that could never be described or defined.

The slow pace had her panting. She tugged at his hair, then slid her palms down his back only to rake her nails up a moment later. He felt the tightening of her heat on his cock, the quivering of her body. Still, her eyes remained on his, eyelids heavy with desire. Until it became too much for her.

"Oh demon, please!"

He was at his threshold, about to leap off a peak higher and more imposing than he'd ever crested. When she threw her head back and begged, he could not deny her what she needed. What they both needed.

His stance widened as he increased the pace, thrusting harder and faster. Finally, he gave into the frantic heat of their passion.

All he wanted was for her to be happy and safe; nothing else, he realized, was important to him anymore. Only her.

Her inner muscles fluttered and gripped his shaft as shudders wracked her body. Fierce pleasure coursed through him. He reached his own explosive end as she cried out in abandonment, their mutual release amplified by their bond. He pumped his hips, pushing them both beyond. She buried her face against his neck, the sounds coming from her creating a beautiful melody.

The entire world spun, bursting into stars and darkness and light, and then they were panting together. He clutched her to his chest, their hearts beating as one.

He didn't set her down, didn't move, didn't sit. He just stood there, holding her to him, one hand in her hair. If love was real, he wondered if it was what he felt for Aria. It was unlike anything else he'd ever experienced; what else could it be? The only time he'd felt true regret in his long, long life had been when he'd hurt her, and he vowed to himself that he would never let that happen again.

He wished he could say the same about others doing her harm, but he was not all-powerful. Not here on this island where he was stripped of his magic. Baltherus had been forced to fight physically for decades, and had an unknown number of men. But Morthanion would not hesitate to fight for Aria. Not even for a fraction of an instant.

All the things he'd done for her could be taken as proof that she needed him, but in truth, *he* needed *her*. More than he thought possible. She was a beacon in his darkness, a ray of light. Aria made him feel like more than the mindless killer he'd been groomed to be. Made him feel like he could choose to be something more, something better.

She stirred and slowly lifted her head. Smiling, she brushed his hair back from his face. Her touch traveled up, over his forehead to follow the curve of his horns. Dipping his head, Morthanion kissed her again, never tiring of the taste and feel of the simple, but meaningful, gesture. She was everything he could have ever hoped for and more. So much more than he deserved, but he would never give her up.

"I still haven't found adequate words to describe you, woman."

Her laughter warmed a deep part of his soul. She shook her head as she took his cheeks in her hands and pecked a kiss on his lips. "Let us lie down."

He carried her to the furs, his wings dissipating and leaving tendrils of shadow fading in their midst. Lying on his back, he settled her atop him. Aria propped her chin on his chest and simply gazed into his eyes. Something fluttered in his chest, something so profound that he was drowning in it. He knew it was coming from her now, at least in part, but this wasn't the first time it had seized him. It was becoming a familiar sensation, and he wondered again if it really was love.

Turning her head, she tucked it beneath his chin and began to sing. He listened, wrapping an arm around her comfortably. Morthanion could feel her music in his body, in his soul, permeating every fiber of his being. He let himself be carried away by it. Had it been water elementals like Aria and her mother that inspired the legends of sirens luring ships to their dooms with sweet song?

She was amazing, astonishing in every way. And two weeks ago, he'd have scoffed at the idea of one such as her being his mate. Now...now he couldn't imagine wanting anyone else.

"Only you...forever you," he murmured, barely audible. Without realizing he had spoken the words of his heart aloud, he let the waves of her song lull him into sleep.

Aria's eyes opened the moment those soft words were spoken, and they almost made her voice falter. She remained still, too afraid to move as she continued to quietly sing, feeling his body relax, his breath growing deep and even.

They were the first words he had spoken that made her think he cared on a deeper level. She knew he was concerned for her well being, that they enjoyed their time together – there was no doubt of that – and he was very possessive, but those things didn't mean that he loved her. Could he? Could he come to love her, too?

Carefully, she lifted her head to look down at him. The hard lines of his face were soothed and relaxed in sleep, his brow soft, and there was a degree of contentment in the way his lips curved. He was so beautiful, her demon.

She kissed his lips lightly, careful not to wake him, and lay her head back down. In his arms, the fear from her earlier ordeal melted away.

"Only you," she whispered softly, repeating his words like a vow. There would never be another for her. No matter what happened on this island, she would keep to that.

Her gentle hums filled the cavern, fading as sleep claimed her.

Chapter Seventeen

Morthanion stood near the mouth of the cave, one shoulder against the wall and his arms folded across his chest. Between two fingers he held a bit of the sail, peeling it back just enough to watch the storm outside. It had cut his earlier attempt at reconnaissance short. He'd managed to find evidence of at least two more groups in the area, putting his current count to twelve men, but little else.

It had been hard leaving her. Incredibly hard. Baltherus was out there somewhere, undoubtedly angry and enacting his next move. That knowledge had kept Morthanion distracted; all he could think about, it seemed, was her safety. Had they discovered the cave? Would this be the moment when the sanctuary was flushed out?

Two days had passed since their last encounter with Baltherus. Morthanion couldn't understand why there'd been no overt retaliation yet, why it had been so quiet. Perhaps he was thinking on his own terms? He was rarely capable of patience while he was angry. Was Baltherus different?

The dark clouds that swept in, setting the trees to swaying in a strengthening wind, had been all the excuse he'd needed to return to her. The warmth of her presence had grown steadily as he neared the cave, engulfing his entire being. She was in the right place. That in itself had been a massive relief.

Though their time together was proving the high point of his life, he knew there'd been something on her mind before he left in the morning. It had been on her face, and he could feel it flowing from her, but he couldn't identify it. How could he, when he wasn't even certain of his own emotions?

Was it simply because he'd gone his entire life without meaningful companionship? Was what he felt for her fleeting? All he knew was that he couldn't talk to her about it. He didn't want to hurt her, and he knew he was all too capable of that. He wouldn't know what to say, anyway. How could he put into words things that he could not yet identify? The storm outside could be witnessed, felt, heard, even smelled and tasted, and so it could be easily described. The storm inside of him, though, was not so simply explained.

He watched the dark water churning, highlighted every so often by a bright, jagged line of lightning. Waves crested, their white heads smashing into one another, spraying foam and mist into the wind.

The sight reminded him of something, and he had to focus on the blurred memory to draw it back to the surface. He'd taken no time to reflect upon it, thanks first to his overwhelming anger at Baltherus and then his extreme relief at getting her home safely and finding her relatively unharmed.

It had been no action of his that had freed her from Baltherus. The demon had already released her before Morthanion was anywhere close, but Morthanion had seen something in the instant before she was free-falling. It had looked like the crest of one of the waves he was watching now.

Had the crimson haze that settled over his vision simply deceived him? Had the panic, fear, and fury coursing through him tainted his memory somehow? Or was Aria far more powerful than she appeared, more than she realized?

Even over the roaring storm, he heard the faint sound of her stirring behind him. The soft, contented sigh, the gentle brush of her skin over the furs. He could picture her in his head, smiling as she turned over and reached for him in her sleep.

MAKE ME BURN | 195

But she wasn't sleeping. She came toward him, the extra sense he'd developed flaring in delight with her growing nearness. Her little feet slapped softly on the stone floor when she stepped off the pallet.

Morthanion smiled when she slipped her arms around him from behind, pressing her cheek to his back, between his wings.

He marveled at her easiness with him. He'd never met anyone who could be so casual around a demon. Even others of his kind were typically wary and cautious of one another. None of that fear remained in Aria, not for him. Warmth radiated from her, and his body absorbed it greedily, setting him to throbbing.

Ignoring his increasing desire, he instead focused on the new questions that had occurred to him.

"What did you do that got Baltherus to let go of you?"

She pulled away from him, slowly. "I...do not know."

He turned to face her, letting the canvas finally fall back into place. She was looking at her hands, frowning. He decided it had been the second of the possibilities; Aria was more powerful than she knew.

"Try to figure it out," he said, not unkindly.

"I was fighting him...and something just pushed through me. I panicked after he clawed me, because all my efforts to break free did not work and I could not change. A rush of...I do not know what it was, but water came from my hands."

He tilted his head. "Do you think you could do it again?"

"I do not know how."

"If for some reason I'm not around, it may very well be the only thing that can protect you from Baltherus and his men."

"That does not change the fact that I do not know what it was or how to make it happen, Thanion."

That name almost tore apart his resolve, almost convinced him to bring her back to the furs. It was too important that she had some way to defend herself. Too important that he not allow himself to be distracted. She was half water elemental; the power had to be inside of her, just waiting to be released. There was only one way he could think of to force that release.

"We both know you're not that useless, Aria," he said, ice in his gaze, "though Laudine sheltering you almost made you so."

She looked at him as though he'd struck her, and his chest tightened painfully.

"I never said I was useless. I might not be as strong as you, or as fast, but I am not useless."

"If you can't even control your own body, you might as well be," he replied, hating himself for it. Maybe, if they had more time, there'd be a different way. If it weren't crucial to her protection, he'd not be pushing her. She'd probably come into her abilities naturally, over the course of months, or years. "What will you do if Baltherus gets a hold of you again? Cry out for me, or fight him?"

Aria scoffed, taking a step back from him. "I fought him the last time he came! I did not call for you before, why would I do so if it happens again?"

Her words produced a surprising sting. Though he didn't want her in a position to have to cry for aid from anyone, he wanted to be the one she turned to. The one she relied upon. The one that she trusted to keep her safe, no matter what.

"Then show me, Aria!" The next words caught in his throat, thick with the weight of the blow they'd inflict. Damn Baltherus for forcing them into this situation, damn him for making this necessary. *It's for her protection.* "Are you going to lay down and die like your mother did when they come for you?"

Her skin paled immediately, features going slack with the shock of what he'd said.

Then she pressed her lips into a tight line, and he could see the anger spark in her eyes. Her hands trembled at her sides. The fire sputtered, wavering, and the air in the cave cooled. He had been so used to flames, to fiery rages. The chill that pulsed at him with her emotions was foreign, powerful, and he wondered if he had pushed her too far.

He dropped his gaze, long enough to see frost crystals forming on the floor beneath her bare feet, spreading across the stone toward him. For that fleeting instant, he could make out the feathery, intricate patterns in the ice. He'd never seen beauty in it before. Another thing he now owed her.

If it keeps you safe, I cannot be sorry.

Then he lifted his gaze to her, and she hit him.

There were geysers back in Talikar, where steaming-hot water blasted up from the ground twenty, thirty, forty feet into the air. That was what her magic reminded him of, but there was no heat. Only bone-numbing cold.

Water hit him in the center of his chest, spraying into his face and up his nose. The force of it lifted him off his feet. He felt the sail resist as he passed, and he somehow heard the canvas tearing through the din of the storm. Then he was in open air, the wind whipping through his hair, rain pelting his skin mercilessly.

"What have I done?" she cried from within.

Twisting himself, he reached out and buried his claws into the stone just beneath the mouth of the cave. His body jerked to an abrupt halt. Pain throbbed from his chest, spreading not unlike the ice crystals had been. He hadn't felt anything like that since the old times, when the war between Light and Dark had been waged openly.

He dragged himself up, his skin starting to prickle as feeling returned. She was there, in the entrance, and backed away as he crawled to a point where he could stand. Water dripped from him, pooling on the stone below.

Morthanion laughed. He rolled his arms at the shoulders, working out the kinks, a grin on his face. At the center of his chest was an angry red patch of skin, and he was still trying to even out his breathing. But he laughed.

Her eyes were wide in her pale face as he tried to move closer to her. He staggered, catching himself on the wall. "Have I mentioned…Aria…that you are…incredible?"

She stared at him, and irritation swept into him almost as strongly as her magic had.

"You did that on purpose?" she demanded, and turned to stomp deeper into the cave.

He followed after her, though more slowly. He could only imagine what Baltherus had felt, taking that square in the face. The thought sparked another bout of laughter, and it didn't fade until he eased himself onto the bench. By the ache the blast had left in its wake, it would probably have snapped a mortal's ribs.

"Try to summon it. Again."

"No," she snapped, crossing her arms over her chest. There was more emotion coming off of her, though it was confused. A sprinkling of guilt in her frustration, perhaps. That was one he'd only recently learned. He would never have guessed that a woman barely past her second decade could teach him so much.

"Try. For me." He smiled as sweetly as fangs and firestorm eyes allowed.

She sighed, narrowing her eyes beneath furrowed brows. Her hands came up, fingers slightly spread, and she pointed them toward the mouth of the cave. She inhaled deeply, pursing her lips again, and then shook her head. "I cannot."

Morthanion rose, hiding his wince as best he could, and walked to her. She watched him warily, but didn't move as he stepped behind her. He slipped his arms around her waist, drawing her rear against him. Despite what had just happened, despite the soreness in his chest, his manhood was already semi-hard. Mouth close to her ear, he spoke softly. "Pretend that Baltherus has me. Standing right there." He lifted a hand to point a claw toward the canvas. It was half torn down, twisting and flapping harder than ever. Beyond, the storm raged.

"Claws at my throat, poised to tear it out. He's already wounded me, and he's about to kill me. What are you going to do?"

Lightning flashed, illuminating the entire cave with white light for a single instant. The thunder on its heels made the stone beneath their feet rumble.

She was quiet, but he could feel the turmoil in her, feel certain emotions starting to gain strength over others. Her fear, her devotion, simultaneously a leaden ball in his gut and a delightful fluttering in his chest.

Magic crackled over his skin, flowing from her, just before the jet of water burst from her outstretched hands. Even though her power was cold, it sent a thrill through him, and reminded him of the old spark he used to carry.

The stream hit the wall near the entrance, hard enough to break away a chunk of the stone. This time, it had been the thought of him in danger that had fueled her. Did that mean that she felt for him more deeply than either of them would admit?

"You need to be able to summon that at will," he said. "Not to kill. To protect. Most importantly, yourself."

"Promise me you will not let him kill you." Her voice was soft enough that he almost didn't hear it.

"Promise me you won't stop me from killing him."

She hesitated. "You know I will not."

Fingertips running lightly over her cheek, he drew her hair back behind her ear and kissed her neck. "And you can rest assured that I'll never let anyone kill me. I promise. It's not in my nature to be so giving."

Shivering, she tilted her head to the side, giving him more room to nuzzle his face, to taste her. Her skin was flushed, its heat flowing freely into him. Nothing else in the world, nothing else in four thousand years, had captivated him like she did. He knew nothing else ever would.

"Every day, I learn something new about you. Every day, my wonder grows," he said, running his fingers through her hair, over her shoulders, and along her arms. "There is great power in you...and you are one of the rare people in this world who will not abuse it. Will not turn it toward selfish goals."

He laced their fingers together. She guided their hands up, pressing his palms to her cheeks. Morthanion leaned his head against hers, his mind awash with her scent, with the scorching heat of her skin, with the curve of her ass against his cock. Nothing would be sweeter than to take her again, to slide into her and pretend everything would be all right simply because they could enjoy the bliss of each other's company here and now, in this moment.

Soon, though, Baltherus would make a move. It would likely be a consolidated one, bringing together a large portion of whatever strength in numbers and armament he had at his disposal. All that Morthanion and Aria could do in the face of it was remain cautious, stealthy, and prepared. They were too outnumbered for much else.

More than anything, he desired Aria, to go through the remainder of eternity at her side. But he longed, too, for the moment when Baltherus's blood ran hot and wet down his arms, when the horrified flash of realization wiped the smugness off the other demon's face. It would be killing to protect Aria, to protect the only thing Morthanion had ever cared for...and it would be done with no small amount of glee.

"I know neither of us want to dwell on this, Aria," he began, denying himself the satisfaction of having her again. If they could overcome the obstacles before them, they'd have a lot more time to enjoy one another in the future. "But they will come for us. Soon. When that happens, and I tell you to run...please. Swear to me you will. Get away from here, go beyond the barrier, and live free of fear."

She turned around to face him, brows lowered over her bright eyes. "No. I cannot promise that, Thanion."

He settled one hand on her shoulder, the other lingering on her cheek. "You need to."

Shaking her chin out of his gentle grasp, she pulled away. "I will *not*. I am not weak, and I will not leave you here."

"I know you're not weak." His arms dropped to his sides, feeling empty and cold suddenly. His stomach churned; was she really going to fight him on this? "That's why, if I tell you to run, I want your word that you will. You're strong enough to survive out there. To take care of yourself. If there's no other choice...if there is only that chance for you to live..."

He dropped his gaze, clenching his jaw. Frustration balled his fists, provoked by his inability to articulate his feelings, by the weight of those emotions and the words meant to express them.

"I have lived a long, long time. And in the eyes of most, that time has been spent committing terrible, terrible evil. I do not regret any of it." He met her gaze again. "But *you* are pure. Innocent. And you deserve time to enjoy being alive."

"It is your past, Thanion. Should you get free of this island, would you continue down that old path?"

"Only if I was without you." His voice was thick, coming from a dry mouth. "Then I'd be back on that path."

My life would no longer be about survival, only my own destruction.

She frowned, and seeing that expression on her face hurt almost as much as the conversation itself. Did she not understand that it was for her? That even if he were to die, it will have been worth it if it saved her life?

"I am not going," she said, a crushing finality in her voice. Breaking their gaze, she walked past him.

There was no way for him to explain that wouldn't make him sound like a fool. No way to say it that she would understand. No words that could convey his concerns without also betraying feelings he was not ready to share.

"So you would allow yourself to die needlessly?" he asked, turning his head to watch her over his shoulder.

"It would not be needlessly." Rummaging through her belongings, she picked up a coil of thin rope. She moved past him again, avoiding his eyes.

"If my death would give you time to escape and live, yours would be quite needless." It was the strongest instinct burning in him now; he had to keep her safe from all harm, even if it meant giving his own life to do so. He'd never thought that way before, even when he was a chosen lieutenant of the mighty Morgalien, The Incinerator. Without a doubt, he knew he would never have sacrificed himself to save the elder demon, much less anyone else.

"You promised you would never let anyone kill you, Thanion. I trust your word in that. I wish you would trust in my ability to survive, too." The sail trembled in her hands as she pulled it back across the opening of the cave. Using the rope, she began to tie it back into place. He couldn't help but notice how the tunic slid up when she stretched her arms, revealing more of her creamy thighs.

Absently, he ran his tongue over his lips. *Focus, demon.*

"This doesn't involve *letting* anyone kill me. It involves me killing as many of them as possible to give you enough time to flee."

"It is growing late," she said, tying off a final knot. The sail swayed more in the wind than it had before, but was secure enough to work. She looked at him, finally, and then walked by again. "We should rest."

His gaze followed her, hungrily. "We don't tend to rest much when we lie down together."

She glanced at him over her shoulder, smiling. Morthanion's heart increased its pace, pumping heat through his veins.

Turning her head away, she slowly slipped the tunic down at the neck, revealing her shoulder. She did the same with the other side, sliding her arms out of the garment. Holding it at her chest, she peeked over one bared shoulder again. Her smile took on new meaning as she let the tunic fall, the fabric whispering down her body, to pool at her feet.

Somehow, he maintained enough self control to keep from charging across the room and tossing her on her knees. Instead, he walked to her casually, letting his eyes roam over her slender back and heart-shaped bottom. He wrapped his arms around her from behind, cupping her breasts, and drew her to his chest.

"I must be rubbing off on you," he said, brushing his erection against her. "You play as dirty as any demon."

Aria laughed, turning in his arms and locking her hands in his hair.

He saw his own fire smoldering in her eyes.

"Make me burn, demon."

*****

Baltherus eased back on his throne, slipping a tart berry into his mouth. The fire in the great hall was roaring, but there was no feast. He'd sent even more men to the west to watch for Morthanion and the woman. He could sense her in that direction, faintly, though focusing on it did not narrow down her location from this distance.

It was only a matter of time before Baltherus discovered their hiding place, whether by searching it out or Morthanion making another mistake. Staring into the flames, he'd considered Ithoriel's counsel for a long while.

Once, Morthanion had been one of the most powerful and feared of their kind, his affinity for hellfire second only to Morgalien's. But what did that mean here? Nothing. They were all on equal ground, stripped of their magic, and Baltherus had never used his magic to fight. His had always been more subtle...no, he'd had to bloody his hands directly in the days of old, and had been damned good at it.

That arrogance, that instability, that savagery, all made Morthanion too much of a danger to keep around. It was a hard decision to make; though they were not friends, the two demons had once battled the light together, fought for the same cause, and that meant something. Not enough to risk sparing the elder demon, but enough to create a nostalgic, wistful pang in Baltherus's chest.

"Send the elf to me," he called to one of the men at the door, plucking another berry from the plate. The human nodded and made his exit.

Without his fire, Morthanion was just another threat to be eliminated. The true power here was in water. He'd tasted it from the woman. Real magic! How long had it been since he felt its tingle over the surface of his skin, that skittering current that eventually burrowed deep into his core?

He needed to charm her, to get her to come to his side willingly. Already, he'd tried to plant seeds of doubt in her regarding her mate. Would they take root? It was impossible to know how the bond would affect an individual, impossible to know how close she might have gotten to the elder demon. Because what was there to admire in a being like Morthanion, if not his blatant disregard for life?

The choice had been clear. If it were between the girl and the demon, Baltherus had to choose the girl. The thought of controlling the only one on the entire island who could use magic was too tantalizing, the possibilities too tempting to forgo.

The door guard returned, ushering Ithoriel inside.

"Master," the elf said, bowing, "what do you require of me?"

"Has Morthanion attempted to summon you?"

Ithoriel seemed surprised at the question, his eyes rounding for the briefest of moments. "I may have felt the merest hints of it, but *his* blood holds no sway over me."

"You will go with the next group heading to the western shore," Baltherus said. "That is where you first encountered him, yes?"

"Indeed, master. Though I do not see what difference I could make. My martial skills are…lacking."

The demon chuckled. Even if the elf were a veteran warrior, he would be hard-pressed to stand against a demon. "You seem less than enthusiastic about being sent out there, Ithoriel."

"I was forthcoming with you, sire, when I spoke of my desire to survive. That has not diminished since our last conversation. I only survived my first encounter with him *at his whim*." The words came through gritted teeth, the elf's lip curled in disdain. "I have no wish to tempt his good will a second time."

"Come now, Ithoriel, there's no need to fear. I told you to have faith."

"Is this meant as a test of that faith?" The elf's eyes were dark with malice. Apparently, Morthanion had made quite the impression on this one.

"Not at all. It is simply the next move. He doesn't know what he's up against, so he will seek all the information he can through whatever methods are available to him. You are one of those methods. If you feel him call you, send word to me with one of the others and answer the call."

"And what will this accomplish, master? A lamb to sate the lion's hunger?"

"He won't kill you, Ithoriel. So long as you make it worth his while. No need to lie to him. He probably won't even think it possible for you to lie to him, confident in the power of his blood. As long as you can get him to come out, we'll be able to find where they are hiding.

"And once we have the girl...we will deal with the demon."

The elf's eyes flared, his lips quivering somewhere between a grin and a grimace. "As you command," he whispered.

"Go. Take what supplies you require."

Ithoriel nodded and left quickly, keeping his eyes averted from the demon.

Picking up another berry between forefinger and thumb, Baltherus studied it contemplatively. The elf had offered sound advice, and been bold enough to speak his mind. Admirable qualities, under the right circumstances. Still, if he were to die – and a meeting with Morthanion meant a pretty good chance of it – there would be no loss. Ithoriel had been a warlock, once, and such creatures never really changed. Sniveling, subservient, scheming things, useless without power being funneled into them by their betters.

The warlock was just another means to an end, simply another tool to be used by Baltherus's expert hands to shape the future of the island. When it was all over, he would stomp Morthanion's charred corpse into ash and rule unopposed, his power solidified by the girl's magic. The elder demon's arrogance would lead him directly into the moves Baltherus needed him to make.

The berry burst between his fingers, and Baltherus smiled. With just a little patience, it would all be too easy.

Chapter Eighteen

She let the waves pull her beneath the surface, the water embracing her like it knew she belonged there. It caressed her, soothed her, rocked her on gentle currents as though it wanted to ease away the turmoil that weighed heavily on her mind.

Opening her eyes, Aria gazed upon the wonder and beauty of the sea. The last of the sun's light streamed through the crystal clear surface, refracting into beams that illuminated the ocean floor. Where there wasn't sand, there was coral of every shape and size. It was filled with bright patches of color, little things that swayed on the currents. She had thought they were plants when she was very young, but discovered that the spongy tentacles moved when touched. Fish of all kinds swam in and out of view, always maintaining some distance from her, even when she went completely still.

Today was a day of freedom. A day to feel the sun on her face and water on her skin. The last storm was more than a week behind them, and she had longed for the caress of the ocean.

Morthanion had been strict about how much time she spent away from their sanctuary, his fear growing stronger each day. He often brought up the matter of her leaving the island; she responded sometimes with vehement refusal, and others by ignoring him outright. Her refusals annoyed him, but her complete lack of a response upset him fully.

On other occasions, she chose to distract him instead. Like her, Morthanion could not get enough. He was as powerless when it came to her as she was to him. They made love. Often.

He also pushed her to use her powers. That was less successful. It was no different than when she turned to water; it took great concentration and left her feeling drained afterward. No matter how hard she tried, she couldn't reliably tap into the magic she held within. Occasionally, he had tried to rile her up, just like he'd done the first time. She didn't feel so bad ignoring him then, even when she could feel his frustration. The situation frustrated her, too.

When Morthanion would leave to scout the area, Aria missed him. Even in his absence, she could sense him near, but her soul cried out for physical touch.

She didn't understand this connection and was wary of bringing it up. He spoke no other words from his heart, and never directly expressed any tender emotions. Not since the night he'd muttered as he fell asleep, his words searing themselves on her heart to echo over and over.

Only you…forever you.

Did he mean them? Or had he only said them because he was sated by sex and on the verge of sleep? Morthanion was old. Sooner or later, he would tire of her. How could a young, inexperienced woman, naïve in the ways of the world, possibly hold his interest? For now, Aria was all he had for sexual release. How long would that last?

All of it frightened her. She knew she cared about him. Very deeply. And she knew that he cared for her, too. But love? Love terrified her. She knew, deep in her heart, that she loved him. Why else would she refuse to leave? Xani had died for love. Had loved Jasper so much that she remained by his side, knowing the fate that awaited her. But Jasper had loved his wife back, fiercely, until the very end. Could it be that Morthanion loved her, too? Or was it simply the powerful, all-consuming bond they had formed?

Would he have cared for her had that bond never existed?

She didn't relish the thought of herself and her demon meeting the same end her parents had. No. Aria would find a way, somehow, for them to live in peace. But in the meantime, she refused to waste any moment she had with him.

With a kick of her feet, Aria broke the surface. She pushed wet hair out of her face as she took a deep breath. She immediately sought Morthanion. He stood on the shore, no longer concealed in the shadows from which he had been watching her earlier. His back was to her, wings partially spread, his legs braced shoulder length apart. Possibly keeping watch on the tree line.

She wasn't sure why he brought her here, but she wasn't about to waste this little bit of freedom. Submerging again, her hair gently waving around her, Aria allowed the water to cradle her.

Her eyes followed a flittering yellow fish as it darted around rock and coral, and was momentarily blinded by a bright flash of light. She flinched and lowered her brows as she sought the light again. As she moved, it blinked, and she realized it was an object reflecting the sunlight.

Swimming deeper, Aria's fingers brushed aside the sand, pebbles, and broken shells, uncovering the item that had caught her attention. When the cloud of sediment settled, she was looking down at the grip and pommel of a knife. Wrapping her fingers around it, she drew it out. It was a small weapon, the blade not quite as long as her hand. She twisted it, enchanted by the way the light caught on the jewel at the end of the pommel.

Aria let her feet touch the bottom and kicked herself back up to the surface. There, in the open air, she raised the dagger to inspect it as she bobbed with the waves. She had never seen its like before. Every weapon Aria possessed was old and weathered, the salt water leaving the blades rusted and brittle. Weapons made on the island were of either stone or bone. There was no way to know how long this blade had been buried on the sea floor, but it shone bright and beautiful, the blade still polished.

She raised her head to look in Morthanion's direction and frowned uneasily. He was still turned away from her, but she could see someone move at his front. Their body language spoke of a conversation, though there was a stiffness to both men's movements.

Slowly, she began to swim back toward the shore. Morthanion had told her to remain in the water when they arrived. He knew it was where she was safest. But to see him there, conversing with another prisoner, was unsettling.

When his *guest* arrived, Morthanion stood in the long shadows cast by the setting sun. He had sent out his summons numerous times over the course of the day, but never felt his blood draw any nearer until now. He knew the elf was in the region, knew that he was amongst Baltherus's men. What was taking the creature so damned long?

The elf hadn't seen the demon at first, and scowled as he looked out at the ocean. Morthanion turned his head to follow the elf's gaze, and saw Aria surfacing. He squeezed his fists, claws pressing into his palms, and reminded himself that he needed the elf alive. At least for a little while longer.

"You will look at me and nothing else, mortal," he commanded through bared fangs. Stepping out of the shadows, he placed himself between his woman and the warlock, not bothering to shroud his features. "You've certainly taken your time."

Any surprise the elf betrayed was fleeting, his eyes narrowing and his scowl quickly falling back into place. "I rather value my own life, and leaving any sooner would have drawn Baltherus's eye. I am here now. What service may I provide you, oh lord and master?"

"So, you are in league with *him*," Morthanion said, ignoring Ithoriel's tone.

"As it is the only way to guarantee having food, water, and shelter, yes. To stand apart from him would have meant death."

"Not surprising one such as you would latch on to the first demon you found. You will tell me what you know. His location. Armament. Numbers."

From behind him, Morthanion heard the sound of something breaking the surface, and knew Aria had come up again. There was all manner of music on and in the water, and he found he was already getting better able to detect the subtle shifts in its songs.

The elf's eyes strayed, and he leaned to the side, looking past the demon and to the water.

In an instant, Morthanion had his claws poised at the elf's throat. He would not tolerate this filthy, parasitic creature looking upon Aria again.

"Eyes. On. Me. Understand?" Hot blood welled on the demon's rough palms, where his claws had punctured the skin. It would take so little pressure to draw more from Ithoriel's soft neck. Just a tiny squeeze.

The elf tilted his head back, throat bobbing, but there was little fear on display in his eyes. "She is out rather far. Do you not worry she might drown?"

Morthanion made no response, save to infinitesimally press his claws more firmly to the elf's flesh.

"He has built a settlement in this forsaken place. Those willing to work their share are allowed to live there and take part in its comforts. There are supplies enough to last weeks, maybe even months, and many, many weapons. Some salvaged from shipwrecks, but most made from materials here on the island. They don't see much use. Who would challenge a demon?"

"Another demon," Morthanion replied, grinning. "Where is this place located?"

"Near the center of the island. There's fresh water and easy access to everything."

Much as he did not want to leave Aria alone, the demon knew he would have to find the place eventually. Hiding was not the only option. He could attack Baltherus on his own turf, and rattle the spirit of the other demon's people. It wouldn't take much; if they were already so dependent on their demon lord, a little bloodshed in their home camp could easily have them doubting just how safe they really were there.

"And how many people?"

"I do not kn—"

The elf hissed through his teeth as one of Morthanion's claws broke skin.

"I speak truth! He never has everyone there at the same time, constantly rotates all of us through different outposts and camps. At least a few dozen, though there could be more."

"He's got almost a score of you in this area. I see your fires in the night, and sign of you everywhere. Why have you not made a move?"

"We are here only to observe," the elf rasped, his features drawn tight. Still, his eyes burned not with terror, but loathing. "He has runners reporting to him daily, but he has forbidden anyone from searching. He sees you and your woman as a threat, and only desires the protection of his people."

Morthanion stared at the elf for a long while. There were few mortals that would long hold his gaze, but this warlock was not looking away. Something about it gave the demon pause. There was truth to the information the elf had given, Morthanion knew there was, but he couldn't help but feel there was more missing.

And the hatred in Ithoriel's eyes...

It is an expression many folk wear when they are being threatened. The few who do not collapse into cowardice, anyway.

He opened his hand. The elf stumbled back, immediately pressing a palm to his throat. The scent of Ithoriel's blood mingled with the briny air.

"Be gone. Know that if I see you here without having summoned you, I will kill you."

The elf bowed, and then quickly turned and hurried back toward the trees. He did not make eye contact with the demon again. Morthanion watched him off, listening to the sounds of his passage through the thickening undergrowth. He could understand the hatred the elf wore. The demon knew what it felt like to be powerful, fearsome, and then be stripped of everything and tossed into a cesspit where the strongest, most savage were the rulers. It was the hatred of a shattered pride clinging to its final, broken pieces.

He scanned the tree line and the surrounding beach for signs of others before he turned to the ocean again, immediately picking out Aria.

Her dark hair was floating around her as she swam gracefully back to the shore. Smooth and effortless, her movements verged on the sensual, and the water embraced her, carrying her where she wanted to go. Around her, the surface sparkled with the dying sunlight, casting an ethereal glow on her face.

She rose once the water was shallow enough, moisture cascading off of her and reflecting more light, her dress sculpting to her alluring curves. Morthanion found it suddenly difficult to recall what he'd just been dealing with. Aria was a vision, an otherworldly being more stunning than any angel.

Her eyes darted to the trees. "Who was that?"

"The elf who tried to get you drunk some time ago," he replied.

She halted. "Why was he here?"

"I bound him to me to use him for information." He moved closer to her, watching her carefully. "He's told me some things, but admitted to open association with Baltherus. I doubt it's as forced as he claims it to be."

"Bound him to you?" Confusion marred her brow. After a brief consideration, she seemed to move on from the first question. "Do you believe what he told you?"

"I believe the majority of it, yes. Just as I believe he is going to report every detail back to Baltherus immediately." Morthanion glanced contemplatively back to the jungle, where he knew there were at least twenty men settling into their camps, roasting food over open flames. "Should have killed him that night."

When he looked back to her, she was frowning, searching his face. He couldn't tell if it was disappointment or concern that was coming from her, but it didn't really matter. Within a few moments, she discovered her smile again. She lifted her hand and turned it over. "I found this."

She held a dagger, the blade pressed along the inside of her arm. It was small with a jeweled pommel and shining metal.

She handed it to him, and the demon raised it to study the weapon more closely. Despite its adornment, it appeared functional in design. "It must be crafted of a rare material, to show no rust." He lightly brushed a thumb over the edge. Blood immediately oozed from the cut it opened. "Still sharp, too."

Changing his hold on it, he offered it back grip-first. "Keep it. Another just-in-case measure."

She nodded, and gripped it with the blade flat against the inside of her wrist when she lowered her arm again.

"Are we returning?" she asked.

"Yes. It's too dangerous to stay out here much longer." He grinned. "Unless you want some lessons in how to kill a man in such a way that he screams as loudly as possible."

Holding his gaze for an instant, she looked away, face paling visibly. "I do not care to hear you speak like that, Morthanion." Without looking back, she began to walk toward the incoming tide.

"My humor oft goes unappreciated," he said in a tone of mock mourning, following just behind her. Before the water rolled over her bare feet, he took hold of her arm and spun her to face him. "Be safe. I'll be watching."

He leaned down and kissed her. When he pulled back, that soft smile had returned to her lips.

When the pair left, one by sea and one by air, Ithoriel followed them with his keen eyes. The demon was the easier to mark, silhouetted so strongly by the sunset. They traveled north and slightly west, toward the rising, jagged cliffs that made the area so difficult to traverse.

Soon, the girl was lost to him, her constant and prolonged time beneath the water making it impossible to track her movements. But the demon, low as he remained to the sea, still stood out. Morthanion glided toward a promontory that jutted like a knife from the mainland, little more than a speck as he followed around its end and disappeared behind it.

One heartbeat passed. Two. Three. By a count of thirty, the demon had not emerged anywhere within sight.

His lips split in the first grin he'd worn in a long, long while. The brush around him rustled as the others arrived.

"We lost them. They went too far out," one of them said.

"I saw," said Ithoriel. "I saw very well. Let us return to camp; I must leave to inform Baltherus immediately."

Chapter Nineteen

Aria wondered if Xani had felt this happy while she was with Jasper.

Sated from making love, Morthanion lay with one arm behind his head and the other draped around Aria. His fingers idly massaged a small circle on her lower back. She listened to the music of the ocean outside and the tandem beating of their hearts, pumping in perfect unison. She smiled, content.

When they were together, time slipped away; minutes, hours, even days lost meaning. During these quiet, intimate moments, she could almost forget the danger. That only a few days before, Morthanion had met with Ithoriel to obtain information about Baltherus's plans and people.

She could almost forget that all of this could come to an end at a moment's notice.

Her thoughts returned to her mother. Had Xani felt this happiness, even though the other islanders had been a constant threat in the back of her mind? It was clear to her why Xani had refused to leave Jasper.

Love.

It was such a binding force. It had threaded itself right through her heart and soul, and tied them to his. Aria couldn't even contemplate leaving Morthanion, especially knowing he would be here alone, standing against so many others. It made her feel ill.

"Did you pack supplies like I asked you to?" Morthanion inquired, as if sensing her turbulent thoughts. His fingers stroked lightly, absently, making their way up her back to cup her shoulder possessively.

"Yes, Thanion. They have been packed for some time now."

"Every day, Baltherus sends more men. You need to be prepared to leave if you must."

You, not *we*.

Aria sighed. It was a tired, frustrated sound, not the one of contentment she had released moments before. "I am not leaving."

"You may not have a choice, Aria," he said, his voice hardening. "You're not going to throw your life away."

The moment was ruined.

She lifted herself, hands braced on his shoulders as she narrowed her eyes on Morthanion. He had continued to insist she leave, if it came to it, and each time her response was the same. She would *not* leave. "No, I am not. My mother did not throw her life away when she chose to remain with my father. She lived. Even if her life was taken, she *lived*."

She *loved*.

Snatching her dress up from the stone floor, Aria withdrew from him and stood. She yanked it over her head and tugged it down her body. "I am not leaving, Thanion. I am staying here with you."

"Do you think your father would have preferred her to die?" he demanded, getting to his feet. He seemed not to notice his nudity; she tried to do the same. "Why would he have wanted that, if there was a chance for her to get away?"

"Of course he did not. But it was her choice. What else was he to do? Fight with her until the end," she accused, glaring at him pointedly, "or savor each moment? They enjoyed their time together, until their lives were taken just after my birth. They were *happy*."

"I savor each moment with you, but I will not have your life endangered if there is a way for you to escape. I refuse to allow it."

"And I refuse to leave!"

"Why are you so eager to die?" he demanded, moving close. His eyes blazed and shadowy wisps writhed around his body. "What do you think it will accomplish? That there is something romantic about dying together? There is nothing glorious about death, nothing good about it!"

"I am not eager to die. I am *living!*" She stared into his eyes, unflinching. She wasn't frightened of him, no matter how many shadows covered his form. "I could die out there, past the barrier, just as easily as I could here. But at least here, I have you."

"I will not have the only person I have ever cared for die for no damned good reason!"

"And we are *not* dying today!" she snapped.

"All I want is for you to keep living, no matter what happens to me. Is that too much to ask of you? Too much to hope for?"

Yes it is.

"If I should die today, my life will have known true happiness at its end. Yours has only just begun. I want you to live. You need to open your eyes to the situation we're in," he said, lowering his voice. He touched her then, his fingers wrapping around her upper arms. "At least half the damned prisoners on this island are looking for us, hoping to be the one to tell Baltherus that they found us. I cannot go beyond the rocks. We need food and water, and we have to expose ourselves to get it.

"It's only a matter of time before we are found. When that happens, do you think we'll be able to fight our way out? Do you think that I can take twenty, thirty, a hundred men on my own? The best I can hope for is to keep them away from you long enough for you to escape. Is it too damned much to ask that you take that opportunity?"

"I am not leaving you," she said quietly. She couldn't leave him. The thought of it broke her heart, made it ache.

Despite how softly she'd spoken, his fury flared and swept through her. He abruptly released his hold on her and moved away, pacing.

"Do you think I want it to come to that?" he roared, turning to stalk back toward her, but she stood her ground. "Do you think I won't do what I can to keep things from getting to that point? I will fight the entire world to keep you safe, to stay with you, but if I had to die to keep you alive, I would do it without hesitation."

"You have my answer, Morthanion." She refused to believe they would die, especially so soon. She would give up everything in this cave if she had too. They'd run. There were places to hide, she was sure, where no one could find them. There had to be.

"Clearly," he replied, and turned away from her to pull on his clothes.

Aria watched him silently as he dressed, feeling anger waft off him, seeping into her. It was potent, but she had gotten better at suppressing it. He stepped into his boots and started toward the exit.

"Where are you going?" she asked, frowning. It was evening, the sun still in the sky.

"Scouting."

"You already did that."

"Well, I'm doing it again," he said, pushing the sail aside.

She followed him. "You are acting childish!"

"I disagree. Stay inside and keep quiet."

"You should stay inside and keep quiet as well! The sun is still up and I am sure the entire island heard your shouting."

"Then I'll just have to kill the entire island so they don't say anything."

"Stop it! Why must you be like this? Why can you not just accept my choice?"

Morthanion turned to her fully, his head angled down so that his eyes bore into hers. "Because it is the *wrong* choice. What did your mother accomplish by staying? She might as well have killed your father herself. You too, since you'd have died were it not for Laudine."

Aria glared at him. Had her mother left, Xani would never have known the depths of love she discovered with Jasper. Aria would never have been born here. Would never have met Morthanion.

"It is not the wrong choice," she replied, her voice quavering.

"Again, I disagree. Seems we'll just have to come to terms with having different opinions on the matter."

"You are the one who cannot stand my choice to stay. My answer will not change, no matter how many times you ask. You know this, yet still you persist."

"Yes. You're not the only one who can be stubborn." He turned away again and moved closer to the cave's mouth. A mass of shadows swirled and solidified to form his wings. "Be safe."

Then he was gone.

Aria watched him go. There was a loud growl, and it took a moment for her to realize it had come from her. She stomped her foot and turned back into the cave, letting the canvas fall back into place.

Why couldn't he let it rest? She knew the dangers, and was willing to face them. There had to be some way. Morthanion was so sure he could eventually get free of the island. He didn't know how long it would take, only that he would. He was stronger than Laudine. If anyone could escape the island, it would be him.

Nothing had to end now.

She hated fighting with him. They had argued so many times about this, and her answer would never change.

She wouldn't live without him. She didn't think she even could.

There was still lingering sunlight on the horizon when Aria heard the sail being brushed aside. Relief flooded her; Morthanion had decided to come back. She'd feared he might have been gone all night, or worse…that he might not have returned at all.

She turned away from the small fire, a ready smile on her lips.

"You are ba—" That smile died and her eyes widened when she saw the bulky figure silhouetted against the canvas. "No!"

Her heart stopped, cold dread filling her. She stared at Baltherus as he slowly advanced, and she retreated, snatching the dagger from where it lay by the furs. The little blade felt inadequate now.

The demon's eyes made a slow perusal of the cave before they came to rest on her. He smiled at the dagger and spread his hands to either side. "I'm here as a friend. No need for that."

His gaze crawled over her, devoured her. She shuddered in revulsion. When he took another step toward her, she raised the blade.

"You are not a friend. The last time I met you, you hurt me." She continued to maintain the distance between them, glancing at the mouth of the cave. If she could get by him, she could hide in the sea. Could cross the barrier.

"That's not going to work," he said softly. "Best to just give in now. Put the dagger down. Come to my home. Be my guest, eat at my table. You and I have many things to discuss."

"The only thing we have to discuss is you leaving us alone."

"You really don't know anything about him, do you?" he asked, pity glimmering in his eyes. "I suppose he wouldn't tell you much about what he is, though. Not while he has use for you, anyway."

"I know plenty about him," she said. *Where is Morthanion?*

"That he was second only to the eldest of our kind? That he has murdered countless thousands and burned entire villages to the ground? And oh, the glee in his eyes as he did all of this. He seemed to be at his happiest when he burned his victims slowly. He and Morgalien would make a spectacle of it."

He paced to the side, getting no closer nor any further from her. His body was relaxed, his motions smooth. Blocking her exit.

Aria pressed her lips together, glaring at the demon. "I know all this."

She hated how he enjoyed the things he had done in the past. But he was changing. He *had* to be changing.

"Do you realize how many other women he's had? How many he's used to get his thrills, only to throw them away? I can't call myself a good man, I can be honest about that, but compared to your Morthanion, I am a saint. I want what's best for you. I don't want to see you hurt. You are too special for that."

You are too special for that.

Morthanion had told her she was different, that what they shared was unique. A bond deeper than anything most people ever knew. Yet, he himself had mentioned other women.

He is trying to put me off guard.

She shook her head sharply. "You do not care if I get hurt. You are out to harm Morthanion."

"Morthanion is unstable. He has been for a long time. Centuries of war unhinged him, and he has never been able to adapt well to a life of hiding. There was never enough burning for him. He's dangerous — to you, and me, and ever—"

"He would never hurt me."

He paused at her interruption, though he betrayed no anger. "He already has, hasn't he? Hasn't madness consumed him, darkness controlled his actions? We're just trying to live our lives, and we get on well enough. Peacefully enough. You can be a part of that. You can join us, and reap the benefits."

"You call sending men to track us down a peaceful act? *We* are trying to live in peace. You just refuse to leave us be!"

Baltherus smiled wistfully, though the emotion didn't reflect in his eyes. "Come with me. I can show you peace and plenty, with real walls. All the food you could want, servants…claim your piece of this paradise."

"I am not going with you."

"What is your name? I feel so disrespectful, not knowing, especially as I'm inviting you to be my guest" he said, as though he'd not heard her refusal.

Aria pressed her lips together, offering only silence, keeping her eyes upon him.

"You are stubborn. I can appreciate that. But refusing to see the truth…well, that can be…*dangerous.*"

She had seen Morthanion move with preternatural speed so often that she had grown used to it, almost didn't notice it anymore. It was simply another thing to love about him, especially when he would sweep her off her feet and down onto the furs that way. But when Baltherus moved – a demon half again as wide as Morthanion and half a head taller – she couldn't help but be amazed by the quickness of it. Had she not seen him do it before, just a touch faster than Morthanion seemed able to manage, she would have been caught completely off-guard.

Now, she had anticipated his attack, following more of his honey-laced words. She brought up her empty hand and forced magic through it. The jet of water caught him on the shoulder, spinning him around and knocking him back despite his size and momentum. Various objects clattered to the ground, and she wasted no time.

Still clutching the little dagger, she turned and ran to the rear of the cave. Shoving the panels aside, she plunged into the tunnel. The sound of her racing heart amplified in the constricting darkness, urging her feet to move faster, kicking up the muddy water that seeped in during the rain. It was only her intimate knowledge of the passage that kept her from hurting herself in her flight.

She was already panting by the time she could see the sliver of light coming through the boards that hid the exit. At any moment, she expected a huge, clawed hand to come down on her shoulder or cover her mouth, to drag her back into shadows that provided her no comfort.

Pausing only long enough to punch the panels aside, she burst into the open air. The sun was setting over the ocean, and its reflection on the shifting waters blinded her, turning everything white.

As forms darkened in her vision, she realized she wasn't alone. There were at least four men, large and rough-looking, their compassionless eyes locked on her as they advanced. Her gaze darted to the edge of the cliff. Maybe if she ran, now, she could jump…and she might miss the rocks below.

"There's nowhere for you to go."

She turned to see Baltherus emerge from the tunnel, twisting his bulky frame to fit through. He brought a hand up, combing his fingers through his hair. Victory sparkled in his emerald eyes.

A branch crunched behind her, and she spun. One of them had crept up from the right side, and lunged at her.

She didn't think; there was no more time for anything but instinct. The magic came more easily, hastened by necessity. There was nothing behind the man to stop his tumble backwards when it hit him. He screamed as he went over the side of the cliff, and the sound ended abruptly.

Her stomach lurched and twisted on itself, ice filling her veins. What had she just done?

Motion flickered in the corner of her eye. She jerked her head to the side, the muddy ends of her hair slapping against her arms. She lashed out with the dagger, throwing her weight into it as the man reached for her.

He swayed back, the blade catching only the fabric of his shirt. His hand moved much quicker than hers had, the back of his balled fist connecting with her jaw. She hit the ground in a daze.

Face throbbing, she looked up to see Baltherus strike down her attacker, blood gushing from the man's nose.

"The next one to harm her loses a hand. All of you know the law."

The demon swung his gaze between the remaining men before moving to Aria. Crouching, he picked up her fallen dagger from the ground, tucked it in his belt, and lifted her to her feet. He clasped her wrists and forced them behind her back.

"It didn't have to be this way," Baltherus said. Someone else hurried over, and bound her forearms together tightly. "I want you to know that you will still be considered my guest, and will be afforded every convenience I can offer."

What will you do if Baltherus gets a hold of you again? Cry out for me, or fight him?

She struggled against the bonds, throwing her body weight away from Baltherus in an attempt to break free of his grasp. There were grins on the faces of the others, like none of them cared that she'd just killed one of their own. And now she was not naïve to the meaning of the hunger in their eyes.

Lashing out with a foot, she caught the nearest one between his legs. He grunted, the sound pitching higher before it trailed off, and fell to his knees.

Baltherus laughed, loudly, and she thought there was genuine pleasure in it. She twisted and thrashed. The demon took firm hold of her face and gagged her before clasping a hand on her upper arm. He started to walk, half-dragging her as she tried to bury her heels.

"You have fight in you. That's good. Life would be boring without that." The demon turned, looking past her to his men. "Come on, then. We've a lot of ground to cover and little time. He'll be coming for her."

He continued on, the lone tree atop the promontory slowly shrinking with distance. As much as she could, she fought against his forward motion, trying to jerk her body away from him, locking her knees to halt his advance. The only result was him tightening his grip on her arm, finally making it painful.

If she knew how to curse him, she would have. Even behind the gag.

Not once did she cry out for Morthanion.

The sensation struck Morthanion just as he thought he'd found Baltherus's stronghold. He'd pushed himself high, scanning the jungle below, and finally spotted a huge clearing filled with thatched-roof huts, all ringed with a wall of logs. Before he could reflect on how easily Ithoriel had given the location away, his stomach sank.

Unease grew in him, slowly crawling up his throat. There was no time for uncertainty. Everything would be over soon, and he wouldn't have to argue with Aria anymore. Her stubbornness – and his, too – would have been for naught.

But the feeling would not leave. It only deepened and spread, thickening into fear. Its icy tendrils came up against the fiery lashes of his anger, and the emotions thrashed within him, battling for supremacy – one with creeping subtlety, the other with graceless brutality.

This fear is not mine.

The realization numbed him. He was deeply concerned for Aria's safety, but what just crept into him was something entirely different, something far stronger. Within the space of a few heartbeats, he had claimed that mounting terror as his own.

Aria!

Hot and cold twisted together, not destroying one another, but coalescing into a fuel as he sped round and pushed himself back to the cave. She was in trouble. The fear was hers. He'd been a damned fool again and left her alone in his anger, and now she was in trouble. How could he have been so senseless, so selfish?

Be all right. Be all right. Please, gods, let her be all right.

The landscape passed with blurring speed beneath him, but his racing thoughts made the journey back to the promontory feel endless. He couldn't feel her anymore. Why was that sense failing him now?

Morthanion burst into the cave, tearing the sail down and casting it aside. His heart did not want to believe what his eyes were showing him. A fire faded to embers, partially knocked out of its neat ring of stones in a smear of ash across the floor. Shells and unique bits of driftwood and smooth little rocks strewn across the furs, one of the makeshift shelves knocked down and split. The bark strips she drew on were scattered, too, some of them smeared by water.

At the rear of the cave, the screen she used to change behind had tipped, and the mouth of the exit tunnel gaped at him mockingly.

Blood oozed from his palms where his claws bit into his flesh. He felt none of it. Baltherus had come. He'd waited for Morthanion to leave, for Aria to be alone, and had taken her. Why wouldn't there be eyes watching? Why would

Morthanion be so arrogant as to believe he could fly off in broad daylight and not be spotted?

Maybe they hadn't gotten far. Baltherus could move quickly if he wanted to, but his men had to go by foot.

Morthanion raced through the tunnel, rocks scraping his skin as he dragged himself out at the top. Frantically, he spun, casting his gaze in every direction. Nothing but trampled grass, some of it darkened by blood, surely left by her struggles.

Cry out for me, or fight him? She'd fought, but what good had it done? He should have forced her to leave, shouldn't have given her a choice!

Tossing his head back, he roared his rage and pain and regret. Her name echoed through the island sky, stretching out and reverberating with bone-chilling sorrow.

He dropped his chin to his heaving chest. The necklace lay against his skin, splattered with mud. He closed a hand around it. *She thought this was the only thing I've ever been given. But she's given me so much more.*

"I can't lose her now."

Faintly, there was a prick of warmth in the back of his mind.

There was only one place Baltherus would go. Only one place the demon would feel secure. He forced his breathing to slow, pushed down the warring emotions, swallowed them like rising bile.

Heat danced up his spine, throbbed at the base of his skull, and called him eastward again. She was alive. She had to be. And if she wasn't...

If you were to die, there would be nowhere on this island safe for anyone.

Chapter Twenty

The jungle had been cleared in a wide ring around the town, which itself was circled by lashed-together logs twice as tall as Aria. Straight ahead was a gap in the wall, with a man perched high on each side. Two more stood on the ground at the edges of the opening. Torches cast flickering illumination on the men, and they held their weapons up in salute as Baltherus ushered her through the gate.

Aria stared at this with a mixture of despair and wonder. This was nothing like her home, nothing like the small camps she'd seen these people erect out in the jungle. This was a settlement – just like the ones Laudine had described in her stories – and Aria was going to be trapped here. Locked behind that huge wall, surrounded by rough-looking men.

As they passed through, she couldn't help but gawk at the people. She'd never seen so many of them gathered together like this. They were all manner of size and coloring, and she knew now that some of them were elves and some humans, but they all shared one common trait: each bore the same mark that Morthanion had on his hand. Most of them seemed to be working, though many stopped and greeted the demon as he passed. Some stared at Aria with unmasked lust in their eyes, and she shuddered, quickly looking away.

"No one will touch you," Baltherus said. He stared ahead, his hand firm on her elbow as he led her on.

Choosing to ignore him, she instead surveyed the surrounding area. All around were smaller structures made of wood, the roofs covered with bundles of grass.

They were homes.

A few of the structures had no walls, only posts supporting roofs under which people worked. They passed by one where a pair of men were roasting a boar over a pit of coals, their skin glistening with sweat in the glow. The smell of the meat struck her in that same moment. She bit down on the gag, willing the pang of hunger away.

The trek down from the rock outcropping upon which they'd captured Aria had been slow, but once they had reached the edge of the jungle, Baltherus had tired of her attempts at stalling their progress. He had tossed her over his shoulder and broken into a run, fast enough that her stomach lurched. She'd been powerless but to rage at him through the gag as she bounced painfully, trees whipping by quickly enough for her to hear their passing. He only stopped when they reached the village clearing and the men waiting there.

It was easier to be angry. She wasn't ready to acknowledge the cold fear that was lodged in her belly.

"It has its own beauty, don't you think?" Baltherus asked, glancing back at her.

Aria grunted against the gag, glaring at him.

"Do not look at me so. You will see that it is for the best. You will have food and protection, and anything else your heart might desire."

But what about freedom?

They approached the largest of the buildings. It was positioned in the center of everything, and its walls stretched long to either side of its central doors. There were two more men standing vigil here, long spears in their hands and knives on their belts. Upon seeing Baltherus, they shifted, each pulling open one of the doors and standing aside to allow the demon in with his *guest*. Both cast curious glances at her as she passed.

Inside, there were large bowls of fire held up on stands, offering bountiful light for the sprawling tables that dominated most of the space. There was a large fire in the center, burning in a stone pit. Directly on the other side of it, a series of broad steps led up to a wide chair draped in fur and cloth that overlooked everything.

He turned right, leading her along the wall. From the corner of her eye, she saw faces turn toward her, but she did not look. This was his home, she guessed, and that made it harder than ever to ignore her mounting terror.

Baltherus plucked an unlit torch from the wall, pausing at one of the fires long enough to ignite it, and then brought her to a square door in the floor at the far right end of the huge hall. He released his hold on her to open it, revealing narrow steps leading down into darkness.

When he reached for her again, she pulled away. She shook her head, but none of the angry sounds she'd made for the entire journey would come.

"I can assure you, it's safe. You'll have some time alone, to think…to consider your options."

He was too quick for her to avoid him a second time, and his grip was firm as he guided her down the steps. The short hallway at the bottom ended with a heavy wooden door. Baltherus opened it and nudged her inside.

The walls were hard-packed dirt, bare wooden supports embedded in them. The empty room smelled earthy, and had no hint of brine like her home. It was dry, and too quiet, and too small.

He removed the gag and stepped back. "Get some rest. I'll be back, soon enough."

The door closed, something heavy sliding into place, and she was alone in complete blackness. There was no sound save the pounding of her heart and the shaky rasp of her own breath.

Morthanion watched the settlement from his tree-branch perch at the edge of the clearing. Soul-shaking fury seethed within him, held in check only by the memory of the many arguments he'd had with Aria over the last week. He'd accused her of being willing to needlessly throw her life away. What sort of man would he be if he were to do the same now?

What good would it do for him to die trying to get in? More importantly, what good would it do her? He had to survey the situation, and temper the heat of his anger with the cold of his fear.

There were six watch towers spaced around the walls, crude structures that nonetheless served their purpose. Even humans, with their weak eyesight, would have little trouble spotting an approach across the stripped land between the jungle and the walls. Though their equipment was crude, like most everything here, he could easily identify bows and spears near at hand for each of the guards.

"She is all right, for now," he whispered. Her presence was near, somewhere beyond those walls. Fear still radiated from her, but her distress hadn't spiked again. He had to count on Baltherus keeping her alive, because she was his leverage. Both to defend against and manipulate Morthanion, he needed Aria.

In the crimson haze that had dominated his vision, he knew he could make it over the wall. He would even make it to the long building in the middle of the settlement, which could be nothing but Baltherus's makeshift palace. He had every confidence that he would look the other demon in the eye.

But how much damage would he take on the way? There were dozens of men inside. Their armament was primitive, but weapons of any sort helped close the gap between mortal and immortal, and these men were hardened by their time here.

Bleeding from a score or more wounds, would he be able to overcome Baltherus?

Thinking about this wrong, he scolded himself, shaking his head. *Brute force is one of* his *strengths. Need to play up my advantages.*

I need to show them fear.

Was it possible to turn Baltherus's greatest asset against him? Was the big demon's charisma enough to hold his camp together?

He took deliberately slow, deep breaths, watching the clouds moving overhead, creeping closer and closer to the moon. Once its glow was shielded, he dropped from his vantage point and slipped forward into the shadow, weaving between the stumps of trees that Baltherus's men had cleared.

Could she feel his presence, like he felt hers? He willed it toward her, hoping it could provide her hope. Though he wouldn't admit it to himself, the sensation caused by her relative nearness was his only remaining source of strength.

He could not lose her. Not when he'd just found her.

There were dull thuds from above, accompanied by muffled voices and laughter. Aria couldn't make out anything they said. She sat on the hard, cold floor, unable to guess how much time had passed. Her wrists were chaffed, the slightest movement of the rope that bound them bringing more pain. The dried mud on her arms and legs cracked and flaked, irritating her skin, and there was no way to relieve the itching.

All the fighting she'd done when they took her hadn't gotten her any closer to escaping. In the end, her struggles – against Baltherus and against the bindings – had only furthered her discomfort. There was nothing else to focus on in the dark.

The room had no opening, not even a window, cutting her off completely from fresh air. Instead of the comforting crispness of the ocean breeze, she had the cloying scents of earth and moist wood. There was only one way out, and it was barred. Her distress grew with each passing moment. In all her life, she'd never been so far from the sea.

She heard footsteps on the stairs, and tensed when she saw light appear through the thin gaps in the planks and along the floor. The heavy piece of wood that secured the door from the outside slid against its surface. Light burst into the chamber, forcing her to turn her head away. She blinked for several moments before her eyes adjusted to it.

Aria lifted her gaze to Baltherus as he entered. He set his torch into the ring near the doorframe. The smile on his face might have been charming if it was worn by anyone else.

"Are you comfortable enough?" he asked, closing the door behind him.

She frowned. "My wrists hurt, and I would prefer to be near the sea," she said honestly.

He approached and eased himself into a crouch a few feet away from her. His forearms settled atop his knees. "I'm sorry, but the magic at your command forces me to keep you bound. I have many other people to keep alive besides myself."

"If I promise not to use it against you?" Could she keep that promise?

"Well," he said, his smile shifting strangely, "I suppose you'd need to offer a convincing argument about why I should trust you."

"I have struck you with it twice, and it has not left any lasting harm. You are strong and fast, and you have many men here. What would be my chances of getting away?"

"Since you are trying to think from my position, don't forget this: I have no idea what the extent of your abilities are. If there are other things you know how to do. If that was as powerful as it gets. It's so painfully little for me to base a decision on."

"I do not even know what my abilities are." Her brow furrowed. "The first time it happened was when you had grabbed me and flew me into the air. Before that, I never knew I could. Do you not think if I had it at my disposal, I would have been a little harder to catch?"

Aria could see his mind working, weighing his options. Finally, he rose and stepped closer to her. He crouched again only a foot away, leaned in, and inhaled her scent. He sighed.

Aria tilted back and drew her legs tight against her. He was larger and broader than Morthanion. Baltherus could crush her with his bare hands if he wanted to.

"You really don't, do you?"

She shook her head.

Before she could react, his arms slipped around her – too similar to an embrace – and he cut apart the ropes holding her wrists together. She moved her hands to her front, shoulders aching, and rubbed her wrists.

"Thank you."

He moved away from her again, allowing her some space, but kept a thoughtful gaze upon her. "I really don't mean you any harm. I hope you will come to see that."

If he lied, he did it well – and hadn't Morthanion said it came naturally to demons? – but Aria detected sincerity in his words. She studied him closely. His eyes were a brilliant green, resting above high cheekbones, and his hair shone in a variety of golden hues. Defined brows sloped toward his straight nose. His lower lip was fuller than the upper one, and he parted them in a grin, knowing she was appraising him.

If she hadn't been drawn to Morthanion, she would have considered Baltherus pleasing to look at. But, unlike Morthanion, Baltherus wore his mask every time he came to her.

"You rule here. Why do you hide yourself?"

"Hide myself?" he asked, uncertain. "I'm not hiding anything. They all know what I am."

Aria looked him over again, just to be certain. There were no horns, no glowing eyes, no claw-tipped fingers. "So why hide your appearance?"

"Does my appearance not please you?" A shadow flickered over his face.

"I simply wonder why you mask your true form and wear the face of a human."

"It is as much my face as the other," he replied tersely. Something about her questions made him uneasy, enough that he wasn't able to conceal it completely.

"I suppose it is." To Aria, Morthanion's true form was the demon. It was the real Thanion, not a pretty mask.

"Are you ready to tell me your name yet? I feel that I have been nothing if not forthcoming with you."

"You have yet to tell me why I am being forced to stay here."

"Survival on this island can be a very delicate thing. It's a careful balance. My people have worked very hard to carve out our place here and keep ourselves alive. You and Morthanion threaten to destroy that balance utterly."

"We threatened nothing. It was your men that came to our side of the island and tried to do us harm. For all twenty-two years of my life, you had no idea that I even existed, and did not know my guardian existed before that." Aria tilted her head, eyes locked with his. She paused briefly as something occurred to her. "Was it your men who killed my parents?"

Baltherus's eyed widened and his brows rose. "Amazing. Simply amazing. Their child survived, then." He spoke mostly to himself as he scrutinized her. He reached out and brushed the back of his finger across her cheek. She couldn't help but flinch from his touch. "Jasper's daughter. I see him in you, but there's more of your mother there." His hand dropped away. "The men who killed your parents are themselves only bones, now."

Aria narrowed her eyes. "Why are you not among them? You are master here, and you think I would look past you being part of that?"

"It was...regrettable." He did not look away, but there was remorse in his expression. "Were I there, I would have stopped it. Men get urges. Powerful urges. Have you ever wondered why there are so few women on this island?" He tilted his head and inhaled slowly. "Men are beasts and are usually driven only by lust. Your mother was a very lovely woman, and some of the men had been without a female's touch for decades. I...arrived too late."

"If it is such a danger for me as a woman, this is the worst place for me to be, surrounded by your beastly men."

"They dare not lay a hand upon you," he said, his voice hardening. "They know you are my guest, and that punishment for disobedience is swift. All women here are under my protection."

"Why? Why am I here?"

"What is your name?"

"What balance do I threaten?"

"I feel that I have answered enough of your questions. You could at least do me the courtesy of answering the single one I've posed to you." He rose from his crouch. "I don't want to force it out of you. All I want is for us to be friends."

"A friend would not have tied me up and dragged me here against my will. Do you blame me for my mistrust of you? How do I know that you will not use my name against me?"

Baltherus sighed softly, a sad smile on his lips. "I don't want to hurt you. I mean that. I wasn't threatening you. Is it so much for you to simply give me your name? It's like you said before; there's not much I couldn't do to you right now, if I wanted to."

She looked away from him, holding her tongue. It was true. He'd had every opportunity to harm her, but all he had done so far was lock her in this room. Not once had he stricken her, even when she fought her hardest against him. He hadn't even punished her when she had...killed that man. The only punishment he'd doled out had been to the man who struck her.

"Aria."

"Aria," he repeated, and his smile grew. "I am very glad to finally make your acquaintance."

"Why am I here?"

"Because I would like for you to take a place at my side. Be my right hand. Rule this island with me, and reap all the benefits of it. You will want for nothing and you will never have to know fear again."

She frowned as he spoke. "I already want for nothing. And I do not wish to rule."

"Just imagine the things we could accomplish together, Aria. The civilization we could craft. A new society; a tribute to your people, who were driven out because of what the mages of the mainland decided to do to this place. A new utopia in their memory."

"A society filled with rapists and murderers."

"Some of them, yes. But we could impose law and order. I have done well in building this place, keeping these men under control, but with you, we could do so much more. Many of them have made mistakes in their past, were misguided. We could show them the way to repent. We could use the example of your father to show them they can change."

"What of Morthanion?" she asked.

"Morthanion? If he is willing to talk, to adhere to our rules, he is more than welcome amongst us. Though Morthanion has never lived by any rules but his own."

"I do not want to rule," she said again. "I do not see why you would care to have me, much less need me. You have already built your own society, and you already lord over it."

"There is strength in you, and power," he said, his eyes intent upon her. "You are tied to this place in a way no one else is. This is your place of birth, the home of your ancestors. Who could dispute your right to reign over it?"

"You."

"Why would I ask this of you, only to refuse you later?"

"If I wanted to rule, Baltherus, it would not be with you."

"You are so confident in Morthanion?" His expression darkened, his full lips tilting down. "He is using you, Aria. You provide him a release for some of his urges. Gave him a safe place to hide. If he had a chance to get off this island, he would take it, and wouldn't even think twice about leaving you behind. No matter what you are to him now, you will always be nothing to him in the end. That is the nature of our kind. We can forge alliances, even friendships, but he will never give you love."

Aria turned to the dirt wall, afraid her eyes might betray the doubt that had crept into her mind. She had wondered the same. Morthanion cared for her wellbeing, but did he hold any deeper attachment to her? He wanted her to leave so she could have a life free of danger. But was his willingness to send her away in itself a sign that he didn't love her? She couldn't imagine going on even a day without him. Given the chance to leave the island, would he take it and return to his old ways? He had no regrets when it came to his past. It would be so easy.

Or had he truly changed? Did he care enough to take her with him?

"Much to think on, I would imagine," Baltherus said softly, calling her attention back to him. "Just remember that I seek to take nothing away from you. I only want to give. Power, freedom, luxury. Meaning."

"And use me to have the same for yourself."

"No. It's not using you. It's mutually beneficial. I want to help you as much as you can help me."

"I do not want to rule, Baltherus," Aria repeated, tired.

"You need time to consider what I've proposed to you." He turned and stepped toward the door, reaching for the torch. Glancing over his shoulder, he paused. "And I suggest you really do think about it. You are in a unique position."

He placed a large hand on the door.

"Wait!" She could not be left here again, alone in the darkness while the earth-stench slowly suffocated her.

"Hmm?"

"Might I be placed...elsewhere?"

He regarded her closely, as though trying to puzzle her out.

"Please," she added. She could not bear to be left here much longer. Maybe if Morthanion was with her, it would be tolerable...but he wasn't.

"If you don't mind the thought of it much, you may retire to my quarters."

Aria flinched visibly, his words sparking fear in her belly. "You said you would not use me."

"It's merely the most comfortable room. I will manage well enough in the great hall."

She glanced around the small chamber. It wasn't all that different from her cave, if she concentrated hard, but the absence of the ocean sounds and smells left a hole in her. His room would, at least, make a more comfortable prison than this one. Nodding, she rose. "Thank you."

Lifting the torch, Baltherus opened the door. "Follow me, if you would." He led her up the stairs and into the great hall. She walked closely behind him, feeling countless gazes crawl over her skin.

He led her past the eager, hungry eyes of his men, and it took her a moment to notice the women moving among them, carrying bowls, platters, and pitchers made of clay. Often, the men seemed to pause their conversations to stare at the women, but none ever lifted a hand to touch one.

They left the great hall to enter another short hallway. There was a single door here. Baltherus opened it and gestured for her to enter, offering a warm, kind smile. She stepped inside.

The room was more luxurious than she could have imagined. Handmade pillows covered a low, broad bed, which was ringed with gauzy curtains. Gold, silver, and precious gems were scattered about carelessly. Salvaged from the sea, they came together with a strange uniformity that her own collection never achieved. She'd gathered an eclectic mix, anything unique enough to catch her eye.

Baltherus had only things that signified wealth and power and good taste; Laudine had told her that the sorts of objects she now gazed upon were hoarded for their value in the rest of the world, though they were worthless on the island.

Gems shone and sparkled in the flickering torchlight, and Aria was drawn to them. She reached out, running her fingers lightly over their smooth-cut surfaces. She had seen a few of their ilk amidst bits of wreckage in the water, but the demon had amassed so many!

The weapons he displayed were elegantly brutal, nothing like the rusted things she'd found. In fact, the only useful weapon she'd discovered — the dagger Morthanion told her to keep close – was now on the wall, hanging with Baltherus's collection. Another pretty trophy.

"Do you like them?" he asked, moving up behind her. "All of it can be yours. And more. As much as you want."

She went still when she felt him pressing against her back. "They are beautiful, but only that."

"There is much to be said for beauty," he said, taking up a polished, opalescent pearl. Gently, he touched it to her skin, running it along her arm.

Aria inhaled sharply and jerked away from him. Bile churned and her flesh crawled. His touch was nothing like Morthanion's. It felt *wrong*.

He only smiled and dropped the pearl on the table. "No need to be so jumpy. Make yourself comfortable. If you require anything – food, water, *anything* – you need but let the man outside the door know. And there will be men standing guard, Aria. You are in the center of this settlement, and desire often clouds men's judgment. You are protected here, but only if you do not run."

She nodded, rubbing her arm where he had brushed the pearl. It felt like tiny spiders were skittering over its surface.

"Rest. And think." With that, he stepped out and closed the door softly behind him.

Aria stared at it for a time before she was able to drag her gaze away. There didn't appear to be a lock, but she knew he hadn't lied. There would be men there, even now.

She wandered the room silently, her thoughts in turmoil. Baltherus's words continued to echo in her mind. Was Morthanion using her? Was it to escape the boredom of the island? To have a female body to sate his lusts whenever they struck? She had proven to be a passionate lover, which he enjoyed immensely. Was there more than that?

She stopped and gave herself a mental shake. She was playing into Baltherus's hands by giving his lies any consideration. Morthanion cared for her. She had felt it. She *knew* it.

Aria closed her eyes and focused on the bond they shared. Warmth blossomed in her chest, and she knew by the comfort it provided that it was his presence. She felt more than heard his heart, each beat sending a fresh pulse of heat through her.

Finding a window, she cracked open the shutters, and took in a deep breath. The fresh air was tinged with salt. It was little comfort, but better than being buried below.

There were more thatched roof huts outside, and beyond those, the log wall. A pair of men walked by, carrying spears.

Her eyes rose to the dark sky where the stars shone. Laudine had told her a little about the Gods and Goddesses who had created the world. She had never put much thought into them before, but now, away from her home, away from Morthanion, utterly alone, she could do little more than pray.

"Please," she whispered to the night, struggling to get the words out of her tight throat. "Help us."

A gentle breeze brushed her face, and she could say no more as tears fell from her eyes.

She closed the shutters and turned away, feeling the deep ache in the center of her soul. She missed him. She craved Morthanion's touch, wanted to feel his arms around her, to hear his voice. To take comfort from his presence.

A loud crash, followed by screams from the main hall made her jump, jarring her thoughts. She didn't trust any of them, regardless of the demon's promises.

She took her knife from the wall, slipping the blade beneath a pillow as she sat on the bed. There was a clamor of voices from beyond the door, but they were too distorted by the walls to understand.

The commotion in the next chamber continued for some time. She waited, heart thumping loudly but steadily.

Eventually, the voices died down, leaving only silence. At any moment, the door would open. Baltherus would return and his calm demeanor would slip, and he'd hurt her. She had to be ready when it happened.

It was exhaustion that finally forced her to lie down. Curling on her side, she wished for the furs in her cave and the music of the ocean. Most of all, she wished for Morthanion.

Slipping a hand over her heart, she felt its steady beat, knowing that, somewhere nearby, his beat in time with hers.

Chapter Twenty-One

Baltherus closed the door to his chamber and strode to the center of the great hall. He was beginning to realize he might have underestimated the difficulty in swaying a woman, even a mortal, from her mate. With a few quick hand gestures, he set a man to guard his door, and placed four more outside to ensure she did not attempt to flee through the window.

He may have pushed her too hard, but the seeds of doubt had been planted. Given enough time away from Morthanion, they would take root and grow, and her resolve would crumble whether they were bonded or not.

As he passed the crowded tables, he offered greetings and patted shoulders, wearing the smile he had perfected over the centuries. He didn't notice any of their faces, didn't bother calling any names from memory. There would be blood; some of these folk would die, but so would Morthanion. All that mattered was that Aria understood it was an inevitability, brought on by her mate himself, and that Baltherus was more than willing to provide her with anything she needed. He would gladly fill in any void she suffered.

Mounting the dais, he eased himself onto his plush throne. The air was fragrant with the scent of roasted meat and fresh fruits, filled with the sounds of his people. He let his eyes roam over them slowly as they laughed and jested and ate, celebrating merely because he'd told them they'd won a great victory this evening. None of them truly understood what had been accomplished, what was at stake. What was to come.

His thoughts returned to what Aria had asked him. *Why do you hide yourself?* It had caught him off-guard. Most of these people had seen the only face of his that mattered, hadn't they? He wasn't hiding from anything, or from anyone.

What the hell kind of question was it, anyway?

More intriguing was her parentage. He'd never guessed that Jasper's child had survived. The men who had committed the atrocity claimed to have never seen a babe. He had looked at the broken, battered corpses of Jasper and his woman and called the men liars. The things they'd done to her...

He had more than his share of blood staining his hands, but their brutality had been disgusting. Even he, a demon, had been taken aback by the savagery of mortals on that day, and he had not let it go unpunished. When the perpetrators were still, their own blood congealing, he'd returned to his settlement and instilled new rules. They needed women just as much as they did any other resource, and they would be treated with the proper respect and care.

His thoughts were shattered by the sound of cracking wood and rustling grass. People shouted in alarm, the entire room thrown into chaos.

Baltherus rose, gripping the arms of his throne tightly enough to splinter the wood. Two bloody corpses – guards from two of the watchtowers – lay in a heap atop a third man, who moaned and slowly stirred.

The demon angled his head back, looking up to the gaping hole in the roof.

"Get out there," he said, leveling his gaze on the stunned men staring at the bodies.

They looked at him with bulging eyes. None of them made any move to obey.

"Go! Everyone damned one of you is on watch now. All but you lot." He gestured to the two guarding his chamber. "You remain here."

Men scrambled to gather up their weapons and headed toward the door, their footfalls heavy on the floorboards. Within a few moments, it was silent again. He remained where he was, still clutching the arms of the chair, his hands trembling now.

I knew this was coming. It is simply the price of the power I stand to gain.

But he hadn't counted on the fear in their faces, on their hesitation, on their disobedience.

"I warned you that the girl was a danger to all of us," said Ithoriel, once the majority of the men had cleared out.

Baltherus crossed the distance between himself and the elf in a flash. Wrapping a hand around Ithoriel's throat, the demon lifted him off his feet. He could feel his shroud slip, just a little, but made no effort to correct it.

"I have kept you close in my councils, warlock, but do not presume to question my judgment." Somehow, he kept his voice calm.

The elf's face was already turning a deep red. He choked and sputtered, hands clawing uselessly at Baltherus's forearm, and managed to squeeze out "Ah...pll...gize."

The demon sneered and opened his hand, letting the elf drop to the floor like a sack of grain. "There are great rewards in serving me well. But do not mistake my kindness for weakness."

"Thank you, master," the elf rasped. He regained his feet shakily and withdrew from the hall. Baltherus didn't watch him go. There was no reason to be so agitated; he'd known Morthanion would strike back. He'd known, from the moment the elder demon had refused his offer, that it would come to bloodshed. For the sake of everyone here, for the sake of what he had built, Baltherus could not allow that to shake him from his plans.

His gaze drifted to his chamber door, behind which waited the key to all of this. For what? The death of her lover, or the death of her captor?

*****

Sitting tense upon his throne, Baltherus took another mouthful of the sour wine his men were so fond of. If only it would dull his senses like it did theirs, at least he'd have respite from his mounting agitation. Even with every man on alert, they'd lost two more before the night had ended, and none of the living had seen anything more than shadows. The light of day had brought with it whispers, and he could feel a difference in their gazes when they were turned upon him.

Few had voiced them within earshot – which had been wise – but most disappointing, most irritating, was that Rogar was the most vocal. Perhaps it was the human's size and strength that emboldened him.

"Got us out hunting a demon for you," the man said. "Ain't that something you should be handling yourself?"

Was their loyalty to him, their faith in him, so easily disrupted? Didn't any of them know what it meant to sacrifice anymore? Perhaps he'd been too easy on them.

There were murmurs of assent following Rogar's words. It was all fueled by fear, Baltherus knew. But they were fearing the wrong demon.

Baltherus grabbed Rogar by the back of his head, forcing one side of the human's face into the coals of the central fire pit. Flesh sizzled, its stink overpowering the aroma of roasting boar. The man struggled with all of his considerable power, shoving against the stones that circled the pit, screaming.

"You hunt a demon for me, yes. Another of my kind. But he is no warrior. He is weak, and has always relied solely upon his magic. He has not yet learned to be strong without it, like all of you should have by now. If you cannot subdue him, perhaps you are not men at all.

"Are you men?" None of them would meet his gaze, collectively murmuring an ambiguous response. "Are you men?" he shouted.

They answered more strongly this time. It was enough.

"It is the responsibility of all of us to defend what we have made here. There is no threat we cannot band together to overcome. So make your choice. Stand as men, or scurry into the undergrowth with the rats."

He pulled Rogar's face from the coals, tossing him back against the steps of the dais.

"Nobody does anything alone. You don't walk alone, you don't eat alone, you don't take a piss alone. Is that understood? If you are by yourself, you *will* die. Groups of four, minimum.

"This bastard will overstep himself, and we will have him by the balls. Now go. Keep our home secure."

He ignored the unease in his gut as they shuffled out, and walked to his chamber. The guards were ashen-faced, but nodded to him as he approached. Sending them to get something to eat – as if they'd have any appetite now – he entered the room, closing the door softly behind him.

"Good evening, Aria."

She turned to look at him, twisting in the chair she'd moved to the window. Her face was pale, eyes wide. "What happened?"

"One of the men was wounded in an accident. I had to use fire to cauterize it."

It was clear that she saw through the lie. "Morthanion is here then?" There was a hopeful gleam in her bright eyes.

"No," he replied, struggling to keep his voice even. "From what my scouts have reported, he is still pilfering supplies from our camps on the west shore."

Aria looked away from Baltherus, to the gathering dusk outside the window. The feeling had been so strong; Morthanion was near.

"Have you considered my proposal?"

"My answer remains the same," she said quietly. Despite her adamant refusal, she had thought about it as the hours crept by. This room was far more comfortable, but was no less a prison than the first had been. And the thought of remaining here, living with the same sort of people who killed her parents, made her uneasy. She didn't want power over others. All she wanted was her freedom...and Morthanion.

"Then help me solidify my rule, and I will take care of everything else."

She frowned. "Help you how?"

"Do you know what the mages use this place for, Aria? What they do to the people they send here?"

"They strip them of magic and banish them to this place, from which they can never escape." She thought again of that symbol, burned on the back of Morthanion's hand. All the others bore it, too.

"Yes. And you are unique of all the people here. Because, even though magic was taken from your father, you are still birthed of a line that possessed it. He passed it down to you, and you were never branded. It's awakening in you. I could teach you how to use it, to hone it...to turn it into a tool that would keep this island a safe place for the rest of your days."

She listened, weighing his words. Was the magic really the result of her father's blood, or had it come from her mother? Laudine hadn't explained how any of it worked; neither of them had ever known Aria had it within her. Maybe...maybe, like Aria herself, the magic was a blend of Jasper's and Xani's, another part of their love and legacy.

Still, she knew that Morthanion could just as well teach her to use it. He'd already started to, though the circumstances were unpleasant.

"A tool?" she asked. "You seek to use me. The only being on the island capable of magic."

"Think about it, Aria!" He moved closer to her, his emerald eyes alight. "With your gifts, we could make this a better place for everyone here. And what possible threat could I pose to you once you've mastered your power?"

"I do not even know what power I have. I would also be a fool to depend solely upon magic." Hadn't that been the state Morthanion was in, when he'd first arrived? Stripped of the one thing he'd relied on above all others?

"As everyone here did, at some point. But you will only gain from this, I promise you."

There was something in his voice that she'd never heard there. It was in the way he was talking, his words more rushed than usual. She realized it was a hint of desperation. But why? What were his real motives?

"I am tired, Baltherus," she said, her thoughts too confused and clouded to continue.

"Very well." The hint of a frown played at his lips for an instant. "I will leave you to rest."

He walked back to the door, pulling it open. "If you are sitting at the window, waiting for him to come...he's not. A mate to a demon is nothing more than a means of procreation. He had his fun with you. I doubt he considers you worth the risk anymore."

Then he was gone, closing the door behind him.

She looked back out the window, where the sky was now fully dark, ignoring the pang his words caused. She had been hoping, waiting, and hadn't a single glimpse of Morthanion. But she felt him, she knew she did.

Her life had begun with the loss of her parents, taken from her before she even knew them. And, precious as her time with Laudine had been, it ended suddenly and far too soon. Her home had been taken next. The one place she'd felt safe. If she lost Morthanion, too...

Closing the shutters partway, she put out all the candles save one and crawled into the bed. It smelled of Baltherus, which was disturbing, but at least it was comfortable.

She laid her head down and closed her eyes, pushing aside all thought of her captor to seek comfort in her bond with Morthanion.

The door opened, startling Aria. Sitting up quickly, she reached beneath the pillow and took hold of the dagger. She stilled when a woman entered with a tray of food. Without so much as a glance at Aria, she placed the tray on the table and exited. One of the guards reached in to close the door.

Aria slipped off the bed and padded to the table. Her appetite was diminished here in Baltherus's luxurious prison, but he always had food delivered to her even though most of it went untouched. The variety of sliced fruits reminded her of the food Morthanion had brought to their cave, and could never match the flavor of what her demon had provided for her. These seemed tainted, somehow.

She lifted the wooden cup, swirling the dark liquid inside. Its pungent smell brought to mind the drink Ithoriel and Mikel had given her on the beach. She could get by on little food, but thirst was more dangerous a thing. She allowed herself a sip.

This was far sweeter, the potency masked by the taste. Still, she only took one more drink before setting the cup back down. Plucking a handful of berries from the tray, she sat on the bed and ate, tasting little.

Her limbs slowly grew heavy, each small fruit bearing the weight of a rock on its trip to her mouth. Her stomach felt as if it was growing emptier as she ate. A dull throb coursed through her, tingling at the tips of her fingers and toes.

Perhaps exhaustion was finally taking its toll. She'd slept poorly the night before, and her mind was racing without cease.

She meant to ease herself down onto her back, but her muscles refused to hold her body upright any longer, and she slumped over. She hadn't lied to Baltherus; she *was* tired. But she hadn't been so weary that she should be falling over. Was it just a different effect from a different drink?

Aria struggled to sit up. Everything was too heavy; her head rose a trembling inch off the bed before falling again. This wasn't right. Why would anyone consume something that did this? Why would–

The drink was sweet, and she realized now it was a familiar flavor. She'd tasted it only once, when she was young, before Laudine had stopped her. A single bite was all it took. Aria had to be carried back to the cave after sampling that juicy red fruit. Even Morthanion had fallen after two mouthfuls.

Oh gods, no!

Ithoriel watched from a bench as the serving woman stepped out of Baltherus's chamber. She'd not questioned his additions to the meal – what harm could there be in a few drops of *flavor* in the cup? The woman looked at Ithoriel for only a moment now before bowing her head and scurrying away, relieved to escape any further attention from him. What care did she have for the woman in her master's chamber?

The word had already spread; Baltherus valued the strange girl in his chamber over anyone else in the settlement. How many had already died because of their master's infatuation with Aria? The elf didn't care, and wasted no time counting.

He'd been promised his vengeance, and that would be enough.

As he approached Baltherus's chamber, the guards posted there exchanged a questioning glance with each other.

"The master bids you rest yourselves awhile," the elf said.

"We weren't supposed to leave the door," one of them ventured.

They'd all seen him speaking to Baltherus regularly by now. Many had heard him voice concerns they themselves harbored. With their faith in the demon shaken, it seemed to be enough. Ithoriel wasn't in charge, but he was close enough to the leader to levy some amount of obedience.

Some of the people had already begun to flee, anyway. No one looked forward to death at the claws of a demon.

"Baltherus wants her on our side. I am to continue his work to that end. He entrusts her care to me while you refresh yourselves."

The two hesitated, but at length nodded and shuffled away. Ithoriel quietly opened the door.

Only one small flame provided the chamber any light, but it was reflected by the numerous polished gems and metals within. It was the bedchamber of a king, surrounded by peasant hovels on all sides. Baltherus had not built this place with his own hands, but it was he who reaped all benefit of it. Smiling to himself, the elf closed the door and quietly slid the bolt into place.

He approached the bed, removing several lengths of rope from his pocket.

The vision of Aria that first night came to him clearly. She'd been so vibrant, and her laughter and song had stirred something in him he'd not felt in some time. He recalled emerald eyes, lush as the forests of his homeland.

Hair like spun gold, glistening in the sun as it spilled over his arm, the delicate brush of his lover's touch. And misery, the only thing she'd left when she betrayed him.

He had to fight the urge to draw his blade.

"Remember me?" he said, meeting her fearful eyes. Her lips parted to release a weak moan as she stirred, her head barely making it off the pillow. He smiled at her efforts. "Oh, but I remember you."

Grabbing her cheeks, he squeezed her mouth open and stuffed a rag into it. He could feel her struggle to pull her face away, but there was no strength left in her.

"And your demon. He treated me like something he scraped from the bottom of his boot." He moved to the foot of the bed and positioned her limp legs, tying them to the bedposts. As he walked back to her side, he trailed his fingers along her calf and up her inner thigh.

She moaned again, the sound muffled by the gag. That was more beautiful to him than her singing ever could be.

He climbed onto the bed and straddled her hips. Aria turned her face away, shutting her eyes as Ithoriel leaned forward to tie her wrists over her head, looping the ropes around the headboard bedposts. Satisfied that she was secure, he hooked a finger around her chin and forced her to look at him.

"Now I will bring *him* low. Using you."

Chapter Twenty-Two

Hate filled eyes stared into hers, and Aria recognized them too clearly. Cold fear wrapped its skeletal fingers around her heart and squeezed. She panted against the gag. Her fingers curled as mobility returned, and a painful prickling spread through her limbs. The ropes binding her wrists went taut when she tugged on them. It only widened the grin on Ithoriel's face.

"Wearing off already? Excellent. That means we can start sooner. I want you to feel *everything.*"

She bucked her body, hoping to dislodge him, sending more pinpricks across her skin. He fell forward, hands sliding on either side of her head to catch himself. He paused, still smiling down at her. Then, slowly, he drew her dagger from beneath her pillow and pushed himself up.

"Your little sticker is doing you a lot of good, isn't it?" he said, chuckling, and gripped the handle between forefinger and thumb to wiggle the blade, the point dangling over her chest. "This will make the loveliest marks…"

She stilled, staring at the weapon, breath caught in her throat. Calm. She had to calm herself and focus. If she could just blast him, throw him off, it might be enough to draw the attention of Baltherus. Twisting her hands, she turned them toward him and inhaled deeply.

"Ah, ah," he scolded. He leaned forward and held her knife between them, the blade catching the light of the single, low burning candle. He stopped only when the edge was mere inches from her face.

Aria's body trembled as the weapon dominated her view. She had no misconception what he meant to do.

"Blood is life. It's everything. It's so very beautiful." There was a mad gleam in his eyes. Leaning closer to her, he lightly traced his finger over the slope of her shoulder. "Does yours flow a sweet crimson?"

He slid the blade beneath the strap of her dress, cutting it with a flick of his wrist.

With the knife away from her face, she snapped her head up. Her forehead smashed into his mouth. He whipped backwards with a curse as something warm and wet splattered on her face, one hand clamping over his mouth.

Ithoriel laughed, the sound muffled by his hand until he pulled it away. Blood stained his grin, oozing from mangled lips down his chin. He ran his tongue over his teeth. Her head throbbed dully.

"Feisty. Makes it so much more satisfying to break you."

She felt it then, the cold steel against her skin, and she flinched with a cry. Shaking her head, eyes filling with tears, Aria pleaded. No discernable words made it past the gag.

The blade pressed harder, and Aria's voice rose in pitch before it cut her. Crying against the gag, she jerked with the flash of hot pain. The elf trailed the knife slowly from her shoulder to her upper chest, applying a little more pressure with each moment. Every nerve lit up in agony. Her vision dimmed momentarily, and she felt herself losing consciousness. He lifted the blade, and the pain eased, but didn't cease.

Aria stared up at him, as aware of the warm tears on her face as she was of the hot blood on her skin. A wicked, hungry grin split Ithoriel's face, the candlelight playing upon his features in a way that made him horrifying to behold. He raised the knife to his lips, and ran his tongue over the flat of it.

The elf hummed appreciatively, shifting his body so that his hard shaft pressed against her stomach. "Possibly the most delicious thing I have tasted."

Her chest rose and fell rapidly. She tried to move, to bend her legs, but between his weight and the ropes, she was trapped. Every tug scraped the rough fibers against her already raw skin. That pain was nothing compared to what he inflicted with his blade. She tried again to call upon the power gifted to her by her parents, but the only cold she could find within was the product of terror, not magic.

The blade settled on her collarbone, and Aria screamed as it bit into her flesh. She clenched her teeth on the cloth and raised her head, staring at Ithoriel.

His eyes were intent on the blood flowing from her wound. When he pulled the weapon back, he dipped his head to lick directly at her skin, running his tongue along the length of the cut. There was crimson smeared across his thin lips as he leaned back, moaning like he was approaching climax.

Ithoriel's free hand dropped, resting on her bare thigh just above the knee.

No! Waves of panic shot through her and she fought him. She twisted, bucking her legs. Her struggles only aided him as he pulled the hem of her dress up over her hips to expose her stomach.

The elf chuckled. He ran his hand over her abdomen and wrapped his fingers around her side. "How about here?" he asked, delicately touching the blade to her soft skin. He watched her face as if awaiting her answer, and no matter how much she shook her head, no matter how much she begged him to stop, she knew he would not listen.

"I think yes. So beautiful. I wonder," he continued, lightly tapping the blade against her, "what they will think seeing you covered in *my* marks? There's little as thrilling as watching the light fade from a person's eyes while they die."

Aria cried out, her throat raw, body shuddering against the agony as he applied slow pressure. Her flesh yielded, and the edge cut deep. She cried Morthanion's name, but the gag made it unrecognizable.

Ithoriel panted above her, his hips rocking. He shifted the knife, and simply cut, and cut, and cut. He always stopped before the darkness could take her, leaving her in agonized wakefulness.

With a grin, Ithoriel ran a bloodied finger along her cheek. "So weak," he muttered. "This will be so much better if you hold on till he comes for you."

A roar broke through the quiet of her shallow breaths. The elf paused.

"Not much longer now."

The blade touched her inner thigh and she *screamed*.

The human groaned as Morthanion took a fistful of his hair. He raised the head from the ground, blood oozing from its broken nose. Despite the danger, despite their fear, they insisted on breaking away from one another to relieve themselves, or to eat a secreted-away piece of food, or to flee and never return to Baltherus's camp.

It was almost sickening how easily they fell. Almost sickening that he was staining his hands with so much blood again. But he knew he was powerless but to fight for her. Every man left alive was one more potential threat to his mate.

Panic flared inside of him, setting the little hairs on his arms on end. Bile rose to his throat, his stomach cramping with dread. The feeling was so powerful, so overwhelming, that his entire body tensed. Aria. Something had changed. Borgeln's balls, something had happened while he was out here playing cat and mouse!

Searing pain sliced through the chill of fear. His mouth went dry, his breath catching in his throat. Was it retaliation for the lives he'd taken, for the chaos he'd sown? Baltherus knew what would happen if Aria was harmed. Did he *want* Morthanion to come?

"Doesn't fucking matter," he growled. She was consumed by fear and pain. Nothing else was important. She needed him. And he couldn't imagine survival without her. His blood caught fire as his own rage swirled into the mix of staggering emotions.

Aria.

Baltherus had refrained from doing her any harm since she was captured. The other demon knew better; her safety was the one thing keeping Morthanion at bay, the only thing that gave Baltherus any bargaining power. But now…

He released his hold on the human, letting the man's face drop to the dirt. The jungle was silent around him, its vegetation thick and stifling. He leapt into the air, crashed through the canopy, and turned for the village.

No more plotting, no more games in the shadows, no more patience. He existed only to care for Aria, to protect her, to have her near. There was room for nothing else. The fires his mate had kindled inside of him were stronger than any he'd known, and now they blazed out of control. He roared to the stars and earth and sea, the sound layered with the call of a savage beast just freed of its cage.

The clearing came into sight below. His heart pounded wildly, and he knew that down there – in the largest of the buildings – hers did, too. The dozens of armed men on the ground meant nothing. There was only Aria. Could be nothing else but her. Anything – and anyone – between them was an obstacle to be destroyed.

Subtlety had never been a strong trait of his. He'd now leave that all to Baltherus, and see how well it helped him.

He dove, wind rushing past him, angling himself for the front entrance of the palace. The unfortunate man standing guard in front of it scarcely had time to look up before the demon slammed into him. Momentum carried

266 | TIFFANY ROBERTS

them through the door, shattering it, producing a single grunt from the human.

Morthanion paused atop the limp body, crouched low, and swept his eyes around the room. She was here, he knew, and she was in pain. But the fire burned high inside of him, fueled by anger and fear, its heat overpowering his instinctual ability to locate her.

He met Baltherus's stunned gaze from across a long, wide table. The large demon had halted mid-stride. In one of his hands gleamed the naked blade of a sword.

If not for Baltherus, Morthanion and Aria could have known happiness. They would have been left to enjoy every moment together, wouldn't have argued over her leaving the island. He could have learned to cherish her without the threat of death looming over them like an unyielding specter.

He trembled with anger. He had known hate in his long life, an overabundance of it. But nothing he'd ever experienced was stronger than the hate he bore Baltherus. Nothing...except for what he felt for Aria.

Like a meteor streaking across the heavens, Morthanion leapt at the other demon.

The force of it carried Baltherus backwards, slamming him into the far wall. Wood splintered, and the entire structure groaned at the blow. Stunned, Baltherus's head lolled backwards, his eyes rolling up behind his eyelids.

Morthanion buried his claws in his foe's sides. Baltherus's face contorted into a grimace.

"Where is she? What have you done to her?"

"She's safe," Baltherus growled through clenched fangs and struggled to raise the sword.

"Lies!" Morthanion roared. "I can feel her pain even now."

Surprise flashed through Baltherus's eyes. "I haven't harmed her! Haven't touched her!"

A fresh pang of agony rippled through Morthanion. That was from her. It had to be.

"You're not even bold enough to dirty your own hands," Morthanion snarled. "Where is she?" He savagely twisted his hands, digging his claws deeper into Baltherus, who crumpled. The weapon clattered to the floor as his legs gave out beneath him.

"My chamber," Baltherus rasped, tilting his head toward one side of the hall.

Morthanion ripped his claws free and heaved Baltherus aside, blood dripping from his fingers. Instinct was dominating him. The other demon didn't matter. Aria was being hurt *now*, and he had to stop it. Had to prevent her from suffering any more.

He'd wasted too much time already. Approaching Baltherus's chamber, he punched a hand through the door, latching onto it with his claws. The wood groaned and splintered as he tore it off its hinges.

The pungent smell of blood hit the demon immediately. There was only a single light in the chamber, cast by a squat candle.

Ithoriel twisted to smirk at Morthanion over his shoulder. He was straddling Aria, only her legs visible from the demon's position.

"Ah, hello *master*," Ithoriel said, and climbed off of Aria to sit on the bed beside her. Every muscle in the demon tensed.

There was no way to tell how many wounds she'd already sustained; crimson flowed from her freely, a stark contrast to her too-pale skin. Blood covered her torso, staining the pillows and blanket around her. It was smudged over the elf's skin, covering his hands and forearms, with more of it on his face around his nose and lips.

Aria lifted her head, her watery eyes meeting Morthanion's, and fresh tears spilled down her cheeks.

Alive. But for how long? He could survive such wounds, but she was not a demon.

He stepped forward.

Ithoriel clucked his tongue, tapping the point of a knife against Aria's throat. Aria's knife. The bloody blade caught the candlelight and glistened.

"Get away from her!" the demon growled.

"I've long wondered what could bring a demon so low. Such arrogant, deceitful beings you are. How happy an occasion when I discovered what mates meant to your kind." The elf twisted the blade slightly, pressing the tip into her delicate skin. A drop of blood welled there.

The heat of the flames burning inside Morthanion took on a more familiar intensity. Seeing her in such a state, not ten feet away but still utterly out of his reach, sent tremors through his limbs. He clenched his fists. The symbol on the back of his hand began to glow.

"Is it simply instinct," the elf said, "or do your black little hearts grow fond of them? I cannot help but wonder." He applied more pressure on the knife, lengthening the new cut he'd opened infinitesimally.

Aria closed her eyes, whimpering weakly through the gag.

"Do not harm her further!" Morthanion roared, but he didn't move. He couldn't stand to see her hurt. By all The Six, she could be mortally wounded. He'd spared this creature's life, had shown mercy for the first time in memory, and this was his reward.

Something inside of him was rising to a boil. They'd come all this way just so he could watch her die, so he could stand by, powerless. Everything was getting so damned hot, and his heart was pounding thunderously. How could he think straight? Now he knew what it felt like to be nothing. It wasn't his capture or the sealing of his magic that had broken him. No, his lowest point, his true terror, was right here, playing out before him.

Heat pulsed in the palms of his hands, crackled across his sweat dampened skin.

Ithoriel tossed his head back and laughed. "Ah, but that black heart must have a tender place for this fragile little thing. If you didn't, you would have come at me already." The elf leaned down, keeping his eyes on the demon, and his tongue slid out to sample the blood that had begun to trickle down to her collarbone.

Glancing over Morthanion's shoulder, the elf's grin broadened. "Master Baltherus! So glad you saw fit to grace us with your presence. She's the taste of her mother. Shame there's not enough time to enjoy this one in the same fashion."

This creature had been there when Aria's parents died? Had been causing Aria hardship and suffering since the very day she was born? She was an innocent. She was *his*. He was supposed to protect her. He was supposed to save her. Something inside the demon broke.

He raised his trembling fists. The branded flesh sizzled and erupted with flame. Within seconds, it had burned away, and the fire crept up his arms, dancing with the shadows that already flowed over his skin.

"No," Baltherus gasped, just behind Morthanion. "That's not possible."

A sulfurous odor mingled with the tang of blood.

"This is the revenge you promised me, *master*. The key to your power, and his mate...all taken away at the same time." The elf laughed again.

The power coursing through Morthanion was one he'd known intimately for four thousand years. It had been a source of strength, of pleasure, of dominance. His chest heaved, heart still pumping as furiously as Aria's. He had the magic to save her at his fingertips.

He had the magic to destroy them all, her included, if he gave in.

"You've no idea what you've done, you fool. How could you possibly understand?" Baltherus said. His voice retreated slowly. "I didn't. Not then."

"I know what I'm doing," Ithoriel snapped, "and I remember. Remember the mages who refused me in my youth. The demons who promised me control, power! Who promised me use of the magic that had always been mine to begin with. Where were they when I was imprisoned? What makes either of you better than me, that you treat me like an insect?"

The elf dropped his gaze back to the blood trailing from the knife point, his eyes shining. "Now you'll be brought low with me," he said, distracted.

"Blood calls to blood," Morthanion intoned. The flames sheathing his arms cast strangely shifting shadows in the room, set the gems to sparkling like the ocean surface at sunset.

He could feel it inside the elf. Even if the binding had not produced the intended results, he had given his blood to the mortal. And his blood bore his fire.

Through the torrents swirling inside of him, he sought out that little piece of himself he'd instilled in Ithoriel, and he focused on it.

Sweat beaded on the elf's forehead, and he jerked his head to the side. Flesh began to bubble on his cheek, and faint tendrils of smoke flowed from it. Ithoriel scrambled back, uttering a startled cry, and brought his hands up to his face.

Morthanion lunged forward in a mass of shadow and flames. He stabbed his claws into both of the elf's shoulders, swinging him off the bed and across the chamber to slam into the far wall.

Baltherus shouted, but Morthanion paid no attention to the words. Here was the real threat to his mate, here was the one who had hurt her more than any other in her entire life. He loosed his tenuous hold on his magic, directing it into the elf's body.

Ithoriel screamed as flames burst from him, filling the room with the smell of charring flesh. He flailed and clawed at the demon, frantically patting to extinguish the flames. Skin melted off his bones as he scraped at his own face with bony talons, fire licking from empty eye sockets. The elf's jaw remained agape, his screams silenced. Blackened bones fell in a heap on the floor, still burning.

Morthanion turned, narrowing his eyes against the brightness of the flames that spread along the walls and floor. The blood-soaked bed was empty. He flexed his claws, ashen remains drifting off them. Rushing to the open window, he peered out.

Baltherus crouched in the dirt some thirty paces away, leaning over Aria. He was the one who'd taken her. He was the one who had set this entire course of events into motion. And he had allowed one of his own to harm her.

Chapter Twenty-Three

Morthanion is here. He came, for me.

The elation that spread through Aria quickly succumbed to the cold creeping into her limbs. She made no sound as Baltherus cut away the ropes that bound her. Her feeble cries would have been drowned out by Ithoriel's agonized screams, anyway.

The demon lifted her. He was gentle, more so than she thought him capable. Cradling her limp body to his chest, he backed away from the flames that were beginning to engulf the room. His bronze skin glistened with sweat, but Aria felt chilled.

Baltherus turned and kicked the shutters open, leaping through the window into the night.

She felt herself falling and tried to call for Morthanion, but his name lodged in her throat. Baltherus laid her on the ground, away from the burning building, and dropped to his knees beside her. He cupped the back of her head with one large hand, holding it up.

"I truly didn't mean you harm," he said.

"I know," she whispered, "but you never meant for me to be free, either."

He looked up suddenly and Aria turned her head, to see Morthanion standing near. His eyes were brighter than she'd ever seen, licks of flame rising from them at their corners. Shadow covered him entirely, obscuring his features, hiding all those scars and tattoos that she'd loved to trace as they lay together, impenetrable even to the raging fire that radiated from his hands. Horns curved from his head, and his wings were arched, feathers flaring. The burning building behind him only made his silhouette appear darker.

274 | TIFFANY ROBERTS

Carefully, Baltherus let Aria's head down. He stepped over her and put his arms out to either side.

"I never meant for her to be hurt, Morthanion," he said. "As hollow as those words sound, I never meant for *this*."

"But here we are," Morthanion said, and there was fire in his mouth when it moved. "*This* has happened. Because of you, because of your greed, because you took her from me!"

Fire roared over the roof of the great hall, lighting the night orange.

"Do not hurt him, Thanion," Aria pleaded softly, her gaze upon him. This was Morthanion, the Keeper of the Flame. This is what he had been before arriving here.

"After all he's done, you defend him?" he demanded.

"Not him, *you*."

He snarled, teeth bared, but she could see his restraint.

"Please, demon."

Morthanion stared long and hard at Baltherus, the firestorm inside of him far more intense than the one burning behind him. Hellfire consumed everything. It left no room for compassion, no room for mercy, no room for anything but a conflagration. Before he'd met Aria, it was all he needed. It was enough, and he was content to allow it to dominate him.

But since meeting her? He'd tasted the chance of a different life. Tasted happiness. Together, they'd glimpsed the man Morthanion could become. He wanted to be that man.

He inhaled deeply and the flames retreated down his arms. The person he used to be did not deserve the woman before him. The fire reached his hands, and he curled his fingers closed, snuffing it out. Before this island, he would never have stopped himself. Before Aria.

Something stronger consumed him in the absence of fire. Love for her. It was more than mere instinct. More than lust or compulsion. He loved her. He could not imagine living without her, not anymore.

"You owe her your life, bastard." Morthanion's fierce gaze bored into Baltherus.

Baltherus bowed slightly, backing away. The muscles of his jaw ticked. "I'm indebted to you both, forever." He stepped carefully over Aria, facing Morthanion, and glanced at her once more before he took to the sky.

Morthanion rushed to her side, taking her in his arms. "Gods, Aria," he said, voice thick. This close, he could see just how badly she'd been hurt. "I've failed you. Failed to protect you…"

She closed her eyes, nuzzling her cheek to his shoulder. Though the movement clearly pained her, she wrapped her arms around his neck; her skin was cold and clammy, sticky with blood.

"I am sorry…"

He leaned down, pressing his forehead against hers, and held her. "No. You have nothing to be sorry for. I'm the one that is sorry. I'm the one that has failed in what I was meant to do."

"I doubted you. I did not…know if you would come."

His eyes stung. Still, he smiled down at her. "I told you before that I will always come for you. No matter how far, no matter what's in the way. Whether you want me to or not."

An eternity stretched between each heartbeat. She'd lost so much blood…

Aria opened her eyes, more tears spilling from them. "I want you," she said gently, reaching up to touch his cheek with a trembling hand. "I love you, Thanion. I will always want you."

He could feel her strength fading, could feel her growing colder despite the heat that raged inside of him. All his power was back, and what could he do for her? Nothing.

Tears rolled down his face to land upon her cheek. They were the first he'd ever shed.

"My demon cries for me?" She smiled weakly.

"Yes," he replied, throat tight, "you are everything. Aria...you...the things I feel for you I've never had words for. I..."

He sagged forward, his arms suddenly empty. All that remained of Aria was her blood staining his hands. It was the only sign that she'd even been there. He flexed his claws, as though opening and closing them would somehow bring her back. Firelight glistened on the moist crimson that coated them.

More teardrops fell, this time to the dirt, claimed by the earth. Gone. Was she dead? Did her kind simply vanish when their lives ended? Or had she been the imagining of a deranged mind the entire time?

No. The blood on his hands was real. Aria had been real. He'd felt her presence in his soul, felt it fading, and now there was nothing. The void inside of him could only mean she was gone.

When he turned back toward the burning building behind him, he made no effort to control his rage. It erupted from him like a volcano, a surge of anger and bitterness and sorrow and hatred. Damn the gods and damn fate for letting him find her, letting him have a taste of her and the man he might become, and then tearing it all away.

He let the heat flow through him, focusing it on the great hall. The explosion rocked the ground beneath his feet, sending fire dozens of feet into the air and a thousand bits of wood even farther. Before the last debris hit the ground, he shaped that pillar of flame and thrust it at the other makeshift buildings, the thatched-roof huts and open-air workspaces, the night shining brighter than day as everything burned like kindling.

He didn't realize he was shouting, screaming at the top of his lungs and beyond. Anguish, fury, pain; it was a release of unbridled emotion. It brought him to his knees, and he threw his head back to look skyward, at clouds tinged orange by the inferno around him.

Aria would frown at him if he told her he would burn the whole world because of his pain. What would she want of him? What would have made her happy?

She would want me to continue on, he thought, *and wouldn't want a single innocent to suffer because of any of this.*

You choose what you are, you are not born to it. Her words echoed in his mind. Resonated in his soul.

He let his head drop, chin against his chest, the fury rapidly draining from him. Even after everything, she had asked him to spare Baltherus. After everything, she had held to her convictions.

After everything, she'd still loved him.

He swallowed thickly, knowing his pain was too immense to be rid of so easily. It would be with him always. And there, in that suffering, he felt...an echoing heartbeat?

Morthanion's eyes snapped open. Her heartbeat, in time with his. Accompanied by a flutter of heat in his spine, it was terribly faint, terribly far off. But he could not mistake it. Could not doubt what he felt.

She lived.

*****

Aria had felt Morthanion's arms around her, his teardrops warm upon her cheek, and then he was gone. Her insides twisted, but she was too weak to empty her stomach. Instead of the familiar heat of his embrace, there were now many hands upon her. As her vision cleared, the faces of

278 | TIFFANY ROBERTS

strangers loomed over her. But she didn't care. She only wanted Morthanion. Needed him, before...

"Morthanion?" one of them asked, turning to look at his companions. Had she spoken aloud?

"He did this?"

The fingers that ran over her skin were cold compared to her demon's touch.

"She is unmarked."

"Impossible! She came from the island!"

"Look for yourself. She does not bear the mark of the condemned."

"That would explain why we received the message."

"Why was she there?"

"We would not have sent an innocent," one of the voices snapped.

Her vision blurred, darkness encroaching at its edges. Their voices were too similar in the haze that was settling over her, and she couldn't tell who was talking, or which of them was touching her. Where was her demon? Why couldn't she feel him anymore?

"Enough! She's lost too much blood already. See to her, and when she is healed, she will answer our questions."

The other voices answered. All she could make out were murmurs as darkness embraced her, making everything – even their prodding hands — seem far-off and unimportant. Aria closed her eyes. She imagined the darkness was the caress of Morthanion's shadowy wings, and let it carry her away.

Her mind was fuzzy, thoughts clouded. Only his name was clear, lingering on the tip of her tongue. Where was he?

"Morthanion," she mumbled. Her body was burning, but it was not the delicious fire her demon produced. Every inch of her skin thrummed with agony. Chills wracked her, racing along her spine and out through leaden limbs. Something soft but impossibly heavy was draped over her, sealing in the stifling heat, pinning her to sweat-dampened cloth.

With surprising exertion, she slit open her eyes. The light blinded her, driving painful spikes into her temples, and she squeezed them shut again. Tears rolled over her cheeks.

"Why are you awake?" someone nearby said in surprise. "You've only been asleep a few days. It shouldn't have worn off so soon." The woman's voice was closer now. A cool hand came to rest on her forehead. "You're burning up! You must sleep now. Sleep and rest."

"No, I need—" Aria tried to say, but the words caught in her dry, raw throat.

"Quiet now. Sleep."

Calm flooded her, wrapping around her mind to drag it back into darkness.

She slept.

Chapter Twenty-Four

Though her head felt like it was bobbing on rolling waves, Aria's entire body was heavy. The scents of sulfur and smoke lingered, and the spot where his tears had fallen tingled with remembered moisture.

Had she died?

Her eyes shot open. She blinked repeatedly against the blinding light. Her vision blurred as she lifted a hand to her shoulder. Phantom pain skittered across her at the remembrance of what Ithoriel had done, raising the little hairs on her arms. But there was no open wound.

Slowly, an unfamiliar ceiling came into focus. It was the gentle white of summertime clouds, unbroken by the blue of the open sky. Brow furrowing, she turned her head to the side. The wall was the same color at its top, but the middle was painted, depicting a landscape wholly alien to her. Low, gentle hills with pale grass and strange, tall flowers in orange and red and purple.

"You're awake!"

Aria flinched, jerking her head to the other side. The motion made it ache sharply.

There was a woman in the room, her face lined more heavily than Laudine's had been, white hair up in a neat bun. Aria kept her wide-eyed gaze on the stranger and started to push herself away. Had Baltherus moved her again?

With a gasp, she tumbled over the edge of the bed. Her bottom took the brunt of the fall, and that hurt more than her head did.

"Oh dear!" the old woman said. She rushed across the room and bent to help Aria extract herself from the tangle of bedding. "You must be careful. Your body's been through so much, and healing has taken a lot out of you.

Now, back into bed with you, and I'll go fetch the High Mage."

The woman's hand was soft and gentle when she took Aria's arm and helped her back into the bed. Too exhausted and confused to struggle any more, she simply watched as the woman rearranged the blankets, draping them over Aria's body and tucking them around her.

The woman left the room with small, quick steps that set her skirts swaying. For several moments, Aria could only stare at the closed door. She was alive, but only had more questions now.

Angling her head down, she peeled the covers back enough to look at her shoulder. That had been the first place Ithoriel cut her, and the agony of that particular wound resonated most strongly in her memory. She brushed her fingertips over the pale, smooth skin. There was no evidence of any cut.

Unwilling to look, she slid her hand under the blanket and over her chest, her stomach, everywhere she knew Ithoriel had marked her. The white-hot pain was still fresh in her memory, but all she found was more smooth skin. Not a trace of scarring, or stitches, or scabs. She'd always healed quickly, but she had felt her life slipping away, between Morthanion's fingers. How could there be no trace of the damage that had been wrought upon her?

The door opened, claiming her attention. The old woman came back in, her steps not slowing despite her burden, and set a tray of food on a stand beside the bed. Behind her followed a tall, broad shouldered figure.

Her heart thumped rapidly. Baltherus. She had told Morthanion to spare him, and he had taken her again. And if Morthanion wasn't here…

The large man stepped fully into the room. Aria let out a shaky, relieved sigh. He was easily as large as Baltherus, but the resemblance ended there. He had pale blue eyes, sharply angled cheekbones, thick black hair, and pointed ears.

"So you have awoken again," he said.

"Where am I?" Aria asked. He wasn't Baltherus, but she had no reason to trust him.

"You're safe."

"Where am I?" she repeated. The blankets seemed too heavy now, too hot. That answer had been too much like the demon's: vague and uninformative.

"Shh now, dearie. You're all right," the old woman cooed, raising a cup to Aria's mouth. "Here, have a drink."

Aria knew it was water without looking at it, and was suddenly aware of how dry her mouth was. She sipped at it, never removing her eyes from the large elf. It was crisp and soothed her parched mouth and throat.

"We acted as hastily as we were able after hearing your call," the elf said.

"What...call?"

"It was more of a whisper, really. 'Please help us'. By the time we were able to scry your location and gather enough mages to teleport you here, it was almost too late."

His words seemed to swirl around without order inside her mind. She had to squeeze her eyes shut, trying to force some meaning out of them. *Please help us*. It had been a plea to the sky, to the gods, to anyone who might have listened.

The mages – the same ones who had put the prisoners on the island – had taken her off of it.

"Morthanion?" she whispered breathlessly. No! He was still there, still trapped on the island!

The elf's face hardened. "He will harm you no further."

"Are you mad? Send me back!" It took all of her strength to hurl the blankets aside and draw herself into a sitting position. If he was alive, she had to go back. He *had* to be alive. He promised he wouldn't let anyone kill him.

When the elf moved closer, instinct kicked in. Aria extended her arms, her open palms directed at him, and surprise flickered over his eyes for an instant. Then she blasted him. The force knocked him back into the wall, cracking it. The old woman screamed and tumbled backward.

Aria swung her legs over the side of the bed. The stone floor was cold, but solid, and that comforted her a bit. She stumbled as she ran for the door. She had to get back to him, had to find him again, had to hold him.

"Stop!" the elf shouted. Aria didn't intend to obey, but her body halted immediately. She strained against it, but her arms and legs wouldn't move.

"Send me back! You have to send me back!"

He approached her slowly, one of his hands extended before him. His lips were pressed in a hard line, his brows low over narrowed eyes.

"Calm yourself. I will answer your questions as long as you answer mine."

Grunting softly, he shifted his position – she guessed it was because of the blow she'd struck him – the elf scooped up her traitorous body and carried her back to the bed. He carefully laid her down, but his face was expressionless when he stepped back again.

"I am Keric Ornthalas, guardian of this tower and High Mage of The Order of the Justicars. We brought you here because of your plea for help. We rescued you and the unborn child you nearly lost due to the severity of your wounds," he said.

Aria's breath rushed out of her, leaving her chest tight and on fire. She stared at him.

"All I ask is for you to remain calm and answer my questions, so I can ensure we help you in whatever way we are able," Keric continued.

"What did you say?"

"I need answers."

"No, I…my…child?"

His dark brows fell low again, and she saw his jaw muscles tick once before he turned to the woman.

"Of course, dear," the old woman said, and she cautiously approached, straightening the covers and pulling them to Aria's chin. "You nearly lost the babe, but the tower's healers are very skilled – and you're rather resilient, aren't you? Your little one will be just fine. It's fortunate they found you before the demon killed you both."

A baby. Morthanion's baby. Aria didn't know what to think. The possibility had never crossed her mind. Not once. She looked down her body, toward her stomach, and placed her hands there beneath the blankets. It was flat.

"I did not know there was a baby," she began, still in a daze. Her gaze rose to Keric. "Morthanion. Where is he?"

"The demon? He is on the island, where he belongs, and can cause you no further harm."

"You do not understand! He did not do this. He saved me!"

"Saved you? That creature is vile, and has not so much as considered performing a selfless act in all his existence."

"This is his child!"

The room went quiet. The older woman stared at Aria with her mouth agape. Keric's eyes flared. "Morthanion's? The fire demon?"

"Yes! He saved me from the one who hurt me until…until…" Her breaths were rapid and ragged. She was surrounded by strangers in a strange place, with no sign of Morthanion anywhere. "Until you took me. He had been holding me before I…I need to go back!"

"You need your rest. We will talk again."

He lifted a hand and waved it over her. Aria's eyelids drooped, that now familiar heaviness draping over her body and her mind. She fought against it, struggling to remain awake. Morthanion was still there on that island. She couldn't remain here.

"Impregnated by a demon?" the woman asked with a shaky voice.

"I don't know if I can believe what she says is true or if it is result of her mind trying to cope with what she suffered at the hands of those monsters. She would have to be his mate to bear his child…"

"Poor thing."

"Come, Agatha. She will sleep for some time."

Morthanion's mate. She was…Morthanion's mate.

And he needed her.

Morthanion landed on a nearby hill, crouched in the grass, and settled his attention on the mage's compound. Walls surrounded a single tower rising like a knife jabbed into an unsuspecting back. Figures patrolled the battlements, and the windows shone in a variety of colors, their stained glass panels illuminated from within. The gray banners embroidered with gold bore the snake, eye, and dagger symbol of the Order. The same the mages had been burned onto his hand.

Aria was inside. He could feel her presence, a delightful heat that flickered and beckoned him onward. Though raging fires burned within him, he was calm on the surface. She was sleeping, he guessed. That was the only reason he was still in control.

He could only speculate about how or why they took her, and had done so frequently during his journey. How many days had he traveled? Five? Seven? He'd stopped counting. There was only room to focus on Aria, on her distant heartbeat. It grew clearer to him with each mile, infinitesimally, but that gradual increase was a powerful driving force.

Focusing on her, he let his eyes slide shut. The tower. That was where they held her, inside their accursed tower, in the center of their damned stronghold.

Exhaustion tugged at the edges of his consciousness. It would be so easy to lie down here, to let sleep take him, to drift into oblivion.

No. Have to save her. Have to have her back.

Was that his instinct, or a conscious thought? He couldn't tell the difference anymore. Didn't care either way. What he felt for her would drive him beyond the limits of any living creature's endurance. He would always come for her.

Long before he'd met Aria, before he could sense her instinctually, he'd learned to manipulate his own arcane energies, to use them to seek out their like. It was only prudent to do so now.

The fortress before him radiated magic like a beacon in the darkness. Wards lined all the walls, all the windows and doors, and would alert those within of any unexpected arrivals. There were pockets of utter emptiness, the same magic-cancelling fields the mages used to capture him in the first place. And of course there were the mages themselves, dozens of them, each pulsing with their own arcane energy – and here, most of them would be battle mages, Justicars trained to deal specifically with beings such as himself.

It would be suicide to go in.

She is so close…

He had to go in.

The last thing a rational being would do was burst into a mage stronghold. And it was his only chance, the most unexpected move. Their defenses were bolstered to scare would-be enemies out of attacking before a single move was made. They would never think anyone foolish enough to charge in alone.

He would burst in, take her, and escape before any of the mages realized what had happened. He refused to go another day without her. No more waiting.

Spreading his wings, he inhaled deeply the crisp night air, made sweet by the grass all around. It would be another night for fire. He thought of Aria again, so pale and weak, of her blood on his hands. The flames that roared back to life within him were the ones she had sparked.

Morthanion leapt forward, pumping his wings to get well clear of the walls. The instant he crossed their perimeter, shouts of alarm rose. Figures scrambled on the battlements, and within moments the air was rippling with unleashed arcane energies. The demon sheathed himself in fire, weaving between ethereal projectiles, reaching out to the piece of his soul that she harbored.

He could collapse when it was all over. When she was in his arms and away from this place. Until then, all he could allow himself was victory.

Magic sparked across his skin, shot in jolts through his limbs. The fire around him wavered, unable to defend against all of it. His muscles tensed painfully at unseen blows. His flesh cracked and charred as it was licked by arcane energies. He shrugged it off and increased his speed, angling toward the window that had to be hers. *Just a little farther. She's so close...*

The window shattered when he hit it, and he folded his wings back to fit through the entry. He landed in a crouch amidst shards of glass. His own blood was hot on his skin, oozing from countless minor wounds inflicted by magic and glass, some of which already itched as they healed. Aria's heartbeat thumped along with his, oddly steady given what he'd just done.

He lifted his gaze first to the footboard of the bed, and then to the broad-shouldered elf standing beside it. The face was vaguely familiar. Kerwin? Kargic? Keric. Another battle mage. Morthanion rose slowly, bits of broken glass falling from his body.

Aria was motionless on the bed, looking so slight beneath the blankets.

"You took something of mine," Morthanion said.

"We won't allow you to hurt her again, demon." Keric stepped around the bed to block Morthanion's view of Aria, smoothly drawing his sword. "I don't know how you escaped the island and restored your power, but you *will* be going back."

"Stay away from her," the demon growled, the flames around him burning brighter. "She belongs to *me*."

"You'll not lay another hand on the girl. You've done enough, I think. She was close to death when we answered her plea for help."

"And I'll not let another elf bastard hurt her again," Morthanion roared, darting forward.

The mage stepped up to meet him, displaying no fear, no hesitation. Claw and blade blurred through the air as Morthanion attacked, trailing fire behind his arms. Keric parried the blows, matching the demon's speed, and thrust his offhand forward.

A blast of energy struck Morthanion, spinning him around and backward several feet. He stumbled into a chair, barely keeping his footing, and snatched the chair up as the elf advanced. The wood crackled as flame spread over it. Before Keric could react, Morthanion swung.

The mage turned his shoulder at the blow. Cold pierced the air around him, a sheet of ice materializing to absorb the impact of the improvised weapon. The chair shattered, flames and ice vanishing in a cloud of hissing steam.

Keric's blade made another quick arc. He was an obstacle between Morthanion and his mate. A potential threat to her. And every moment spent in this place reduced their chances of getting out.

The demon raised his hands, catching the flat of the blade between his palms. His muscles strained to halt it, and he could feel the force behind the weapon as the elf strained to follow through. Exertion reddened Keric's face.

"You expect me to believe you care for anyone other than yourself?" the elf said through clenched teeth.

Muffled voices called from the other side of the door, followed by pounding.

Morthanion channeled heat into the steel. Within moments, it glowed. Keric's eyes flashed, and frost crept up from the hilt. The two forces met in the middle, and their advance halted.

"Awaken," Keric commanded.

Morthanion saw movement on the bed over the mage's shoulder. His heart fluttered, and everything inside of him seemed to constrict at once. Ragged breath escaped him, and he found himself unable to draw in more for several long moments.

Aria lifted her head, and her half-lidded eyes went round. He hadn't realized how much he had missed them, the vibrancy inside of them, the way blue and green swirled together to create a color both reminiscent of the ocean and nothing like it at all. Only Aria had eyes like that, and they were the only ones he wanted to gaze into.

"Thanion!" She shifted to crawl off the bed, casting the blankets aside.

"Stop!" both Morthanion and the elf commanded in unison. But the demon knew it was not his word that froze her in place, her eyes wide.

The air between the demon and the mage wavered as the heat increased.

"Release her from your spell, or I will tear your still-beating heart from your chest and incinerate it before your eyes!"

Keric grunted, the blade shifting slightly closer to him as new fury surged into Morthanion's limbs. The demon wrenched the weapon, meaning to twist it from the elf's grip.

The heated metal gave way, bending for an instant before it broke from the rest of the blade. Morthanion's own strength set him off-balance, meeting none of the resistance he had expected. It was a small opening. Keric capitalized on it.

Another wave of force collided with Morthanion. His feet left the floor, body twisting and flipping backwards, and he slammed into the wall to land in the remnants of the window he'd shattered.

The room spun around him for a moment, and he wheezed to refill his lungs.

"Did you speak the truth?" he heard the elf say quietly.

Morthanion struggled to hands and knees. He looked up, and through blurred vision could see that Keric was looking at Aria. *She's mine.*

He stumbled to his feet. "Away from her!" he roared, charging at the mage again. There was piercing agony in his side, a throbbing in his head, but he had to keep fighting. Had to keep her safe.

Keric swayed back, avoiding the demon's swinging claws. Heat from the flames still burning around Morthanion's arms singed the elf's clothing.

"Demon, beware of what you are doing!"

Morthanion ignored his foe's words. No more talking. No more thinking.

"Thanion, stop!"

The fire wavered at the sound of her voice. His back tingled with her nearness, and that was enough to extinguish the flames completely. Her arms wrapped around him from behind and she pressed herself against him. "Stop," she said again, softly.

Keric watched from several paces away, his features tight, face red. "She is your mate, then," the elf said. He tilted his head, eyes narrowed. "I didn't think even that would hold sway over one such as you."

The demon swallowed thickly and tried to ignore the weakness in his legs. Now the mages knew what Aria was to him, and they, too, would use her against him. Why should she always be made to suffer because of the things he had done? He couldn't allow them to take her again, couldn't allow anyone to take her again.

Without willing it, his wings formed, and they shifted back to shield her from the sides.

"Interesting," the elf muttered. "How is it you escaped the island?"

Aria removed her arms from around Morthanion's waist, sliding them to lie along his spine, and pressed her cheek to the skin between his wings. Calm flowed through him like water gently lapping at the shore. He shouldn't allow himself to grow complacent, here in the den of his enemies, but the sensation was so welcome after everything that happened, he couldn't deny it.

"There are things stronger than your magic."

"If you didn't hurt her, who did?"

"He will not hurt anyone any longer," Morthanion said. There was no more he would reveal about it. He didn't want to think of it anymore, to remember the scene he'd burst into back in Baltherus's hall. Reaching behind him, he placed a hand on her side, relishing the feel of her here, with him.

"But you could."

"All beings are capable of doing one another harm. My kind is just markedly better at it."

"Which is why you cannot be allowed to run free," the elf replied.

Morthanion gave Aria a gentle squeeze as she pressed harder against him. He would not allow anyone to take either of them. Not today. Not ever again. "You've taken my freedom once. I assure you, it would cost you much more to attempt taking it a second time."

"You utilized your freedom to murder innocents. Do you think I will allow your threats to keep us from containing you?"

Aria surged out from behind Morthanion, glaring at Keric. "He protected me from the murderers that *you* sent there! The ones that killed my mother's people! You are no better than any of the people you send to that place."

Keric's face paled as Morthanion took Aria by the shoulders and guided her back again. As much as he admired her courage, he couldn't stand for her to be in harm's way.

"We didn't know," the elf muttered.

"He has changed," she said defiantly. "He is no longer the demon you banished."

"The two of us will not be separated again," Morthanion's voice was low, "and she is not returning to that place. Accept that and let us go, or see how many of you it takes to stop me this time."

Keric clenched his jaw, regaining his composure. "You would risk placing your mate and unborn child in the middle of a battlefield? That does not surprise me, demon."

Morthanion's heart stopped. Unborn child? He wanted nothing more in that moment than to turn to her, to look into her eyes, but he couldn't trust the mage. Had to worry about her safety...about *their* safety.

"Aria?" he asked, watching Keric.

"They thought my call for help was for myself and the...baby. I did not know..."

"She nearly lost it – and her own life. Would you like to place her in that position again?"

"Now more than ever would be a foolish time to threaten me, mage," the demon said, fire flaring in his eyes. A child...Aria was with child. *His* child. That protective instinct was surging again, growing to overwhelming proportions.

"Not a threat, demon. A promise. We will not allow you to sow death and destruction any longer. We healed the girl for the sake of her and her babe. Not for yours."

They had healed her? Yes…that made sense. She was so close to death when last he'd held her. He thought he'd seen the last flickers of life sparkling in her tear-filled eyes.

"But…seeing you with your mate, and given the errors the Council has made," the elf continued, "perhaps there is a chance for you to redeem yourself. To prove that you're no longer a threat to our order and to the world."

"I'm not interested in redemption. All I – we – want is to be left alone."

"And you would be, mostly. But we cannot allow you full freedom until you are deemed…safe."

Aria pulled away from him, and he could feel turmoil in her, could feel doubt surfacing. Much as he longed for it to be directed at the mage, he knew she was wondering about him. Would he be able to truly forsake the man that he'd been?

He thought for a long while, trying to look past his rage, beyond the instinct that demanded he fight for her. What would fighting accomplish here, anyway? The mages had already caught him once, and now he was in the heart of one of their strongholds, surrounded by dozens of them. It had taken a handful the first time.

If they were to escape? The Order would hunt them like criminals, like animals. Their life would consist only of running and hiding, no different than it had been with the threat of Baltherus hanging over them. Morthanion would always be hunted for what he was; did she not deserve better than that? She didn't deserve to suffer for what he'd done.

He did not regret the fires of old. Could not summon remorse for the wrongs that he'd done. Because he was selfish. Those things had culminated in his being banished to the island, in his meeting her.

He held his hands out, fists loosely curled. "Take my magic."

Aria gasped, and shock played over Keric's features.

"Demon," she said, placing a hand on his back, "you just got it back..."

"You would give up your power?" the elf asked, shock replaced by skepticism.

"To be with her. With them." Morthanion nodded once.

"You would resent me. Resent us," Aria whispered.

"It led me down the path to finding you," Morthanion replied, turning his head to peer at her over his shoulder. "It's served its purpose. I've no use for it anymore, if I'm not with you."

There was amazement on her face as she stared up at him.

"It may not have to come to that," Keric said, "if you agree to aid us."

"In what way, mage?" Morthanion asked, unwilling to look away from his mate.

"By helping us contain others like you, who spread the same death and destruction you did. Your experience and power would be of great assistance, and it would be put toward making the world safer for your mate and child. In return for your help, the Order will provide you and yours with protection."

The demon arched his brow, silently asking for Aria's decision. A few months ago, he would have simply burned the building to the ground in response. He'd changed in the time since, enough to realize that this decision was not his alone to make. All he wanted was to be with her. He would do it in whatever way he could.

She searched his face for a time. "We cannot go back there," she said finally, sorrow touching her voice. Before she spoke again, she dropped her gaze. "Can you give up the things you have done? That you said you were born to do?"

Morthanion turned to face her, bringing up a hand to cup her cheek. "All there is in my life now is you." He settled his other hand on her belly. "Both of you," he said, wonder in his voice.

She tilted her head back, covering his hand with both of hers. "I meant what I said, Thanion. I love you. And I will always want you...even if...if you do not want me."

"You'll grow tired of me long before then," he replied, brushing his thumb over her cheek, "because there will never be a day, not a single moment, that I won't want you."

Moisture welled in her eyes. Her smile reached deep inside of him.

"What is your answer, demon?" Keric asked.

"So long as you assure me that everything in your power will be used to keep my...my family...safe from those I must hunt, you have my aid, mage." Morthanion couldn't pry his gaze from her. It had been an eternity since he was last able to stare into her eyes, to touch her, to hold her.

"You have our protection, and my hospitality. I imagine having you come with me to arrange a contract is out of the question?"

"I'll get to that eventually."

Aria's smile broadened into a grin, coaxing one onto his own lips.

Chapter Twenty-Five

Agatha led them to their new room, smoothing wrinkles in the bedding, making minute adjustments to the trinkets on the shelves, and talking incessantly. Morthanion bit his tongue to ensure he maintained his patience as he waited for the old woman to scurry off. Once she was gone, he slammed the door, narrowly missing her, and slid the bolt into place with a satisfying click. He turned to Aria and lifted her off her feet. Pressing his mouth against hers, he carried her further into the room, heat blossoming over his skin at the feel of her limbs wrapping around him.

He'd thought her lost to him forever. For an immortal, that was an achingly long time. Now that he had her back and they were safe, he planned to enjoy her.

Arms around his neck, she drew back from the kiss to look into his eyes. "I was afraid I would never see you again," she said.

"I'll always come for you." He kept her body against his, her legs about his waist, unwilling to let her go for even a moment. "I thought you died in my arms."

"How did you get off the island?"

After she'd vanished in his arms, he hadn't spent any time wondering at the return of his magic. Without hesitation, he'd begun to fly, and hadn't stopped until he came to the tower. "Our bond is stronger than the hold they had on my magic. Seeing what the elf did to you awoke something inside of me. The mark burned off."

He leaned forward, running his lips over her jaw line, down her neck.

"I am your mate?" she asked, shivering as he kissed.

"Yes. My mate. My love. My life," he affirmed. Despite the wave of exhaustion that would likely crash down atop him soon, he had to have her. He'd already been too long without her, and wanted to bask in her, to feel her whole and alive. "You are everything."

He laid her on the bed, propping himself up on his hands over her.

"How did you know? How did *they* know?" She was staring up at him, a faint flush of arousal coloring her cheeks, and she ran her fingers up through his hair.

"I knew from the moment I heard you sing for the first time, before I even saw you. And I fought it, because most of us were taught that a mate is meaningless, that it is nothing. Another tool to be used, a means to reproduce…a potential weakness. Little more than that. But each moment I spent near you, it grew harder and harder to believe those things."

"When we made love our first time?"

"Our souls joined forever."

"I *felt* you, Thanion. Everywhere within me."

"And I, you." He ran a hand down through the valley of her breasts, over the flat of her stomach, keeping his touch light. "I *need* you, woman. In every way that counts, and more that don't."

She smiled and laughed. "Everything here is so different from our cave, but at least one thing has not changed." Reaching down, she grasped the hem of the robe she wore and began to tug it up, revealing her legs a little bit at a time. He watched, raptly, as she exposed her thighs, the fabric rising higher and higher.

A growl rolled from his chest. "Yes…you are as addicted to me as always," he said. He settled one of his hands on her leg, following the progress of the robe slowly up. His fingers ran over every inch of her skin, caressing her. There was no sign of the wounds she'd been dealt.

She grabbed his face, forcing his gaze to meet hers. "And you had best be just as addicted to me, demon."

"My delectable little water nymph," he replied, grinning crookedly, wickedly, "addicted doesn't even begin to describe it. You make me burn."

About the Authors

Tiffany Roberts is the pseudonym for Tiffany and Robert Freund, a husband-and-wife writing duo. While Tiffany was born and bred in Idaho, Robert was a New York native who made the decision to fly across the county to be with her. Tiffany and Robert have always had a passion for reading and writing, and it was the dream to write books that they both shared that brought them closer. While they never gave up on this dream, work and kids came first until they were able to focus on moving their writing career along.

Connect with us:

Website:
https://authortiffanyroberts.wordpress.com

Facebook:
https://www.facebook.com/AuthorTiffanyRoberts

Made in the USA
Charleston, SC
23 April 2016